THE RIGHT MAN FOR THE JOB

THE RIGHT MAN FOR THE JOB

A NOVEL

MIKE MAGNUSON

HarperCollins*Publishers*

HarperCollins books may be purchased for educational, business, or sales promotional use. For information please write: Special Markets Department, HarperCollins Publishers, Inc., 10 East 53rd Street, New York, NY 10022.

FIRST EDITION

Designed by Ruth Lee

Library of Congress Cataloging-in-Publication Data

Magnuson, Mike, 1963–
    The right man for the job : a novel / Mike Magnuson. — 1st ed.
      p.   cm.
    ISBN 0-06-018710-7
    I. Title
    PS3563.A35214R54   1997
    813'.54—dc20   96-28396

---

97 98 99 00 01 ❖/RRD 10 9 8 7 6 5 4 3 2 1

*For Bob Clark, Mike Lohre, Bill Pratt, and the
Thursdays we spent talking smart*

What a world that must be
the world that is his
where you can't ask for food
or tell a woman she's beautiful

where you can't pray or sing
or speak drunk to the dead
or cry out in the night for help.

—Bruce Taylor

This October Saturday there is sun beyond the Ohio haze, and I have become a professional asshole here in Columbus, a sweating man who knocks on doors in blue coveralls and a button-down shirt and says, all day, "How could you let your rental payment go past due?" I have become a man who stuffs notes in people's doorjambs, short nastygrams of my own creation that tell the truth: "Your life will be miserable till this account is settled." Or "If you don't pay, I'll take your shit away." I am a man trained to ignore the word *no*. And for each day since mid-August—each new door my knuckles meet, each face I see frowning when I come to collect—I have been paid to forget who I am, a factory man from northern Wisconsin moved to Ohio, the great state where the license plates announce to the world that this is the heart of it all. Over my breast pocket I wear a big plastic tag with a yellow winking smiley face stamped on it. This little face is named Winky. He is the mascot of the company that pays me. On the tag, in a perfectly round talk balloon, Winky says, *I'm Gunnar Lund, your Crown Rental account manager.*

So this is who I really am, part Winky, part chubby guy from Wisconsin: this man who drives slowly down Jefferson Avenue in a gray Ford van with Winky himself airbrushed on the side panels. This is me gripping the steering wheel and gnawing an unlit cigarette, sweating too much from my brow on a hot day in October.

Everywhere along Jefferson Avenue children play. Men stand in groups, drinking forty-ouncers of Crazy Horse or Little Kings. On concrete stoops or on the hoods of purple Oldsmobiles, women smoke cigarettes and hold infants loosely, as if they might be footballs. All these folks are black. I am white, luminous in the van, and everywhere eyes watch me watching them, huge pupils shifting briefly up from a conversation or ogling me from behind a diseased elm. The houses lining this street are identical, HUD duplexes, circa 1968, khaki-colored and square, each with tattered shingles and peeling paint, some sealed shut with particleboard, condemned signs tacked on the doorjamb. None of the yards have any grass, just pebbles, dirt, and broken bottles. And paper trash dots the street: Rally's cups, Wendy's wrappers, empty boxes from Sister's Chicken & Biscuits. Every twenty feet or so, crunching sounds come from under the van tires, small destructions that are part of the constant noise in the hood. While I drive, I listen for silent spaces.

Somewhere up this road is 1726, home of Miss Dorothea Dixon. She rents a washing machine from Crown Rental and hasn't paid for three weeks. I have never seen her. Dewy Bishop, my partner, has told me Miss Dixon is uncollectable, the sort of customer only an expert account manager can take down. He's knocked on her door, left nastygrams, has smooth-talked her some days and told her she's dirt others, but she has not budged. If he can't get her to pay, he's told me, I might as well not even try. But Dewy's off alone in another van now, searching streets in a different part of Columbus. I'm out here to prove to him I've mastered his trade.

What I know for sure about Miss Dorothea Dixon appears on a computer printout detailing her payment history, seven months of an eighteen-month rent-to-own contract, only two weeks of which has she paid on time. Steve Lawson, Crown Rental's store manager, my boss and a white man, has written REPO on the print-out in lime-green marker strokes. He's quick to write this when the customer is black, as is most often the case. Steve Lawson hates black folks, thinks the store's customers are dregs, because they're black or acting like it. Dewy Bishop says Mr. Lawson will burn in hell. When I drive through this neighborhood, I figure we're all in it.

In the back pocket of my coveralls I carry a pair of channel locks—uncomfortable against the van seat but handy in case I need to disconnect Miss Dixon's washer—plus a camouflage bandanna, a sweat-rotten wallet, and a Wisconsin driver's license. I'm wearing the same pair of steel-toed boots I wore three months ago, when I finished my eighth year as shift supervisor at Peterson Products, a plastics factory in McCutcheon, Wisconsin, exactly 770 miles from Jefferson Avenue. The boots are still filthy with hydraulic oil, plastic dust. They are shitkickers, and I wear them because they make me feel like a hick, like I have an honest job in a little town. I migrated to Ohio for love, followed Margaret Hathaway to Columbus when she came here to attend graduate school at Ohio State. She enjoys her opportunity in the city, which is a chance to mingle with the brain trust in big-time women's studies, legions of smart women wise in the ways of the oppressed, women she could never meet in the redneck taverns of northern Wisconsin. But my heart is still attached to those backwoods bars, quiet smoky rooms where the talk is of deer hunting and the fate of the Green Bay Packers, and I want to remain a professional dirtball, as I've always been, a guy who smokes cigarettes and works on machinery. It's only for the paycheck that I've become a professional asshole.

I drive Jefferson Avenue cautiously, looking at house numbers and thinking of the Wisconsin I used to call home. I remember clipped lawns and pine trees and lilac hedges. I remember flagpoles bearing the Swedish flag.

1726 Jefferson is an older two-story yellow New England, a freak single-family house at the end of the

Jefferson Avenue duplex row, a leftover from the white neighborhood that this area was twenty-five years back, and it's surrounded by a shabby link fence. The lawn, like all lawns in this part of the north end of Columbus, consists of a few weeds, some sketchy grass, but mostly pebbles and dirt. Two empty plastic milk jugs lean against the fence. In the middle of the yard stands a small headless concrete deer. This piece of junk, this ruined yard ornament, might be a Wisconsin version of the Venus de Milo.

I open the gate with one hand, feeling the hinge creak through the rusty steel, and I stride up the walkway to the porch, trying to appear tough and rigid, arms motionless at my sides. I don't want Miss Dixon to believe I'm a man she can control. Winky says, *Look confident.*

On the planked porch, roofed over, I give the door five sharp raps, the standard repo knock, and I wait. It is humid, eighty degrees. I feel the itch of sweat breaking on my shoulders. Near the door there are greaseprints on the yellow siding, chunks of food, boogers. A television cackles inside the house, applause, a game show. I listen to someone walking the floors.

When the door opens, before I see anybody, I hear, "What the fuck you want?" The voice has a volatile squeal to it.

I say to what I cannot see, "I'm looking for Dorothea Dixon."

"You found her." She appears in the doorway, barefoot and in jeans. She's slightly taller than me, an even six without her shoes, and she wears a gold halter top, which drapes like a rumpled tablecloth over her thin torso. Bony shoulders and arms, her skin is the deepest shade of brown. Her hair bristles down to her neckline and appears sprayed with something to keep it wet. From behind her comes the smell of good skunky dope and something salty cooking: black beans, I imagine, bubbling in salt pork. Everything inside looks orderly, nothing cluttering the floors, unusual for a Crown Rental customer's home.

She smiles in a lifeless way when she looks at me. "You Crown Rental?"

"I'm here for the washer," I say. "Mr. Lawson wants me to pick it up."

An uncomfortable moment, we look into each other's eyes, neither one of us giving off a trace of emotion. The whites of her eyes are yellow, lashes like tiny pencil tips.

"Fuck his white ass," says Miss Dixon in a monotone. "Motherfucker knows I'll pay him."

Even though this is my second month on the job, day after day in this same situation, I still feel awkward when a customer gets belligerent. On my own out here, knocking on doors, I am timid, a goddam white rabbit, or that's what Dewy Bishop calls me. He always says I'm too softhearted for the inner city. But all I can think is that I am whiter than white (back home, even among nothing but white people, I was whiter than everybody else, all tavern-pale and freckled), and I'm going to get killed over a VCR or a microwave, a sofa, or any of the cheap junk Crown Rental hawks out at a godawful weekly rate. These women tote guns, too, or their man lurks somewhere in an upstairs room, waiting to take out his anger on a white man demanding payment.

"You've been behind on your payments since you rented the washer, Miss Dixon." I focus my concentration on my right hand, attempting to suppress a nervous twitch in my index finger.

"How come you here, instead of that fat Dewy Bishop?" She crosses her arms, in the process flexing her shoulders back. "That man been dogging me no end."

"I'm just doing my job," I say, and worry my voice is cracking.

For this work I make $265 a week, flat-rate, nothing extra for overtime, which is the most a factory boy from Wisconsin can expect in Columbus, and that kind of money, anybody will tell you, isn't worth dying for. But if I'm making repo calls with Dewy—him a black man from Sandusky, a six-foot-six, 340-pound former University of Toledo defensive tackle—I am fearless. Mr. Bishop is my protection, because nobody I've seen yet in the hood has had the guts to fuck with Dewy Bishop.

"That Dewy takes his job too serious," says Miss Dixon. "You'd think that washing machine was his mother's, bad as he wants it back." She places a hand on the doorjamb and slips it upward, accentuating her long thin arm. A few flecks of white deodorant cling to her armpit hairs.

"Dewy takes pride in his work," I say. "No doubt about that."

With Dewy, I have picked up babies, set them down on housing-project linoleum, and repoed their cribs. With Dewy, I have walked into pure-black parties and demanded forty bucks plus late fees on a refrigerator. After ignoring the standard deadbeat's excuse—*you can't squeeze blood from a rock*—I have emptied these people's refrigerators and wheeled them out the door with a dolly. If he's along, I can repossess anything. Without Dewy, if I run into stubbornness, I usually tell the customer I'll be back with him, knowing he's scary enough, huge man enough, to make the snag.

"You shouldn't be sticking up for the man," Miss Dixon says. "He's a menace to the community."

I let out a long breath, calming myself. "If you knew the man better," I say, "you'd probably like him."

Dewy and I are buddies. He's the only person in Columbus, apart from Margaret, I ever shoot the bull with. He's the sort of person who makes fun of my troubles in a likeable way, gives me good-natured shit when I need a laugh, which is what any man looks for in a buddy. Whatever's on my mind I'll tell Dewy, and he must like my company, because the two of us are always scheming to make repo calls together. Sometimes Steve Lawson will threaten to shitcan me because I get along too well with Dewy. Steve thinks I don't repo enough merchandise independently. He says my problem is that I'm "too friendly with the goddam niggers." Really, I should argue with Steve about this. I'm too friendly with everybody, is what I'd tell him. I just like talking to people. That's the way everybody is back home. But I don't want to get fired, lose my already pitiful income. Margaret reduces me to cinder, as she often does, when money comes up, my lack of it. If there are principles with me, money will override them every time. And that, Dewy sometimes tells me, is the first step toward being a man in the city.

"Whatever you thinking," says Miss Dixon, "that fat Dewy Bishop is a horsetooth motherfucker. You ain't convincing me different."

I look away from her, scan around the yard, my eyes resting on the headless concrete deer, and I concoct a ruse. I point at the deer.

"How'd you chop the head off that fucker?" I say in my thickest Wisconsin dialect, a mix of dumb TV lumberjack and immigrant Swede, heavy on the consonants.

Miss Dixon steps onto the porch with me, her face relaxing into a genuine smile when she looks at the deer. "It's always been like that." She inadvertently bumps my hand with her forearm, and I can feel the softness of her skin.

I shuffle my feet, rolling a pebble under my shit-kickers. "Back home, folks would think that's pretty cool."

"You from Ireland?" asked Dorothea. "You talk funny."

"Same thing," I say. "Northern fucking Wisconsin." I take a pack of Marlboros from my shirt pocket and offer her one. She accepts, flashing me the smile people give when they meet a foreigner, extra-courteous and nodding rapidly, and I light the cigarette for her in a backwoods gentlemanly way. I can feel her falling for it. "No shit, Miss Dixon. Wisconsin life, you know, is simple as a goddam spoon. This city living is tough on a Cheesehead."

For a few minutes we talk casually. She asks me why I ended up in Columbus, no less the hood. I tell her it was just one of those things that happen in the dreary space of a life. And she chuckles and rocks herself forward and back from the heels, waving her cigarette in the air.

She says, "If you was a West Virginia hillbilly motherfucker, I wouldn't give you the time of day. Them toothless clowns always coming here to the hood and sponging."

"Is that right?" I say with a grin.

"They the only whites we ever see here," she says. "You the first Wisconsin person I ever met."

I feel a tension between us, but not the repo kind. This is the kind where we might be leaning up against a bar somewhere, picking each other's brains for an opportunity to hold hands, kiss, go home and crack the slats under the box spring. I let her talk and go on asking me questions, and I tell her lies about my life. I say I was raised on a farm in Hayward, way up in northern Wisconsin. Really, I'm from Milwaukee, and I moved two hundred miles north to McCutcheon at age eighteen. All I actually know about farm life is what I heard from folks during my eight years in the factory. But I describe to Miss Dixon an elaborate farm—complete with geese, chickens, and a llama (why not?)—and she seems entertained, smiling when I speak, satisfied with my story. She occasionally touches me on my coverall sleeve.

When I think she's buttered up properly I say, while she's mid-drag on the cigarette, "Fifty bucks'll get you off Friday credit."

An exhale first, then she squares up toward me, her arms loose at her sides. "Twenty-five's what y'all can get from me today, honey."

"Look, fifty's what it is. Otherwise, I'm picking it up." I am doing my best to sound stern now, my voice flattened and serious like a newsman's. "If you want, I'll take it back to the store and hold it till you're ready to pay."

Her pause is the same as it is with every delinquent customer I've seen thinking, a looking downward and fidgeting. I face away from her, watch a group of kids throwing a basketball in the street. They are playing a game of sorts; when a car drives by, they pitch the ball over it, and they all hoot if the ball strikes the curb on the other side of the street. Off in the distance I hear the superbass booming of a rapmobile, probably some lime green Jeep Cherokee modified into a lowrider with bowlegged wheels, gangster gold hubs. I hear the police helicopter that always hovers over this part of the hood, a giant lawnmower in the heavens.

"Okay," Miss Dixon says abruptly. She puffs out her cheeks and rolls her eyes. "Write the motherfucker up."

When I take the receipt book from my pocket, she

takes a wad of bills from hers. She must have five hundred dollars. Women *never* have that much money in the hood, only food stamps and pockets full of coins. She deals or hooks, is what I'm thinking. But I'm too pleased with myself, my little victory, to press her for more cash, make her pay an advance month on the washer, like Dewy Bishop would. I simply write down the figures—three weeks' worth—which catch her up, well, to today.

"You'll be past due again tomorrow," I say.

"You come hunt for me then," she says and places the cash in my palm, brushing her hand across mine in the exchange. She makes a humming sound, runs her tongue over her upper lip.

"Why thanks, Miss Dixon," I say, imagining my voice sounds like a small-town shopkeeper. "You have a good day now."

She reads my name tag and says, "Gunnar, you got a peculiar name. But it was sure nice meeting you. You different. Tell that Dewy to keep his pork ass away from my crib. You come, and I pay."

Her eyes are brown and remote and beautiful. "I'm pleased to meet you, too, Miss Dixon."

I return to the van and drive to the store, the world of garbage and helicopters and people carrying hidden guns all around me, and I imagine I do my job well.

The North Columbus Crown Rental sets on the west side of Cleveland Avenue, between Twenty-fourth and

Twenty-fifth streets. It occupies one of two retail spaces in a red brick and cinder-block plaza, a rectangular building with a flat roof and a dented aluminum canopy that shades a raised concrete walkway. Enormous steel garage doors are mounted over both glass storefronts, thief gates that seal the place at night. Fresh graffiti appears on the building each morning. Next to Crown Rental is an Arab-run grocery called Key Foods, where two weeks ago I bought a carton of chocolate milk that had gone rancid. But it didn't surprise me that the milk was bad. The only items properly refrigerated in that store are the forty-ouncers, which outsell milk by twenty to one. The fresh fruit most always looks withered, and the lettuce, if they have any, is covered with brown spots. Even the canned goods in Key Foods look inedible, coated with dust, as if nobody's touched them in years. What keeps Key Foods in business is a steady food-stamp traffic in cheap white bread, corn wieners, candy, off-brand chips, and Faygo pop, favorite of Dewy's, who each day will wander over to Key Foods for a sixteen-ounce bottle of Faygo Red. In the hood, Dewy says, the people fuel themselves on garbage.

I park next to Dewy's van, surprised he's back at the store before me. Probably he's made a spectacular snag, and he's come back early to tell Steve Lawson all about how ruthless he was, how he repoed that VCR or chest freezer without batting an eye. Dewy's van is identical to mine, Winky smiling on the side panels, but he doesn't drive it much. Most of the time he rides with me, giving me directions from the passenger seat and making me laugh. The third Crown Rental van, an old Chevy we never use because it stalls in traffic, is parked next to Dewy's van, rust on the fenders and tailpipe and grill. Its picture of Winky is peeling and blistered. Since I've worked here, nobody's bothered to start up that Chevy, and for all I know there could be a bum sleeping in its cargo bay.

With some pride I light up a cigarette and step out onto the asphalt, examining my copy of Miss Dixon's receipt. For once, I know I'll be able to walk into Crown Rental and tell Dewy and Steve I've scored on my own. I lean up against my van grill, take long draws from my smoke, and plan out my story of Miss Dixon and how I schmoozed her into coughing up the cash.

Whenever I'm here in the lot, I see movement. People walk, rarely alone. And they never walk quickly. At a saunter, arms loose and feet shuffling, people go by looking around, stopping to make a point or to shout at somebody across the street. When they walk by me, they either scowl at me or don't look at me at all. Everybody in this neighborhood knows each other. Everybody in this parking lot, whether they know my name or not, knows what I do and why I belong here, relaxing with a cigarette in front of my van. Some years back, the entire plaza was a Kroger's Foods, bustling, no doubt, with helpful stock boys and pretty white check-out girls. These days, though five Arabs from Key Foods clean the lot every morning at eight, paper trash drifts steadily over the asphalt like tumbleweeds.

On Cleveland Avenue there is movement, too, a

constant surge of rumbling engines, horns honking, and taillights streaming off into the distance—such as it always is with an asphalt river in the city. Cleveland Avenue runs south for three miles and directly into downtown Columbus, where the Ohio state capitol stands among the skyscrapers, most important of which, according to Margaret, is the Les Wexner Center for the Performing Arts. She's been to symphony concerts there twice without me, because I can't scrape up the dough for a ticket; just because Gunnar Lund is broke, she says, doesn't mean Margaret Hathaway should live in a cave. From the Crown Rental parking lot the skyline looks to me, no kidding, like a few dozen spaceships ready to shoot to Mars. The skyscrapers glimmer even in the daytime haze. At night, they glow and blink as if breathing. Two miles to the north, Cleveland splits into Route 3, which in turn becomes the main drag through the white Columbus suburb of Westerville. Every night before eight I drive to the BancOhio at that intersection and make the store bank deposit, one of my daily responsibilities. Two miles due west of Crown Rental is the nearly all-white student ghetto of Ohio State University, the largest university in the United States and probably the world. Most evenings when I return home from work, Margaret will tell me some anecdote about Ohio State, how smart the people are there, how diverse her classmates are, what the coffee shops are like, and so on; and though I rarely drive through that part of town, I know the university district well, at least Margaret's version of it. I can picture the ponytails and book bags and Birkenstocks and smart conversations about the decline of the world. This Saturday afternoon the Buckeyes are playing Indiana, and I can see from Crown Rental the Goodyear blimp hovering over The Horseshoe. Almost a hundred thousand folks are at the game, hollering and wearing the Buckeye scarlet and gray. I'm sure there's much happiness over at the college, but whenever I think about Ohio State, I tell myself that *that* university is the reason I knock on doors all day. If that university didn't exist, I'd be in Wisconsin this Saturday afternoon, warming my stool at the Liquid Forest Bar, shucking peanuts and debating with my bar buddies about how many days we have left before the snow flies.

Columbus is the big city all right, people everywhere I go, the metropolitan area adding up to over a million folks, more than a third of which aren't white. Back in McCutcheon, a cowpie burg of forty thousand, I remember in the ten years I lived there seeing just three black residents, one of whom I knew, a woman named Tamara, who drank beer daily at the Liquid Forest Bar. She ended up moving south to Milwaukee, because she grew tired of pretending she was white. In the neighborhood here, I almost never see another white person, not even in the cars driving up and down Cleveland Avenue. Still, I haven't decided to pretend I'm black. But I think about being white all the time. I can't help it. I wish I could take these neighborhood people I meet for who they are, how they think, just the way, back home, I dealt with my crew in the factory or folks I would drink with at the Liquid Forest. But I look at my freckled hands, my pale pink palms, and I know I'm forever a blob of glorified rice, funeral potluck dish of Wisconsin Scandinavians, absent of color and flavor. All that crosses my mind in this hood is that everybody is different from me, and I'm alone among them.

When I open the Crown Rental glass door and stride into the air conditioning, I screw a big prizewinner's smile on my face and hold my receipt book in the air. "Look at this shit," I holler. "I got Miss Dixon to pay up."

Dewy and Steve are standing by the counter at the back of the store, looking at each other. Dewy is nearly three times as big as Steve.

Steve Lawson says, "Hot damn, Mr. Cheesedick finally learned how to work."

Dewy says, "I told you my guy's got it going on."

"You ain't shitting," I say, and I walk through the store like a repo champion, my strides struts, hamming up extra because no customers are in the store.

Up and down the cream cinder-block walls are rows of refrigerators, chest freezers, sofas, stereos, televisions, lamps, even enormous plastic trees, each item tagged with a yellow piece of cardboard bearing a picture of Winky and his weekly and monthly rate. The show-room floor is filled with living room suites, all arranged at odd angles to slow the customer down on the way to the counter. While I walk the furniture maze to Steve and Dewy, my shitkickers make scratching noises on the carpet, which is all-weather red and the consistency of Astroturf, the sort of carpet that's easiest to vacuum spotless after our customers have tracked it with dirt.

When I reach the counter I slap my receipt book down, and Steve says, "No more putting up with crap from that bitch, right?" He's a tiny man, five foot five and 140 pounds, with brown slicked-back hair and aviator glasses. He wears a pressed white shirt, a thin gold tie, and gold slacks. He looks like a shoe salesman crossed with an ankle-biter dog. When he opens his mouth to smile or speak, he shows a line of gray misshapen teeth. "It's about time you did something on your own."

He examines the receipt, runs his small hand over his hair, and says, "Fifty bucks! Jesus. Is that all you could get? She'll be past due again tomorrow. You shouldn't have left that cunt's house till she paid a month in advance. See, when I write repo on the fucking printout you gotta pick the shit up. I don't want to hear about none of this take-what-cash-she's-got crap."

Blood rushes to my face, one more fuck-up, one more day I can't please the man.

"I'll do better next time," I say.

"You're fucking me and you're fucking the store," Steve says, and he turns quickly, takes an agitated stride to his desk, opens a drawer, and produces a yellow booklet that I've seen many times before: *Winky's Rules for Account Managers*. "If you'd ever read the goddam book, you wouldn't be fucking me all the time." He tosses me the booklet like a Frisbee, but I miss. It drops to the carpet at my feet. I crouch to pick it up.

"Why you always harping on my guy?" Dewy says, his voice deep and friendly but whining a touch at each word. "That Miss Dixon's pure uncollectable material. My guy did good taking a payment."

"You stay out of this," Steve says, and he points to the booklet in my hands. "He should pay attention to the book instead of you."

"Tiny Steve, I wonder if you ever gonna figure out what the fuck's going on," Dewy says, and I can't help looking up at Dewy with a smile. Dewy is monster-huge. From his size-fourteen EEE feet to his size-eight head, he's one big motherfucker. But I'm no slight man, either. Dewy is the first person I've ever known who outweighs me by more than a hundred pounds. His Schottenstein's green double-breasted suit is a size fifty-eight; that's ten sizes on me. He wears a fourteen-dollar tie imprinted with a beach scene, Hawaiian women dancing in circles, hands rubbing their tummies. Dewy refuses to wear the Crown Rental coveralls, because Dewy is store employee number two, the assistant manager, which doesn't mean much, really, except that on Thursdays he gets to close out the till and lock up the store.

I'm the only man doing Winky's work in uniform.

"I know enough," Steve says, "that I'd be better off if I canned both your asses."

Dewy steps behind the counter and looms over Steve. "You sure as fuck ain't out knocking down doors all day. You too chickenshit for that. At least my guy's got the guts."

"Fuck you," Steve says, his face reddening. This guy's a poodle. I swear to God.

Dewy laughs, wise and mocking. "Now you know better than to talk that shit to me if you was on the street. Tiny Steve, you lucky you the company man behind this counter." Then Dewy turns to me and winks, rotates his shoulders in their sockets, and he walks over to the row of display-model stereos on the far wall, produces a tape from his pocket, and pops it in. He turns the volume up good and loud. The tape, as it always is when Steve and Dewy are bickering, is Rev. Milton Brunson & the Thompson Community Singers, gospel music, which pisses Steve off no end, because he's a country-and-western man through and through. Dewy claps his hands and does a dance step, sings "Jesus Is a Rock" along with the choir. He shucks and shimmies.

Steve yells, "Paybacks are a bitch, fucker."

"Come on, Tiny Steve," says Dewy. "You can cut me better than that."

"I'll cut you out of a job," Steve says.

Dewy says, "What you should do is find a dentist to cut out some of them fucked-up teeth." And he cracks a belly laugh, does a few Egyptian movements with his arms and head.

Steve purses his lips into a blue anus, puts his hand over his mouth, and rotates away, flushed red and quivering. He moves to his desk, pulls out his swivel-back chair, sits and begins looking over some papers. His small hands tremble.

Dewy watches Steve, and Dewy's face relaxes into a frown. He walks to the stereo and turns off the tape. The store falls silent, save for the fans blowing cool air through the ductwork.

"You don't need to get all hurt and shit, Tiny Steve," Dewy says, his voice earnest and flat. But Steve does not turn to face him. "Just wanting you to give my guy some credit for getting the job done."

Dewy steps to me and socks me slow-motion in the shoulder. "I'm pleased with the payment, man. Fifty bucks from that bitch is like a million."

In my head I run through the whole Miss Dixon story I wanted to tell, but I look into Dewy's eyes, that friendly glint they have, and all I can do is grin.

"Read the book for a few minutes. That'll calm Tiny Steve down some."

I see Steve at his desk, his head nodding.

"Besides, my sweaty brother, you look like you need some air conditioning. In a bit, you and me gonna snag some serious shit out there. You best be cool for that."

And Dewy tramps off to the back room. I hear him opening up one of the repoed refrigerator doors, and he says, "This motherfucking stinks. That's all there is to it." Refrigerators always reek when we bring them back.

Steve turns to me with a forced smile, and he points to the booklet in my hands. So I open it up to page 3, which is the page Steve usually tells me to read; for there's no sense, he says, reading the intro. On the top of the page Winky smiles and says, *If you remember these rules out in the field, you'll be well on your way to success.*

And a numbered list begins, which fills the remainder of the booklet, an even thousand rules long. I skim the first few.

1. A Crown Rental account manager is a courteous professional.
2. The customer has a contractual obligation with Crown Rental.
3. Never let the customer take control of the account.
4. If the payment is received late, you must apply the late fee.
5. If the customer cannot pay, you must pick up the merchandise.
6. It is not your fault that the customer cannot make payment.

The list goes on and on, each rule brief and easy to keep in mind, maxims for the rental trade. When I first got the job here, I was sent for a week of training in Canton, a hundred miles north of Columbus, and during that week I was tested daily on various rules in the booklet. Here's a test question I remember: *Word for word, list ten of Winky's rules between 700–750.* Off the top of my head I can think of a couple from that range. Winky says, *Never deliver scratched merchandise.* Winky says, *Rapport is crucial during the first two months of the rental.* In one way or another, Winky's rules pop up in my head all day. If a trainee doesn't score at least 80 percent on each test, he loses his job, gets sent back on the

bus to Columbus—or Chillicothe or Cleveland or
Dayton or Wheeling, West Virginia, whichever Crown
Rental city the trainee represents. There are forty-three
Crown Rental stores in twenty-six cities. That one was
on the test, too. I barely passed the five portions of the
test I took, but I passed them all the same. I learned
enough in Canton to know how the business works.

Each Crown Rental item pays for itself after four
months, which is generally as long as any customer can
afford paying; although to own a given item, a customer
has to make payments for eighteen months. Rule number 380: Winky says, *Four months of payments means fourteen months of profit.* Most of the merchandise is rented
out as new, and officially we are to mark merchandise
previously rented if it's spent even an hour in the customer's home, but almost nobody who'd rent from us in
the first place can make the complete schedule of payments. So we pick up their stuff—their fridge,
microwave, electric stove, and so forth—recondition it
in the back room, make it shine as if straight from the
box, and rent it out again, more often than not tagging
it as new.

Above Steve's desk hangs a four-by-six-foot silk banner of Winky, which says, HOW ABOUT RENTING A
BRAND-NEW STOVE TODAY? Next to the banner there's a
round schoolhouse clock, in the middle of which is a
picture of Winky emerging from the mouth of a dryer.
Every ten feet along the store walls Winky smiles on a
different banner. He's mounted in neon on the glass
storefront. He's on our name tags, stationery, business

cards, pencils and pens, delivery dollies, the vans; his face even appears on the van key chains.

Winky is everywhere. Still, I haven't met a customer yet who knows him by name.

After a few minutes, Dewy wanders from the back room and steps behind the counter, eyeing me up and looking amused. He says, "Tiny Steve, me and my guy got some business." But Dewy doesn't look at Steve, nor does Steve look up from his paperwork. He merely grumbles.

"Today," Dewy says, "we snagging Leslie Britton's shit." He clasps his enormous chalky hands together and, like an aristocrat, cracks his knuckles. "Boondog that white bitch. How's she gonna play me?"

When Dewy reaches under the counter he grunts at the restriction of his threads. He produces a yellow megaphone, fingers its trigger, and raises it to his mouth. "LESLIE BRITTON." The Vader voice gives off how funny Dewy thinks he is. His two coal eyes widen at me over the megaphone's bell. "CROWN RENTAL'S GOT YOU SURROUNDED. WE KNOW YOU'RE A DEADBEAT. NOW GIVE ME BACK MY MOTHERFUCKING TV."

Leslie rents a Magnavox twenty-seven-inch cable-ready color console, and Dewy talks about snagging it nearly every day, though he can't manage to make her crack. She made the first month's payment, the story goes, when the TV was delivered. Three months later, she hasn't coughed up one more thin penny, won't answer the door when Dewy knocks. A week ago, Dewy says, he got cussed out by Ms. Britton's next-door neighbor. He had pounded so hard on Leslie's door he knocked a picture frame off the neighbor's wall. Winky says, *We always knock.* And Leslie's phone is disconnected. He can't harass her with calls. Winky says, *We always call.*

"I'm telling you, man," Dewy says, and he raises the megaphone again. "Miss Britton, you store deadbeat number one." Then he presses the megaphone to his chest like a Bible and stands solemnly upright.

"Both of us are going, motherfucker," he says. "Walked up to her crib this morning, bitch just rolled shut her venetian blinds."

"You ain't shitting," I say, Wisconsin thick. Several times I have had customers do this to me. I know that loping up the walkway, all tight jaw and sternness, then seeing that slight movement in the blinds, the slits narrowing to nothing. Two months beating on doors and leaving nastygrams have made me a pro.

"How's she gonna play me?" says Dewy Bishop, raising the megaphone. "YOU'RE SURROUNDED." His megaphone voice is blaring and tinny, and it reverberates through the store, bouncing off a thousand pictures of Winky.

Dewy's plan, as always, involves stopping at United Dairy Farmers for a jelly doughnut and his signature half-stolen mixture of cocoa and coffee, which he calls

Bhagwan, after Bhagwan Rajneesh, famous, he says, for duping a lot of rich honkies. When we stop here today, I get a bottle of Mountain Dew and a pack of Marlboros, worrying, as I often do, that Dewy will get caught putting Swiss Miss into his cup and get charged for it. But I've done it—in fact, usually do it. Bhagwan is good, blows the doors off the gourmet grinds my long-haired and lentil-eating friends brew back home. Maybe it's too hot today, too warm for October, too far from home for coffee and cocoa. When Dewy pays he tells the woman at the cash register, by my white estimation a chunky girl with linebacker hands, that she should stop in the store sometime and see him. Me, I just pay and head back to the van.

I am Dewy's driver. He has been a rent-to-own man four years now, ever since he graduated with a business degree from Toledo State. Before hiring on at Crown Rental in June, two months before I did, Dewy managed an America Rents outlet on Morse Road, which is just north of the hood and in one of the few Columbus shopping centers where both blacks and whites shop. Two years before that, Dewy had been an account manager at a Rent A Center in Toledo. Educated man that he is, the rental business is the best career he can find, though from time to time he talks about finding a paper-pushing gig in one of the skyscrapers downtown.

"Experience, brother," he says, maneuvering his mass into the passenger seat. "That gives me the king seat. Drive, my prince." He says that every time. He likes me, says we make a good tag team. On certain days he'll name us: Regents of Repo, Sultans of Snag, the Bishops, of course, of Back Rent, or the Kings of motherfucking Sling, which is to say we deliver the stuff, too.

We head north on Cleveland Avenue, toward Morse Road and beyond it to Highway 161 (Dublin Road), which is the northernmost reach of the table-flat city of Columbus. We ebb and flow with the traffic, pass people milling at bus stops, people shuffling along the sidewalks. The people we see gradually change from black to white as we head north. Leslie Britton, our target, is of course white: one of the 15 white customers out of Crown Rental's 750, and I often wonder if that's why Dewy's so obsessed with her account, because she's unusual, a real repo trophy.

While I drive, slurping my Mountain Dew and smoking a cigarette, Dewy raves about the clerk at United Dairy Farmers.

"Now that was much booty," he says. "Gonna fuck that ass." He claps his hands together, then gestures regally toward the van ceiling.

I say, "I just don't see it, Dewbert."

"You got to love that big ghetto booty."

I'm a nerd. "Big, certainly."

"Cheese?" That's Dewy's name for me when we're on the road. "You okay. Just don't know nothing about pussy. Some homegirl should teach you how to fuck."

We have this conversation daily. I play stupid. Dewy instructs me in his way of the Columbus world. But he's always right. Probably, I don't know much about women, what physically makes a good one, if that's how we're thinking about it. When I'm driving with Dewy and see a head-snapper, as he calls it, it's usually while we are coasting through a West Virginia white-trash neighborhood on the west side, the Hilltop part of town, so named after the state mental institution there. I see these mountain women, straight-haired and in raggedy jeans pushing a stroller, and I'm reminded of the dairy-grade trailer-court women I worked with at Peterson Products. It's nostalgia, homesick bullshit, really. Maybe these are the only women, potty-mouthed and lifeworn, I have learned to think about with the huck and spittling anxiety of adult lust.

Miss Britton's neighborhood is mostly white; at least, driving now down her street, that's what I'd guess from the cars here: Volkswagens, Ford Escorts, here and there a pickup with meat tires—whitefolk cars, for sure, plain, practical. In the hood, cars seem made intentionally unique: personalized hubcaps sometimes or something quirky hanging from the rearview mirror; often, for reasons I've never discovered, this will be a cheap gold decoration bought at a Chinese restaurant. In Miss Britton's neighborhood, a curving row of joined-together townhouses, the grass, though brown in the late fall, is free of paper garbage, and the shrubbery is trimmed.

Before we pass in front of the townhouse row, Dewy tells me to duck into the back lot. I stop the van next to a yellow El Camino with crumpled Budweiser cans in its box.

"Cheese, she ain't seen you yet. Go up and pretend you're friendly. I'll be hiding in the bushes." Dewy hands me his repo bag, a cheap briefcase of sorts containing a calculator, a receipt book, some pens and nastygram paper, and the *Graphic Street Guide to the City of Columbus*, a blue paper map book that divides the city into coordinates, so we can find any street we want. While we walk to the corner of the building, Dewy rests his hand on my shoulder and says, "Just relax into it. Be cool. When it's time, I'll bum-rush the bitch."

Dewy follows me partway up a long sidewalk. One door from Leslie's apartment, he attempts to conceal himself behind a tubby and manicured cypress bush. He makes a lot of noise stuffing himself behind it, and I can see his face back among the greenery, jowly and grinning at these proceedings.

The standard repo knock, five sharp raps, and I wait. Upstairs, there is a momentary ruffling of curtains. I hear steps in the house, the jingle of the latch, and the door opens a crack, revealing a plain woman, straight-haired and freckled. She's wearing a black Metallica T-shirt. Her fingers are thin and elegant, the nails chewed. When I look into her eyes, green and blood-shot, I become awkward, because she is lovely, because she is the exact central-casted dirtball woman I imagine my Wisconsin heart loves. My first thought is to tell her to keep the television. *Keep everything*, I think. *I'll bring you more stuff, if you need it. I'll cut you in on my paycheck. I'll bring you back to the land of cheese and snow, and folks will take care of you there.*

"What do you want?" she says, her voice a West Virginia barroom gravel. I love her.

I raise Dewy's repo bag but keep staring at her, her eyes, those arms, freckled and, no shit, translucent. I cannot speak. Rule number 73: Winky says, *Never get involved with the customer*.

"That fat black boy sent you, didn't he?" She opens the door a little farther, revealing her entire stature: a sturdy stick all the way down. Her white painter pants have a vertical rip on the front right thigh. I see paleness, freckles, and an interruption on the skin which I suppose is a scar. She is at once homely, mannish-tough, and graceful as the Appalachian beauty that I figure she is. "He don't give me no rest."

"Look," I stammer, remembering Dewy is watching. "You have to pay on the television sometime."

"It's my sister he wants to see." Something in her eyelids, a little tic, makes me think she's giving me a line of manure.

"Aren't you Leslie?" I say.

She frowns, her eyes fixing on some point over my shoulder, and says, "Ain't none of your business who I am. You can tell that to your nigger friend."

At this, Dewy topples through the cypress, growling and swiftly stumbling toward her. When she sees him her mouth gapes into an oval, and she slams the door.

Like Fred Flintstone locked out, Dewy pounds on the door with both fists, hollering, "Bitch, give me back my shit!"

He eases up after a few more blows and says to me, "Repo bag."

I hand it to him dutifully. Breathing hard, he produces the nastygram pad and a pen, then writes, in print big enough for me to see it, *Next time I bring the sheriff.* He crams the paper into the doorjamb and gestures for me to follow. As he strides back to the van, I notice a near lilt to his gait, a victory walk.

In the van he shouts, "That was the shit, brother." He laughs and bangs his fists into the ceiling. "Did you hear that bitch? About to have a motherfucking hissy. And listen to that bitch say she's her own sister."

Dewy directs me to drive around the block, which I do, taking a nice slow pace. When we pass by her apartment, he reaches to the steering wheel and honks long and aggressively.

"See that?" Dewy says. "The nastygram's gone. How's she gonna play me?"

I wonder the same thing, wonder about me and her—her face what I remember most now, that tough face, the kind that might spit in a lover's face at the point of climax, those lingering bloodshot eyes all scorn and misery—and I hope on Monday I can return here alone, talk to her in our white-trash way, which is dully, our lives forgotten, the television not important, but how we got here, how we ended up in Ohio, why the fuck we stay; that's what we could talk about; that's what could bring us together.

Dewy flips on the van's Philco AM radio to WVKO, rhythm of the city, the black station, and Zap comes on:

"More Bounce to the Ounce." While the tune plays, a dance groove as deep and hard as a limestone quarry, Dewy makes angular movements with his arms. His belly contorts with bliss. In Wisconsin, I would have never heard this tune. In Ohio, I never pass the day without it. For the first time in two months, I absolutely wish I wasn't here, and I want to go home. The music is fine. I bob my head and tap my fingers along with Dewy. But I am growing tired of the daily excitement, the constant movement wherever I look, and I'm tired of everybody I meet wishing I hadn't come. More than anything, I want to be sitting this afternoon in a Wisconsin bar, a buddy there drunk with me, with maybe some Ted Nugent on the juke.

I drive Dewy out of Miss Britton's neighborhood, the road busy everywhere, traffic piling up at each intersection, and I begin to realize I'm forgetting who I am.

Dewy's hands beat time on the dash. He says, "This is the shit, brother."

I agree, without looking at him. My head nods with the music.

A mile south of Leslie's apartment, Dewy instructs me to stop in the Kroger's parking lot on Dublin Road. Here we sit and wait for Leslie to get comfortable for a while. We'll give her enough time to think we're not coming back, and then we'll hit her again. At this time of afternoon the lot is all hustle-bustle. Cars move slowly, easing around for a good parking spot. People mingle over their shopping carts and talk. We watch women— some white, some black—come in and out of Kroger's, and we speculate about the good-looking ones, as workmen in a parking lot will. With each new prospect Dewy laughs and elbows me in the shoulder. Dewy's head is shaved nearly bald, save for a little greased nap on the top, which, combined with the yellowish-red pallor of his dark skin, makes him look somewhat like an enormous cartoon beaver. In the van's rearview mirror I see my orange-yellow tangle, my dirtball hair, and I decide Dewy Bishop and I look as little alike as steak and rice pudding.

"LaKenya was at my crib last night," Dewy says, almost girlishly, and pokes me in the shoulder.

"Was it fun?" I reply with a slight whine. I think about my home life with Margaret, how we never plunge around anymore.

"LaKenya smokes some serious Johnson." He grabs his crotch and happily grunts.

"Dew," I say. "How do you get all those women?"

"It's the threads, brother. You got to show some class to get that ass."

"Clothes never mattered much to Margaret," I say.

Dewy gestures to my coveralls. "Obviously."

"But hell," I say, "I came all the way out here and got a gig and then she quits giving up the goods."

Dewy guffaws. "Ugly as you are, I'm surprised she fucked you in the first place."

"Back home," I say, "I was the pick of the crop. Wisconsin men are usually all green and shit. Some of the fellows have three eyes."

"Still, they looking better than a Cyclops like you," Dewy says, and he slaps his hands on his thighs.

"You got a point," I say, and I close one eye and open the other wide, cocking my head toward Dewy and making gagging noises.

We laugh for a moment together. I wonder what Margaret and her women's studies cronies would think of our conversation.

I venture this: "What ever happened to being a nice guy and all that shit?"

"Face it, Cheese. You a born-natural prick, and that's why your woman ain't fucking you regular."

"I guess I don't give a shit anymore *what* I am," I say. "Doesn't get me laid if I'm Mr. Goddam Sainthood."

"Then you all fucked up, nothing else to it."

"Now, that Miss Britton," I say, "could stand a ride on a Wisconsin buck such as myself."

"That one break your dick off first chance she get," Dewy says. "Miss Britton's all full of cunning."

"Those are the best kind," I say.

"As long as they get the job done," Dewy says, and he makes a few thrusts with his pelvis, chuckling as he does. Then he sits upright, rubs his chin and says, "Drive, my prince. She been sitting up there long enough."

When we get back out on the road, I light up a cigarette, take deep drags, focusing on the ashtray taste of tobacco. Up the road is Leslie Britton's, and I imagine her eyes, the way they seemed so tough and green and doleful, her voice a euphonious twang of the West Virginia mountains I've never seen.

Leslie's street is quiet, Ohio-gray. As before, Dewy conceals himself behind the cypress, and I give the standard repo knock. This time there is no ruffling of curtains, no sound from within. I strike the door again, now with an even and friendly-sounding four raps. There still is no response.

"Ain't here," I say to Dewy, and he extracts himself from his position in the foliage.

"She's playing with us," he says, his voice raised, exaggerated. He winks. "Fuck the note, Cheese. Deadbeat bitch couldn't read it anyway."

I follow Dewy to the van.

Before we've walked sixty feet, I hear a door slamming. I turn and there goes Leslie, beautiful and ragged in a blue sundress, running toward the street, her sandals making a popping noise with each stride.

"Leslie Britton," Dewy yells. "Give me back my shit!"

The two of us begin lumbering after her in our chubby-guy way.

"Be reasonable," I let out.

Too fast, she reaches a gold Mazda RX-7, climbs in, starts it, and she screeches off down the road.

"Follow that hole!" says Dewy.

We beat feet to the van, pulling at our clothes as we go, fat boys on the fly.

"Drive, my prince," hollers Dewy Bishop, and I haul out into the street.

At the first intersection, Dewy spots her. "There that cunt goes!"

Traffic everywhere, I join the flow cautiously and begin after her.

Dewy says, "Cheese, don't be driving like a fucking pussy. Chase this bitch down."

For a second I consider telling Dewy I've never received a traffic citation, some such nonsense, and I haven't come all the way to Ohio just to get a speeding ticket. But something about the way he's perched in the passenger seat—a black Caesar, both hands on the dashboard, a genius repo strategist—something about his sheer fascination with getting this woman's merchandise persuades me to begin driving wildly after her. Maybe I simply don't want to pass this day without looking into her eyes again. It doesn't matter. Dewy wants me to catch her, and I will.

We're heading down Cleveland Avenue now, four lanes wide at this point, and we're closing on her. I'm threading the needle through the slower cars, living out every chase scene I've ever watched on television. We're the new Mod Squad, Dewy and I.

She veers right onto Morse Road, changing lanes, ducking and swerving her little car. I begin sweating with excitement.

"You think she knows we're back here?" I ask.

"Hell yes, Cheese. Bitch knows exactly what the fuck's going on."

I loosen myself behind the wheel, feeling nothing but the contest of it all. I don't worry about Leslie, how she might feel about this. Under the sunless city sky I am hunting her down. This is all I think. She takes another aggressive right, this time heading north on Morse, circling, I figure, back to where she started.

At a stoplight eight blocks up, we catch her at the red. I pull the van directly behind her and can see her in there, wiggling about, her hair seeming to shine as she jerks her head like a jackrabbit in a box trap.

"Watch this shit," Dewy says, and he gets out.

I do watch, registering it in slow motion. Dewy strides casually to her driver's side, reaching into his pocket. Twisting in her seat to see him, she locks her doors. Her hands, from my vantage point, appear elegant, as they earlier did. She barely moves now, looks up at Dewy, who leans down to her window and flashes a smile. Now she is perfectly still, and for some reason, this amazes me. From his pocket Dewy Bishop takes out a business card and wedges it under her windshield wiper. When the light changes Dewy merely waves, positioning himself so she can see him while she drives off. Then Dewy moseys back to the van and resumes his position in the king seat.

"Okay," he says, "we boondogged the bitch enough for today."

I drive a block farther north, back at my hick pace, and pull into a Dairy Mart. Dewy seems ecstatic with himself, breathing hard and softly chuckling. He motions for me to give him a cigarette, which he rarely will smoke. I decide to have one, too.

"You did good, my brother," Dewy says. He hands

me a business card that I assume is a duplicate of the one he affixed to Leslie's windshield. "She's your account now."

On the card is a picture of Winky and some print that says, *Just a friendly hello from Winky and all his friends at Crown Rental.*

There are a thousand tricks in this business.

2

After eight, dark. A stout wind comes from the west, carrying the exhaust and Dumpster smell of the city, and the sky threatens rain. I am walking fifteen blocks south on Cleveland Avenue to catch the Number Three bus out of the hood. My ankles and knees throb, a reaction I've always had when air pressure drops, when the weather takes its downward turn. I am susceptible to rain coming on. But these last two months it hasn't rained much, only a sprinkle occasionally. I remember one thunderstorm, not a very big one, the fifth day Margaret and I were in Columbus. Yet most every day seems cloudy. No sun, no stars, just a constant definitionless haze, it's as if this town is an American version of London, all the gloom but never the elegance.

Though it is fifty-eight degrees—what would be a warm night this time of year, back home—I wear my big green 60/40 parka, my winter coat, as a disguise, and I pull its hood over my head, keep my hands concealed deep in my pockets, hiding who I am.

When I hike across the intersection of Seventeenth and Cleveland, someone drives past and honks, recognizing me as somebody else. My head raises on reflex to the sound, exposing my face, giving up my whiteness. A black woman in the car sees me, a flash of teeth from her, a finger pointed at me. I panic, pick up my pace.

Around me lights shine in the porch windows, the houses tall and ramshackle and square, and I do not peer into any house long, do not look anywhere except the ground, shifting my eyes only up to catch a glimpse of a passing car, or to look for dark figures looming along the rusty fences or between the tottering buildings, every other lot either vacant or containing a house that's all boarded up. Bits of broken glass dot the sidewalk, each bit a purplish reflection of the streetlights. I hear rapmobiles booming in the alleys, that fuzz sound they let off; shouts, too, close and far; and distant sirens. Saturday night in the hood, and it's coming alive the way a swamp does after sundown, noises and sudden movements and things emerging from the hollows.

A block east of this intersection is the Windsor Terrace project, 1,220 units big and the boyhood home of Buster Douglas, the only prizefighter ever to knock out Mike Tyson. The project now is an orange light over the building line. I can hear basketballs bouncing over there, and hooting and stereos and brief chirpings from car alarms. It's a city in itself back there, and nearly every customer I've met in Windsor Terrace has a story about drinking a forty with Buster Douglas, or having him over for ribs and greens, or jumping fences with him during his wild days, running from the project precinct cops. And that's the exact touristy tidbit, when I'm home safe in Margaret's arms, I'll relate about my day. *Imagine that*, I'll say, *great people come out of the hood. They all know Buster Douglas, too. That Buster, he's made an impact on those people.* And I suspect Margaret will say again how beneficial my brush with black culture is, and she'll talk about her struggle to defeat oppression in the class-rooms of Ohio State. She'll tell me how white culture is fucked, and she'll dance limply about our apartment to her Bitches With Problems CD, mouthing happily the words "Eat my pussy like a hog eats slop." I couldn't tell you what Margaret's pussy looks like, or anybody's any-more, although I'm certain she had one before we moved here. Still, I remember those late-July evenings, full of bourbon and dope, us under the Wisconsin Northern Lights—whatever it was about her olive legs and arms that was our falling in love—that parry and dodge that brought me to Ohio.

My way of walking these blocks is a sneak-thief walk, strides like eggshell steps, arms held in tight to the body, heart thumping, each nerve ready to frazzle with the guilt of someone who's where he shouldn't be. I am not a thief, but I am guilty of much in this life, much I can handle, much I can't. The professional asshole part of me: That's bad, but I have to make a living somehow. That I'm a white man: Can't do much about it. But this: I am guilty of jilting. That part, I can't get over. I am a leaver of brides at the altar, or *a* bride, and however I want to look at it, that's what landed me in the hood. Five months ago I was engaged to marry a woman named Sara Weber, and this goes without saying: Sara Weber is not now my wife.

When I tell the story to Dewy Bishop, I say Sara and I were really married, and for many years. I tell Dewy I left Sara for Margaret, which I really did, but there are no divorce papers pending in the McCutcheon courts. There is no judge named Hans Kallstrom whom Sara and I have to face for an hour of signatures and longing looks. Fact is, I lived with Sara for eight years, which might qualify for common-law marriage in some states, but not in Wisconsin. We were live-in single slices of cheese, the way Dewy would put it, if he knew the truth.

I was nineteen when I met Sara at a beach party on the McCutcheon River, and she was twenty-five. In her own way Sara was a good-looking woman, though no head-snapper, and I miss her sometimes. She had pretty blue eyes, an endearing smile, and thighs like birch logs, which is common for Wisconsin women. And when I saw Sara standing that day among the drunks in the sun, I fell in love, not, as I think about it now, because she wore a blue bikini and smoked a footlong El Producto and had a certain raggedness of hair I appreciate, but because she was friendly enough to talk to me that day.

She talked about insects, which is probably as good a conversation topic as any.

And six weeks later, after the usual prolonged muck and thrust that signals the start of love, Sara and I shacked up in a duplex on the banks of Sawdust Lake.

Not long after that I dropped out of the state university at McCutcheon, where I had been a music major—a jazz trombonist, of all things—and I began my career as a Peterson Products wrench. See, Sara had some magic back then, something in the humpty-pump zone that could move me to forget everything I thought I was. I hadn't been a great trombone man anyway, so when I left school for love I didn't feel much of a loss, and as far I can recollect, after I moved in with Sara I never again picked up the trombone. But I felt then, and I feel now, that the nighttime company of a woman is worth any sacrifice. I am a fool for it, and I guess my life is the proof.

These days, though, now that Sara Weber is as gone from my life as happiness, I remember her as a dull woman, a woman-child I could make laugh by saying the word *radish* in a chipmunk voice or by lumbering around our duplex half with a chunk of raw cauliflower in my mouth. I remember if I would bring her a two-buck giant rubber grasshopper she would blush and coo as if I'd bought her a gross of white roses.

It didn't take but a few months in the factory—the long shifts and searing heat of close work with plastic machinery—and I knew goddam well life in industry wasn't for me. I got to that point where my days became ten hours of grease and sweat, five hours drinking, and the rest either sleeping or driving to work or to the bar. Even though I couldn't imagine at the time what else I might do with myself, I fell into a convictlike funk. I was looking at a life term at Peterson Products. What young trombone-playing fellow could be happy about that? What young trombone-playing fellow could figure life-time wrenching was his own fault? That factory was Sara's fault. I figured she had somehow yanked the horn from my hands and maneuvered me into time-card slavery, and for paybacks I sought out other women—women who had nothing to do with my ten-hour-shift life.

But when I look back at my McCutcheon years, which I seem to do all day, I can never precisely picture any event from back then. I wonder sometimes if I've forgotten everything that makes up my life, and I am left with a set of memories that I fabricate as I call them up; some things I make up to entertain Dewy Bishop; some things I make up to fill the empty spaces, when no one is around to listen to me lie. It sure would be easier if it wasn't me who lived those eight years in McCutcheon, sneaking down to the Liquid Forest Bar and concocting bullshit the next day about getting too drunk to make it home before morning; not me forget-ting to buy Christmas presents for Sara or insulting her family or the way she held her spoon at supper like it was a gravy ladle; not me, after eight years living out a shitty love in a shitty duplex, moving with Sara to a big farmhouse in the country outside McCutcheon, an eleven-acre spread full of scrub oak and deer; not me knocking up Sara one mid-March evening in that farmhouse, drunk and in a rare cheery mood, then shuttling her off one May morning to an abortion clinic in Minneapolis; not me, during that long drive home after the procedure, saying, "It'll be okay. I think it's time we finally get married," then setting the date for an August Saturday, and making up a guest list, and ordering the roasting hog for the reception. God, I wish it wasn't me then agreeing to let Margaret Hathaway—the single mother of a ten-year-old boy named Fred—who was my dope dealer, who was just accepted to graduate school in Ohio, have her college-graduation party at my farmhouse. That way, not three weeks after Sara's abortion, some other Gunnar Lund could have been the man, drunk and stoned with Margaret in my toolshed, who listened to her say, "Gunnar, I love you. Come to Ohio with me, and I'll make you happy."

Our lives are better remembered as lies.

Truth: Number Three is arriving now, a big dented bus with nobody riding in it. Number Three slows and opens its doors, and behind me is the orange hue of the project sky, a giant carnival of misery, and I've been there all day.

Truth: I'm a professional asshole made it safe through another stretch on the job. I can live through the hood another day. I know I can. I can do that.

3

Sundays I rest. Each week Winky allows his faithful one free hazeless Ohio day, which this one is—immaculate skies, the morning sun shining over the boulevard oaks and the falling leaves. Winky says, *On your day off, spend time with your family. Renew yourself for another strong week.* But here the relaxing account manager sits at the kitchen table that is not his, with the family that is not his, mother and ten-year-old boy, and Winky didn't pay for the Frosted Flakes the kid's spooning into himself. Margaret did. She bought the spoon, the cereal bowl, the place mat, everything in this apartment, the TV, the bed I defile her on.

Fred is a skinny kid who looks even skinnier in the XXL T-shirt of mine he's wearing. The shirt hangs on him like a smock. He is the son of Paul Hendricks, who once owned a vacationer's resort with Margaret, and who, six years ago, took a glass ashtray and beat Margaret upside the head with it, and that's what prompted their divorce. Margaret's had custody of Fred these last six years, a fact that she would have me believe has drained her ample pockets dry.

"Fred, you eat that cereal like you're loading a scow," Margaret says, and Fred's spoon hand gives off a nervous wiggle. Still, he eats, leaning over his bowl and looking down. Under his lips two drops of milk form into one, and he makes a rhythmic crunching sound like feet scuffling down a country road. Whenever I watch Fred do anything, I think of myself at ten years old, all the friends I had in my neighborhood, how after Sunday breakfast I could always find something fun to do, a kid to play catch with, maybe to ride bikes with. But Fred can't play with anybody, because he's stuck with his mother in an apartment fifteen blocks north of downtown Columbus, where there aren't any other kids around.

"You're disgracing yourself, eating like that," Margaret says.

"You keep eating, my good man," I tell him, "and you might grow the guts to do repos with me and the great Dewy Bishop." And I give him a fist tap on his ribs. He makes a pained smile at me, keeps spooning. If Margaret snaps at the boy, I know better than to speak, for he's not my son, and I don't have the right to interfere, but I most always do.

"Always undermining me," Margaret says, and

reaches for her cigarettes on the windowsill. "No wonder I can't control him."

"Looks to me the kid's controlling himself just fine,"
I say. He spoons.

Margaret says, "And how would you know that?
You're never here."

Her glasses are the schoolmarm standard, bulky rec-
tangles, brown and bifocal, plain glasses that constitute
the principal piece in her women's studies attire. She
wears an orange sleeveless T-shirt featuring a picture of
Nelson Mandela. Her arms are olive, beautiful arms,
hairless and smooth as a schoolgirl's. And she may hate
me just now, but I love her all the same.

She picks up her Zippo and ignites a cigarette, her
fingers slender and chewed at the nails, her wrists and
neck and head shaking the way a political criminal
under interrogation might, nervous and shifty, balking,
preparing to speak, balking and balking again, and she
chuffs smoke toward the ceiling.

She says, "You are a selfish man, Gunnar." She
draws again, blows smoke away from Fred and myself,
and she sits so I can see her in profile. She's developed a
hint of a double chin since we've come here, a bulging
crease her neck makes when she dips her head down,
but her face remains smooth, if a little paler than a few
months ago. When she twitches her head, her hair
flounces like a sock hitting the laundry bin. "I'm in a
bind here, Gunnar, and you don't even care."

"I care," I say. I picture Leslie Britton, the way she
ran from Dewy and me, sandals clicking across her

lawn. "You have to tell me what I should do."

"There's the thing: You should *know* what to do."

Whatever I do—I know this—it will be the wrong thing, but I have a solid idea what's eating Margaret. Her period is a week late, and she's been throwing up, crying over anything, losing her normal enthusiasm for baked chicken and cheese sandwiches and everything else she likes to eat. For several days now, she has tizzied, arms jerking about when she talks, always snapping whenever I'm at home, probably at Fred when I'm not here. She hasn't been sleeping nights, fitful once the lights go out, elbowing me in the ribs and demanding I snore on the couch. She is certain she is pregnant. But these last three months she's been late with her period, which I figure owes to her having a tough time adjusting to Ohio. When she gets used to this place, her bleeding zone will regain control of itself.

I say, "A little patience never hurt anything."

"You don't care what happens to anybody. Do you, Gunnar?"

I do and don't.

"It's Sunday," I say.

The world should be easy, not a bicker festival.

Fred lifts the bowl to his mouth, slurps the milk, and exhales. Like his mother he's olive-skinned, has a nose split into a bulb at the turned-up tip, and I do care that he's hearing this.

I say to Fred, "Maybe you can give your mother and me a moment to ourselves." He looks at me blankly. I am not the first man he's witnessed scrapping with his mom. Since Margaret divorced his dad, there have been four live-in men, all of whom Margaret drove into the shitcan.

Fred slides his chair back to stand, but Margaret grabs him by the shoulder with her cigarette hand and holds him down. Ash falls down into his lap.

"My child," Margaret says, "can hear anything I want him to."

Leslie Britton enters my mind again, that ragged and freckly way she has about her, the way she slammed her apartment door in Dewy's face. Even Leslie Britton I have to fight to get at.

What I want most from life right now is to do something I might have done back home. On a morning like this, if I weren't hungover or working at Peterson Products, I might have taken my bicycle for a ride out in the country, an hour sweating in the fresh day wind. I might have felt for a moment released, my soul made better from the road, my inner life built of my pumping legs and heavy lungs. I want that road feeling, the pebbles popping under my tires, that worryless mind feeling, maybe a spin through the skyscrapers fifteen blocks south of here.

"You know," I say, "the three of us could sure use some quiet time."

"You want to run and hide. Is that it?" She jacks her smoke back in her mouth and takes a mean drag, as if she's injecting the nicotine.

"If I took my bike out for an hour or something, maybe it would be good."

"What about me?" says Margaret, and she blows a cloud into my face, stinging my eyes some. "You'll leave me, your little pretend wife, home with one kid and knocked up with another."

Fred straightens in his chair, looks nervous, his head tilted toward his mother. Watching the kid watch us fight sends an electrical cringe through my upper body. I say, "Margaret, this isn't for public discussion."

"The fuck it isn't," she says, grabs Fred's hand and places it to her stomach. "Feel that?" His hand fixes there, doesn't move a titch. "You have a little brother or sister growing in there, and it's Gunnar's fault, because he's irresponsible."

"Fred," I say. "Your mom's not pregnant. She's not having a good day, is all."

"I'm not having a good life," she says, and pitches her cigarette over my head, and it lands in the sink, a sizzle sound, like a June bug held over a candle flame. Then she makes a kind of ghoulish moan, stands, yanks her T-shirt over her head, and pulls Fred by the scruff of his neck into her stomach. She mushes his nose into her navel.

"Please," I say.

Margaret's torso is bulged somewhat, a few jagged stretch marks visible near Fred's head, old marks she acquired carrying him.

"*Please* isn't good enough."

"Try to be calm," I say.

"I'm beyond *calm*," she says, and her voice is level and whispery.

Outlined in the window as she is, the shirtless view of Margaret is both delicate and terrifying, that sheen her skin has in the morning sun, the tender space between her bra cups, the shudder of rage building from her neck, and over the shoulders shaking, and the prominent veins twitching on the backs of her hands.

Fred's head begins shuddering, too, and he makes a flubbering crying sound into her stomach.

"Go ahead and bawl, Fred," Margaret says. "You have to learn right now how a pecker can ruin a woman."

"Let him go," I say, which is the first thing I can think of saying. "And put your goddam shirt back on." Just as I stand to free the boy, she releases him, and he bolts from the kitchen, his running feet rumbling the apartment walls.

"I can make my own decisions, thank you very much."

"You're not pregnant," I say. "It's nerves or something."

She folds her arms in the manner of Mussolini. "There's probably a fine reason for my nerves."

"Your period will come," I say. "It always does."

She says, "I hate men."

It always ends up with this. Her proof: I am the man who fucks her, whose mental life she believes revolves around a world outside her, those streets I drive, the back-home I always think of, and she's convinced the only reason I'm with her is because she'll give up her physical goods, which, of course, is close to the truth. Love, for me, is muck and thrust and late nights full of languish. But when I see her now, even at her craziest, I know there are times when we get along. She'll discuss with me the nature of her studies at the university, and I will nod and agree there should be equal roles between lovers, that I certainly won't objectify women, or anybody ever again, because she has shown me the beauty and the way. I am her parrot on these matters, and this calms her—some of the time. There is, she probably thinks, hope for improving me. For every woman's secret dream is to improve her man and make him respectable.

Margaret says, "My life would be better off if I never knew a man in the first place."

"It's true," I say. This is my lie to pacify. "You've had a rough go of it."

"You have no idea what *rough* is."

"Look, I'm just trying to help here."

"The best thing you could do is vanish, and I mean all the way back to the sperm that made you." And something goes funny-colored in her face, a redness first, then a grayness. She elbows me in the chest, rushes from the kitchen and into the bathroom, and she begins to retch with terrific volume. Puking for emphasis, I figure. Between horks, I hear her saying "Fuck" or "Shit."

On the wall next to the kitchen window is a framed eleven-by-fourteen group photograph of Margaret's family, taken seven years ago, during a reunion at their yacht club in the Bahamas. Ten of the Hathaways pose happily on a clean beach, three with champagne bottles in hand, and they all wear blue T-shirts with the words TRUE LOVE printed on them. Off on the right side, Margaret, tanned and drunk-looking without her glasses, is standing with Fred. I can barely recognize him that small. He looks like he could be any skinny brown-haired boy on vacation. Paul Hendricks stands there, too, all blond hair and smiles, probably thinking of the fortunes he will inherit someday. The principal Hathaway, George Hathaway himself, sits on the white sand in the middle of the group—bald, tiny, and sunburnt. At fifty-three years old, three years before this picture was taken, he retired from the paper business, selling his ten paper mills in Kaukauna, Wisconsin, for multiple millions my factory heart cannot imagine. Here George Hathaway is pictured with the fruit basket of his entrepreneurial life: an afternoon full of booze and sunshine, family at his side, his future a promise of boating and bliss.

Margaret blats into the toilet again, a trombony sound I hear through the apartment walls, and she flushes the toilet. Fred's bedroom door creaks slightly, which means he's watching the hallway through the door crack. Who knows what the boy's thinking? Me, I'm thinking escape. I've got a minute or two, I figure, while Margaret composes herself, to get myself out of here and pedaling to freedom. So I tread lightly into the bedroom and change into my bike shorts. It's work tugging these shorts on, tighter than I remember, way tighter: too much sitting in the rental van, too much driving around, too much hanging around the apartment and arguing.

After I'm suited up for the ride and heading back to the kitchen for a glass of water, I pass the bathroom door and hear Margaret say, "That's better now. That's all of it."

And I shuffle to the kitchen window—Margaret's window—and overlook the intersection of Neil and Hubbard, which is exactly one mile south of the Ohio State University grounds. Cars pass slowly by. Angled sunshine, a brilliant day—it's all that.

There are four apartments in this building, once a single-family home of someone with unthinkable money. It's a huge building, too, a blond brick Victorian with turrets and dormers the likes of which I'd never seen before moving here, and our apartment occupies half of the second and third stories. Most houses in this part of town look much like this building; that's how they get the neighborhood's name, Victorian Village. It's the rich-student ghetto. Graduate and medical students fill the buildings around us. Some of these folks— earnest J. Crew–dressed Ph.D. candidates in semantics or Native American literature—Margaret will recognize when they stroll down the sidewalk below this window. She will say, "Now that man is no Neanderthal." Or "She's a brilliant lesbian theorist."

As if there could be any other kind.

Behind me now: "Look at your fat ass in biking shorts. You'll up and leave, right? Typical."

And I rotate to the noise and see her eyes, brown and bloodshot looking pukesore behind her glasses, and she locks in on me. I'm pleased to note she's put her shirt back on. I hold her stare momentarily, then look back out the window, because the worst thing, I've been told, is to stare a biting dog in the eye.

The leaves on the streetside oaks are in full fall blaze, fireworks to the morning, and the Victorian houses seem frozen in the century of their construction, ornate and indestructible. If a buggy and Clydesdale would pass, they would not seem out of place.

"God, it's gorgeous out," I say. "Reminds me a lot of home," which this really doesn't.

"Why don't you just go there?" she says, and she thumps across the kitchen to give me a shove. "That's all you ever talk about. Fucking Wisconsin. I'm pregnant and your biggest worry is your long-lost drinking buddies."

"Look," I say. My voice is repo-solid. "You're stressed with your schoolwork."

"I'm stressed because I'm living with an asshole."

I can't hear Fred moving around in his bedroom or the sound of his TV. I know he's still listening to us, probably chewing his thumbnails in some knowing way. What I want is to maintain some decency here; the boy might think I'm a good man, no matter what sideshow his mother's putting on.

"If you can try to stay calm," I say, "I'm sure everything will be better."

"How can I be calm when I'm living with a self-centered son of a bitch?"

Sometimes I can understand why Paul Hendricks whacked her with that ashtray. But I don't want to hit her. I want to get the hell out of here.

"Let me take a spin through downtown," I say, "when there's not so much traffic. I'll only be an hour."

"That's fine for you, big man. You pick up and go whenever you want."

"I'll only be forty minutes. How's that?"

Who knows why I'm insisting on this? I guess it wouldn't matter if I went riding or not. I could as easily take the laundry and Fred to the laundromat, play video games and make fun of the prostitutes on High Street, as we do every Sunday morning. That would make Fred happy, and maybe Margaret happy, maybe even me. The laundry *would* get me out of here. Yet for a moment alone and quiet, that whole inner life of legs pumping and sweat and wind, I think, *Fuck it. I'm riding.* And I stride to the entryway, strap on my old yellow bike helmet, and start unlocking my mountain bike.

Before I make the move down the steps, right when I'm shouldering my bike for the descent, Margaret is on me, tugging at my shirtsleeve.

"I won't let you abandon me in the midst of this crisis," she shouts, and tries to pull me back into the apartment. "I'm not another Sara."

I flounder a second at the mention of Sara, how it's Margaret's doing that I left her, and I lose my balance and my grip on the bike. And the bike falls down the whole flight with a tremendous crash. At the bottom of the steps a pedal spins a few rotations, then becomes still, as if the bike's just breathed out its last.

My only thought is to see if the bike is damaged—no kidding, it's worth six hundred—and on reflex I begin down the staircase.

"I won't allow this," hollers Margaret.

I'm so much bigger than her that I drag her along without noticing her there, barely feeling her, until she pulls so hard on my T-shirt that the sleeve rips clean off, making a riffling sound, like cards shuffling. The gone sleeve releases the pressure between Margaret and me, and she falls backward, thuds hard on the steps, and screams. "You make my life miserable," she says when her screaming's done.

There she is: flush, angry, humiliated because she's fallen. But I don't get worked up or feel sorry for her. She wants to be crazy; she's going to have problems. But she's pathetic in a way, beaten-looking. Her hands are holding her forehead, her hair mussed, her shoulders slumped. We, who were not long ago smitten with each other's love, have arrived at this, brawling and destroying things on a Sunday morning. And while I stand over her I have that predictable spatting lover's flash, an instant motion-picture remembrance of our best times together. This woman on these steps is the same Margaret who I believe I love.

"Here, Margaret," I say. "I'll help you up." And I reach my hand down to her.

She keeps her head in her hands, shivering and making the snuffled noises of the first stage of bellowing.

"Go straight to your little hell," she mutters softly, so I'm not sure that's what she says.

"I'm there already," I say, take the last few steps down to my bike, upright it, and make my way out the door. But before I get fully outside, Margaret jumps on my back, and I fall out onto the porch, Margaret on top of me, flailing and biting like a wild chimpanzee. And in the moment I get my hands under me to push myself up, in the powder-keg space where I fight off the urge to flip Margaret off my back and slap the shit out of her, I see, not three feet in front of my head, splayed on the porch planking, two size-fourteen EEE basketball shoes.

And I hear this: "Looks like my guy Cheese having himself some fun with his Cheesette."

Margaret dismounts me quicker than I can get the full view of Dewy—black sweat suit, gold trim, thin superblack sunglasses—and she introduces herself in a voice so calm she sounds like she just finished a session with a masseuse. Their hands meet over me and shake a moment too long, I think, for introductions.

"The Cheese *will* talk about you sometimes," Dewy says.

Margaret's nostrils flare down at me. "I'll bet he does."

"When we working, you know," Dewy says, "we got to jaw about something." In his voice, which is his dumb black-guy voice right now, all a put-on for her sake, I can tell he's laughing inside.

Margaret says, "It certainly is a pleasure to meet you." And their hands still grip.

I let out a whiner's grunt when I sit up, and I say, "The way you guys shake hands, shit, looks like you're old pals."

"I wish we were," Margaret says, syrupy and full of suggestion. I stand up between them and brush the porch dust from my shirt. My bike lies on its side like a shot deer, but at a glance I don't notice anything ruined. No matter, though; the ride's off.

Dewy's sunglasses are so dark I can't get a fix on his eyes, can't watch him thinking, so I ask him the obvious: "What are you doing here, anyway?"

He says to Margaret, "I got the van here. If I could use the Cheese for a couple hours, we could clean up some business before the week starts." Then he gives Margaret a quick touch on the forearm. That smooth arm of hers, how can he touch her that way? "If it's okay I can have your man for a bit?"

A giant smile's overtaken Margaret, and it's the kind of too-friendly smile, ever-nodding and hiding the inner lie, that lets me know what's thrilling her right now is that she's face-to-face with a genuine member of the oppressed class. This, from nappy head to massive belly to basketball shoes, is a black man, and by God Margaret will treat him well. She strikes a kind of genuflecting pose, looks upward at him, and says, "Maybe if you have a minute before you go, you can come upstairs and meet my son."

Proof. I can't watch this.

Dewy's left shoe taps slowly and evenly. Beyond the shoe three cigarette butts rest in a neat line, probably butts Margaret left out here in the middle of the night. And beyond the porch cars begin the daily steady procession up and down Neil Avenue, churchgoers today, and the cars kick up clouds of fallen leaves.

Dewy says, "Me and your guy here should get to it, if we doing it. But I'd be glad to meet your son."

"Lovely," Margaret says, of all things, and she heads up the stairs, Dewy cludding in tow, and I pause to regard my bike, how it lies as an embarrassment in front of Dewy, how it proves to him I can't control my woman, and how it proves to me I never do anything I used to—no biking, no lounging in bars, nothing—and I don't want to drive around with Dewy and harass customers—I want to be alone—but going with Dewy is the only safe way I have right now to escape Margaret. The bike-seat cloth has acquired a small rip in the tumble down the stairs, and when I hoist the bike, I place my thumb to the rip, and I wonder if I'll ever get it fixed.

Inside the apartment this scene is in progress: Fred in front of Dewy, eyes turned upward and scanning and wide with astonishment; Dewy looking down at the boy, big teethy smile, genuine, sunglasses in his chalky hand; Margaret standing off a few feet, serious face and admiring the moment, which is admiring herself for providing Fred with a moment of true cultural diversity. As for Gunnar Lund in this scene, I am witnessing the frontwards and backwards of my life. And Dewy, bless him, is saying what a buddy should right now.

"Your man Cheese," Dewy says, and he pats Fred's goggle-eyed head, "is a repo champ. Maybe sometime we take you along with us."

Fred shyly meets Dewy's eyes and looks hopeful. "I'd like that," he says.

And Margaret is the last tie to my Wisconsin life. Her way of tilting her head in such a moment of first meeting, the way she stands with her legs wide apart, the slack way she mouths her cigarette—everything about her suggests Wisconsin, the small-tavern and pine-tree backyard life, which is a narrow and white life, and a life she's devoted her days to renouncing. She regards Dewy as she might an artifact, watching him leaning forward and kidding with her son, and she appears to be making mental notes to herself, smiling here and there as if everything Dewy says corresponds with something she might have read about black people in a textbook.

"Is there anything," Margaret says, and she leans over to Fred's ear, "you want to ask Mr. Bishop?"

Fred says, "I don't know." But he keeps staring at Dewy.

Dewy's ears twitch, and he stands upright, looks at me, at my bike shorts, and says, "Get out of your damn underwear, man. Let's go do this thing."

Margaret and Fred laugh a long and hearty laugh.

And I blush and head to the bedroom to change into my uniform, Margaret's laughter like grenades going off in the apartment walls.

4

The city is glass and sapphire towers, and I drive Dewy among them. Here is the YMCA, seven stories tall. Here is the Nationwide Building, thirty-eight stories, with a restaurant on the top floor called One Nation. Here is the Rhodes State Office Tower, forty-one stories, and a week ago I saw a helicopter take off from its roof. Dewy says the city has nested peregrine falcons at the peaks of these buildings, a new way to keep the pigeon population down. I see no pigeons now. Through these early-morning carless streets I coast the van, Dewy directing me down this street or that, and I remember summer Sundays, driving through the Wisconsin countryside, the roadside flowers looking like blotches of paint. I think how it would be now to have wildflowers below these mirrored buildings, and I can't form a clear picture. I am forgetting again who I am, am forgetting the flowers, the birch trees, the sumac thickets, all of it. What it is with me now is this Ohio road, these skyscrapers, this big black man next to me, whatever he tells me to do, wherever he'll tell me to go.

This is what Dewy says: "We fuck around for a while, keep you out the house, and maybe we run a surprise attack on Leslie Britton."

I say, "We're not supposed to run customers on Sunday."

"I don't give a fuck. Bored, my brother. We killing time, is what we doing."

"I wasn't exactly bored, Bud."

"You was. You just won't admit it."

"I wasn't mounting my old lady, if that's what you mean."

"Shit, I got my Johnson wore silly last night. That LaKenya, she's industrial hole."

"And your point is?"

"Bitch tired me fierce, Cheese. Get it? Needing to run with the fellas today."

He points this way or that, directs me in wide arcing patterns around the downtown area, and he hums and taps his meaty fingers on the dashboard. It strikes me that Dewy, like me, doesn't have any friends.

He says, "You living a fucked-up life, ain't you?"

"Who isn't?" I say.

"Looked like your woman was whooping you some, when I showed at your crib. Saved your ass just then, didn't I?"

I don't respond, a matter of keeping a little dignity. What kind of guy admits getting bullied by his old lady? I pull a cigarette from my coveralls and torch it up, the first cloud of smoke I blow all lackluster and sounding like a sigh.

"I know you happy we out here, Cheese. You can't be hiding that shit from me." He laughs deep and long. "I'm your motherfucking savior, is what I is."

"I don't know what I'd ever do without you, Bud," I say, and let out a fake chuckle to hide everything bottling up in me.

"What we need is supplies, my brother. You driving, I'm buying." And he instructs me to take High Street north out of downtown.

Past the Greek Orthodox church on High Street, Dewy has me stop at a Dairy Mart that overlooks I-70, which bisects the city. He tells me to wait in the van while he gets what he thinks we need. It's 9:35 A.M., and I-70 is the road to Wisconsin. My old life exists down that road. And whatever I do to remember my Wisconsin parts, whatever day I try to pick out and say *that was a pleasant day*, I end up thinking about Margaret, or what brought us here, or how it's possible she really *is* pregnant.

A few cars, some rusty, some clean, drive along I-70, heading west, and the lonesome part of Gunnar Lund imagines me in one of those cars, heading home. Seven hundred seventy miles in that direction would put me in McCutcheon, enjoying the Sunday Packer game drunk. Or I could be sitting in a tree in the forest, bow and arrow ready, waiting for a big buck to appear from the thicket. A road can get a fellow anywhere. I see other roads and me driving on them, the truck stops and chintzy billboards, and I recall the day this last May, sunny and warm, when I drove Sara to Minneapolis for her abortion.

I remember sitting in the waiting room of the abortion clinic while Sara was under the hose. Five men were there, all of us knowing somewhere beyond the flowery walls the end of something was taking place. None of us said anything. On my upper thigh that day I had a big welt, because I'd overfilled my Zippo before we left McCutcheon and Ronson fluid had eaten through my pants pocket and into my skin. I can't say now if I was sad, though I recall grinning from time to time. I was thinking all those years, and all that sneaking around and mucky-muck, I had been certain I shot blanks. The other fellows in the room grinned occasionally, too, or rubbed their foreheads, thinking, I'm sure, about lineage, afternoons walking their sturdy children through the woods, guns in hand, or playing catch on a Saturday afternoon: any of those last-minute possibilities that might occur to a man whose brief child is about to be destroyed, then forgotten.

In the middle of the waiting room was a small table that supported a fishbowl full of hard candy and a tiny pink box for donations, presumably coins for the candy. This was the only item in the room that held anyone's attention. From time to time I would see a fellow staring at the fishbowl, not with any sorrow, merely looking forward at something, a way to avoid looking at the receptionist or the other men. At some point, one of the men stood, a guy in jeans, an acetate tavern jacket and a feed cap. He moved slowly to the fishbowl, reached in, and took a piece of candy. After crinkling the wrapper, he turned to the rest of us in the room and said, "Shit, this is the fifth time I've been here. It's about time I get something for free."

Everyone laughed, and for an unusually long time. When he sat down, there was silence again. I thought how crazy it was, this fellow on his fifth trip to the procedure house and making wisecracks, and I thought, maybe with good reason, I was a better man than him, because I was only on my first visit. Knocking a woman up, the inevitable for us trailer-court-and-tavern trash in the Far North, I had avoided it until then, though not intentionally, and when I glanced at this guy, his mouth grinding away at the candy, his face not letting off the slightest concern, I decided that most of us never feel anything about anybody.

Later that day, driving back with Sara, who I remember being very talkative and relieved, I listened to a radio report about the schizophrenic homeless in New York City. There were stories—this man had been a plumber; this woman had run a beauty shop; this woman had sold advertising for a community newspaper—and there were short interviews with each of these unfortunate folks, where they talked about canned tuna, hot dogs, the joys of shelter soup and coffee. While I listened, Minneapolis becoming farther and farther behind us, I thought it was odd that these lunatics interested me more than what had just occurred to Sara, and to me. The sun shone over the highway. The cars glinted. The radio told me what I needed to know of the world and who lived in it.

It's happening to me again with Margaret. The three months her period was late before this I didn't feel it, didn't believe her lateness was anything but her brain sending her body the wrong cues. But I know it now—how the anger rises in her so quickly, how she's puking all the time—and I have made this mistake twice in one year. Everything Margaret's doing now is what Sara did six months ago. Pregnancy, from what I've seen of it, is always the same infection.

When Dewy opens the van door, it scares me, and I holler, "Ho! You can goddam have the TV back, for all I care."

"You a jumpy one, Cheese," he says.

"Spacing out, is all," I say.

"Spacing out's for biscuitheads." And he hands me a grocery bag that clinks when I grab hold of it. "Look at how I hooked us up."

Inside the bag are two forties of Red Bull, an extra-large bag of barbecued pork rinds, two White Owl cigars, and a box of ginger snaps.

Winky says, *Relax, renew*.

Dewy is regal. He says, "Drive, my prince. I'll divvy out the picnic goods."

I say, "You bet." And it's my thickest Wisconsin

voice, because the sight of beer right now somehow makes me happier than I could imagine. I got a decent pal in Dewy, sure enough.

North on High Street we go, slowing at stoplights, coasting block to block, and we pass the first forty of Red Bull between us. A road can get a fellow anywhere.

Here is the corner of Fifth and High, trash on the road and sidewalk, three white drunks sitting at the bus stop, ignoring each other, the strip-joint marquee above them still lit up this time of morning: SISTER WANDA AND HER WHOLLY E CUP REVIEW. I slow the van down at the intersection, swig deeply from the forty, and grab a handful of pork rinds. Here are the hot-dog stubs I see along the curb, and the empty Old English 800 bottles, the rumpled cigarette packs, the drifting front page of the *Weekly World News*. Near the drunks, five sparrows feast on a pile of last night's puke. As always, wind, light and warm, blows from the west, moving the debris. The asphalt seethes. North by ten blocks is Ohio State University, *where Margaret lives, where Margaret's walked with our unborn child*, and on this sloping long street I can see it down there, the college hospital, the upper floor of the law building. Down there is what Margaret tells me makes up the world.

I say, "My woman sure is fond of that university."

"That's what fucks her up, too," Dewy says. "Thing with her, I'm telling you, is she believes that shit they telling her. Look at the way she acts around me."

"Sucking up pretty bad, eh?"

"It's like here's the black guy in the house, and the woman acts like I got a deformity, being all extra-nice to me and shit."

"I'm sorry about that."

"Ain't nothing with you," Dewy says. "Your bitch just listens too much at school."

Dewy swigs again and orders me toward the hood. "We drive where we belong, Cheese. Two sharks in the hood, you and me."

I laugh out loud, because I would belong equally well on the moon.

East on Fifth the buildings fade to industrial lots. There's two huge lumber warehouses, some machine shops, a parking lot full of semi trailers, and everything along this street, even in the morning sun, looks gray and weather-beaten. Ivy grows up the barbed wire fences, but only in patches, and the vines are brown now in this shriveling month of October.

When Fifth Avenue becomes the hood it's easy to recognize. Here I-71 cuts north through Columbus, and on the far side of the overpass the hood begins: White Castle on one side of Fifth, McDonald's on the other. To the south of Fifth lies a neighborhood of tattered old whitefolk two-stories, a quiet neighborhood before the interstate was built, now a hood of its own. We have customers in that neighborhood: Eleanor Green, Callissa Smithers, Lewanda Jackson. And more. Tomorrow I'll be at their doors early, in my Crown Rental coveralls and a button-down shirt, alone or with Dewy, and I'll be leaving these women nastygrams, or taking their twenty bucks, letting them slide on their late fees.

At Cleveland Avenue and Fifth sits a Church's Fried Chicken that overlooks a railroad yard. Maybe at noon tomorrow Dewy and I will eat in the Church's parking lot, watching the boxcars and talking about jumping them. That's what Dewy and I do together; we slum, and watch the slum be a slum.

When I turn on Cleveland, Dewy eyeballs the buildings we pass, nodding and humpfing to himself. Between the two of us we've visited nearly each house up Cleveland to Crown Rental, even the fourplex brick buildings that appear on every other block, ratty and lined-up like old people on a nursing-home verandah. Thousands of dollars of Winky's cheap junk fills these homes, and I know none of it's owned, and nobody will keep up their payments. Here's something Winky doesn't say: *If it ain't broke, don't fix it.* But if he paid attention, he *would* say that. Or maybe he'd say it backward: *Don't fix it if it's broke.* A rental outfit in a hood like this will always thrive. The worse the hood, the better the pickings for Winky.

Dewy tells me to slow up when we near the store but don't stop. Two steel posters for Winky, the two other Crown Rental vans, sit in the middle of the parking lot, and parked in front of the vans is Dewy's copper 1978 Cadillac El Dorado.

"Look at my cruiser," Dewy says. "If we had any sense we'd hit Leslie Britton today with that. We'd be taking her down with class."

"I thought you only wanted to drive around. You don't really want to run Miss Britton, eh?"

Dewy mouths a pork rind, directs me northward with a tomahawk motion of his arm. "We got to. That's the surprise she needs. All Sunday-comfortable and shit, she'll never expect us."

"What is it with her, man? You looking to fuck her, or what?"

"If I wanted to give that bitch the opportunity, I'd have split open her shit weeks ago."

We observe an odd period of silence, pass Hudson and North Broadway, pass the strip malls that mark the slow change from the deepest hood to the white-trash quadrant of Leslie Britton.

"Don't you think," I say, "we could try being nice to her, and maybe if she softened up some we could snag her stuff then?"

"That bitch is never gonna be nice."

"Bitches never are," I say.

"There it is," Dewy says.

And I drive, a fine breeze rushing in through the open van windows, and I think of Leslie's eyes, something hidden in them that struck me as friendly, something on the edge of kind about them, which is the kindness I once thought I saw in Margaret, and in Sara, and in all of them. I wonder if it's men make women mean, or if women are just mean naturally.

Here's Leslie's street again, sunshiny and swept up, and all the whitefolk cars look safe and tidy. Her RX-7 sits directly in front of her apartment, and I pull the van to her car, park nose-to-nose with it. Dewy cracks open the second forty, swigs twice, exhales as if he's just used mouthwash, and hands the bottle to me.

"You sit tight," Dewy says. "When I give you the nod you start blowing the horn."

With a grunt he steps out of the van, walks, hitching up his sweatpants, to her car, and sets his rump down on her hood, sliding himself back into the center, so his legs dangle over the edge like he is a giant toddler in a high chair. He kicks and smiles, points to me to begin honking. I lay into the horn, making a car-accident sound, like the horn's stuck and the driver's unconscious, and I watch her apartment window. A few birds fly off her roof. The morning sun reflects perfectly off her upstairs window.

But nothing. No movement from her, and I quit honking.

I stick my head out of the van window and say, "This ain't budging her, Dewy."

He kicks his feet and rotates both arms in front of him. "Honk more," he says, and I do. Leslie's car hood sags underneath Dewy's weight, and I wonder if he's creating a permanent dent. There's something calming about letting the horn blast like this, a great releasing in me, a formless anger that has the effect on me of standing in a hayfield and howling. I honk and swig malt liquor, and a good part of my unhappiness fades away.

And when I see Dewy clapping with glee, I know we've gotten a rise from Miss Britton.

Sure enough, her upstairs window opens, and she sticks her head out into the morning air. I quit honking and hear this: "You shitass, get off my car." And the voice is twangy and all gravel. And the face is ivory and scowling in the sun. Her hair is raggedy and draping over a white muscle shirt. What a beautiful woman! How can we be fucking with her like this?

Dewy laughs and slaps his knees. "Give me back my TV, and I'll leave your car alone."

"I don't know what TV you're talking about," she says.

"Lie all you want, Miss Britton. You must wanna let your neighbors know you're a deadbeat and a thief?"

"Look who's talking about criminals?" she says. "Your lumpy ass should be in jail for what you do, harassing me like this."

"I'll send you to jail right now, Miss Britton. TV thief."

A strange look comes over Leslie, a dropping of her jaw and tilting her head upward, and she pulls her head back inside. Through her open window I can see the far wall of the room, and it appears to be covered with evenly spaced round objects, hunting trophies maybe; it's hard to tell. Now her head appears again, and she's grinning and holding a beer bottle.

"Mr. Shitass," she says, "you *will* get your butt off my car."

"TV or I'm sitting. That's it."

"Okay then," she says, and her head ducks in for a second, then she holds the bottle out the window, pointing it at Dewy, and I can't help imagining her hand around that bottle as if it were around my penis. Ah, the translucence! Now her other hand reaches to a point past the mouth of the bottle, and I see she's holding a cigarette lighter, and a stick protrudes from the bottle. Now a flash, and there's a loud whistling noise, a trail of smoke, and a sharp bang on the opposite side of the street. The smoke trail lingers a couple feet from Dewy's head. She's shooting bottle rockets at him.

"You crazy," Dewy shouts, and he bolts from the hood of her car, a heavy unbending sound from the metal as he does.

"You daggone bet I'm crazy," Leslie yells, and she aims the bottle and fires another rocket, this one whistling directly to her car, where it pops on the front fender in a flash of silvery light. "Dammit," she hollers.

"Can't aim worth a shit, can you?" Dewy barks back at her, and he runs behind the van and jumps in. "Cheese, bitch is fireworking me," he says, and he's laughing. "That's too good. She wins this round."

Another whistling sound now, and a bottle rocket flies right past the windshield, exploding on the curb across from us. Dewy chuckles some more, says, "Drive, my prince. She takes the championship."

And when I turn the ignition I look up at Leslie, who's all floppy hair and smiles, and she blows a kiss at me, yes, palms up and pursed lips, yes, and even from this distance I detect a hint of greenness in her eyes. I nod my head to her, the old Wisconsin hey sign, and I wink, ease the van into the street and drive off, passing the forty back and forth with Dewy and having a grand time.

Margaret's car is gone from its usual spot on the corner of Neil and Hubbard, and it's me who's forced her to drive somewhere Gunnar-free, but I don't care. I'll get my time alone now. I feel good, have a small beer buzz on, and my cheeks ache from yucking it up with Dewy. A gray Saab sits where Margaret's Taurus sat, surrounded by fallen leaves. My guess is she took Fred somewhere she can act happy with him, the mall maybe, or the arcade on Fishinger Road, somewhere she can pretend she didn't scream and puke and ruckus all morning. She'll cut loose for a while with Fred because he's her son and she loves him. It's hard not wondering if she loves me.

Dewy drives down the street, leaves everywhere descending around the van, and when he turns off Neil

I see him and Winky, smiling together and fading away. The day has become warm, haze returning with the heat. October should not be like this. The leaves should drift in crisp air. But for the moment I am pleased with Ohio. There's beer here, after all, and once in a while a few laughs.

I hum a little tune to myself when I ascend the stairs, "Turkey in the Straw," and jingle my keys in a happy rhythm. My mind is on the shower, with Margaret gone, that I can lengthen out for twenty minutes. She always gets on me for wasting water or electricity, for wasting in general. How's she going to time my shower now? But the apartment door opens for me and there she stands, my comely Margaret, flush in gym shorts and her Nelson Mandela shirt, her arms elegant and smooth as pewter.

"Feel better now?" Margaret says, smiling, looking at me in a forgotten way, as in our first weeks together, when our world was filled with hopes and longing glances.

"Yes," I say.

In his room Fred plays GI Joes. He makes shooting sounds, and he blubbers his lips to move vehicles. He calls out battle instructions and mumbles about bazookas and mortar placement. Plastic tumbles in there, a muted tinkling sound.

Margaret reaches her hand to me, laughs in her low mannish laugh, and says, "My period came."

I say, "Thank Christ." And I move in for a cautious hug, run my hand along her arm to her shoulder to her back, and we are the soul we once dreamt of. We are combined again. Her neck gives off a woodsy smell.

Abracadabra, alackazam: She shoves me away. "You've been drinking."

A magician of moods, my Margaret is.

She bounds to the kitchen for her cigarettes, her feet stamping, and I follow like I'm a bad dog, cower for her in front of the sink.

"I can't believe it. Back to your Sara tricks. And on Sunday morning, no less."

"Me and Dewy just had a couple. A social thing, that's all."

"That's rich," she says. "I'm home with Fred, and you're whooping it up."

"It's not like I was gone all day or anything."

I nod and watch the way her hands shake, how her body sways and bobbles, and I go on the alert for her taking a swipe at me.

"No responsible man would drink on a Sunday morning."

"You don't love me anymore. Do you?" I say this almost under my breath, surprised at myself for saying such a thing.

"I love you," she says, and takes a long drag off her cigarette, holds it in as she would a dope hit. She stares at the floor, her double-chin crease bulging. "I just don't like you."

"There it is," I say, and I throw up my hands.

A silence follows, our eyes not meeting. I am full of wondering. I remember a hundred moments with

Margaret: her getting undressed or holding my hand or resting her head on my lap. I expect she's wondering, too, though probably not about me naked or licking her neck or fiddling with her toes, but about obligation, how she brought me to the city to get me out of the factory. She thinks I owe her for that. Maybe I do. But whatever we're both wondering, I'm sure she has nailed down the truth about us, and who we are together. We don't like each other at all. When I think about her studies at the university, all that women's studies and Black literature shit, I think one word: *fraud*. A woman with a background like hers—country clubs and fat bank accounts and goddam family yacht clubs in the Bahamas—will never understand the hearts of the oppressed. And everything I do appalls her: how I hold my fork or watch football or read the sleazy personals in the *Columbus Dispatch*. Or my worst offense: my constant milk-and-honey world of remembering Wisconsin, the hunting stories, tavern stories, all of it. She believes I'm a slug leaving a trail on her life, proof of where she came from, something it exhausts her to change.

"I'm surprised you're home," I say. "You must have gone somewhere. Your car's not where it was."

She snaps alert now and grabs my arm in no mean way, a light squeeze, apparently forgetting she's hacked off at me.

Quickly, "What do you mean? I didn't go anyplace."

"Car's not there."

"That's great," she yells. "Just great."

She runs down the steps too fast for me to follow. I

stand at the head of the staircase and wait for her to return, which, in twenty seconds, she does, propelling herself like a B-movie monster, arms reached forward but the strides deliberate. She plods up the steps. She does not say a word, passes me, and I walk behind her to the bathroom, which she enters and shuts the door behind her. A silence, a ruffling around with toilet paper, a flush—she opens the door.

"Well, I'll just have to get another car," she says, and lingers before me, showing not one trace of emotion.

"Call the cops. They'll find the thing with a helicopter."

She remains solid, though at the mention of *cops* I can see in her eyes the inner rush of terror she wishes to hide from me. She always cringes when a squad parks in front of the apartment building, worries they're going to come and get her.

"Gunnar, I'm going to leave it go. That's final."

"They won't jail you because your car was stolen."

I extend my hand to place it on her shoulder to comfort her.

"Get off me," she says, and clunks to the kitchen, lights another cigarette. "First, I'll need a paper. Then I'll call Johanna and see if she knows anyone in the department who's selling a car."

"Let me go look for it," I say.

"I'll need to go to the bank tomorrow."

She continues to speak to herself, pacing the kitchen, fiddling with her cigarette. I light a smoke, too, and consider why I don't think she's behaving unusually.

The jerky movements, the bursting way she has of vacillating from one mood to another, I almost never find it strange. Since I've known her, that's how she's been. Before, I chalked it up to genius, her mind so brilliant that it can lickity-split from one subject to the next, from one emotion to the next, and her higgledy-piggledy mood shifts have been something I respect about her. But now she has had her car ripped off. That Taurus must be worth ten grand, a fortune even for her, and she's not thinking this out the right way. I make up my mind to shake her out of it.

"You are a Martian," is the first thing I say.

For a moment she freezes solid, heels snapping together. "I beg your pardon?"

"Try to be rational."

"What I want you to do is get out. Go to a bar again. Stay shitfaced the rest of your life. You will anyhow."

At this, I walk away.

In our bedroom I grab a clean pair of gym shorts and a T-shirt, head to the bathroom, close the door, and strip. Here's the naked Cheese in the mirror: six feet tall, pale and thick about the abdomen, the torso looking like raised bread dough. No woman would want to sleep with me now. It's amazing that Margaret will, rare as that bliss comes. It's amazing that anybody's pounded the bed boards with me, because I have always looked about like this. Maybe that's what keeps me with Margaret, because she's beautiful, and I'm a doughboy.

There will never be another like her, and if I leave her, and God knows I should, I'll never find another woman with the rock 'n' roll qualities of her, never the legs and olive arms and all those hidden delights. Before I turn on the shower, I hear her voice, rapid-fire and deep, talking to someone on the phone, and I wonder what's worth enduring in life, and what isn't.

For Fred's father, whatever grand things Margaret had to offer proved unendurable, and I say, *Good for him.* He owned a successful resort, earned something like seventy-five thousand dollars a year at the end. He had Margaret naked and supplicant on certain of her cheerier evening hours. He had a young son, whom Margaret named after Frederick the Great. An A-frame house in the woods, two four-wheel-drive vehicles, two fast snowmobiles, cross-country skis, a mechanical wood splitter—he had all the fine stuff people with money in the north woods could ever want. But he had Margaret, frenzied, tizzying Margaret, who had dropped out of college to run that resort, and who no doubt reminded him of that every time they battled. And one February evening, when they were drunk and bored by the endless subzero off-season, they had an argument about whether to vacation in Hawaii or Barbados, and Paul picked up the infamous glass ashtray and whacked Margaret upside the head. While she cried and bled on their fine home's strip-pine floor, he emptied a six-pack of Leinenkugel's Bock on her head. "A waste of good fucking beer" is what Margaret told me Paul said during their divorce trial.

So she's fucked up. I can understand that. We're all

fucked up, each in our own lovely and brutal way. In my happier moments here, alone and driving my repo van under the Ohio permahaze, I feel sorry for Margaret. This woman threw aside all the advantage of a college education and a future big inheritance to run a goddam resort in America's equivalent of Siberia. There's a heroism in that. And most days I see myself in something of the same situation, running here to Ohio to start a new life full of hope and love.

But having an ass-load of money never hurt Margaret. In the divorce decree, Margaret got everything: Fred, the house, the vehicles, and the woodsy finery. She sold what could be sold—the resort, too—amassed something like two hundred grand, and she returned to college, enrolled herself at the university in McCutcheon. She did well in school, of course, but was stoned all the time, had one live-in man, and another and another, and eventually a fellow named Don Morgan came along. Don was thirty-four years old, skinny and handsome, though his nose had been broken a few times. He was a student registered with the Wisconsin Department of Vocational Rehabilitation, and he hung around in the university smoking lounge, which is where he met Margaret, who must have appreciated his stories of living the tough life. One night he escorted Margaret to a Willie Nelson concert at the McCutcheon University Arena. Stoned and snorted-up after the show, "My Way" still ringing in their ears, they stood in the parking lot outside her apartment complex and negotiated the terms of love.

"I know people," Don must have told her, "who could make you rich."

Within weeks, Don moved in with Margaret and Fred. And with five grand of Margaret's money, Margaret and Don entered the McCutcheon dope trade, selling quarter pounds for a song, ounces for a fortune, the way all ingenious weed salesmen will.

It was this Margaret, girlfriend of Don and weed supplier to the regulars at the Liquid Forest Bar, that I first met. When I reconstruct how exactly I fell for Margaret, all I see are still-frame pictures: April, Margaret getting accepted to Ohio State one week, her smiling at the bar and telling people what a promising future she had. Then I see her face a week later, after she and Don got busted with an ounce of weed—fortunate for her, because she had a load more than that in her apartment. I remember now only that mournful look on her face, that open-mouthed waiting for the penitentiary. Then I see myself on my mountain bike, shuttling, pound by pound, her fifteen-pound stash from her apartment storage locker to my farmhouse. I see the shovel in my hands, the bags of dope disappearing in the dirt. I see Margaret's face at secret places we would meet then, looking at me as if I was saving her from the rock pile.

It doesn't matter anymore what brought us together—we're stuck here now— although these days I think she picked me for utilitarian reasons. Her being busted wasn't going to stop her from graduate school. A six-thousand-dollar retainer on McCutcheon's best drug lawyer assured that. She shitcanned Don Morgan, who she blamed for the arrest, and who, she found out at her arraignment, had one time taken a fellow who owed him coke money out to a barn at gunpoint, strung him up with clothesline, snipped off his hair, and smeared his body with cat shit. She did not want this kind of man near Fred, no less herself. The way I figure it, she knew her move to Columbus would be trying on her and Fred, and she didn't want to face the ordeal alone, without an adult to confide in. Since Don was out, since she knew I hated the factory, and she knew I cheated on Sara at will, Margaret probably decided it would be worth it for me to get out of McCutcheon. And she was right. I did want to leave. Too many years, I was thinking, too many ruts worth letting go. I had helped her, risked years in prison to move all that weed from her apartment. In her eyes it was a profound act of loyalty. If the cops had found that fifteen pounds instead of the minor-felony ounce they did bust her for, she would have been studying laundry carts and drill presses in Taycheedah Correctional instead of comfortably discussing women's issues in the classrooms of Ohio State.

Maybe I came to Ohio for adventure, simply taking what I figured to be my one chance to get out of Wisconsin and see the country, and whatever hardship I have to endure now is what I deserve for leaving home. But mostly what I remember is deciding how comfortable Margaret's hand felt within mine, or the way, like long-shelved novels, thumbed over years ago, our bodies fit together. My love for her, then as now as it probably always will be, had nothing at all to do with who she was, how her able mind worked, but with how she felt in my hands—slippery in the shower with me, or hard and immutable when I would kiss her, us pinned against her Ford Taurus, what remained of the Northern Lights fading into the Wisconsin summer sunrise. And when she told me she loved me that May afternoon in my toolshed, I realized I had lived out the last eight years of my life badly. I had constantly cheated on a woman who had loved me. I had treated Sara like shit. And there in my shed was Margaret—beautiful, brilliant, crazy in the most interesting ways—and without reflection I decided I could be faithful to her, could treat her decently. I would become a good man for her, however far away from home she would take me.

But I guess I'm not a good man. I am twenty-eight years old now, and I have the right to change my mind about love. I'm ready to move on. All day I knock on doors and talk to women, take money from them. Maybe one of those women, poor and worn-out on the streets of Columbus, is the woman for me. If Leslie Britton isn't the right one, surely I'll find another.

This Monday-morning drizzle falls on Columbus, and I am alone at 8:00 A.M., pounding on Leslie Britton's door. It's the coldest day I can remember here, fifty degrees. In the street, in the same place as yesterday, sits Leslie's RX-7. Leslie is home all right but refusing to answer the door. She must recognize me and maybe feels bad about blowing me a kiss yesterday. Could be she's pissed I'm back again, who knows? The cypress bush near her door is dripping, giving off a strong pine odor, that smell of open air and woods making me think about walking on such a day through the forest, shotgun in hand, waiting for a grouse to thrum up from under a spruce. The cedar chips along the building reek of mulch and worms and loam forming. I pound. Leslie does nothing.

I remove a nastygram pad from my repo bag, and I

draw a mustache and beard on Winky to help get Leslie's attention. While I write her a note, mist hits the pad, making the ink run.

Dear Ms. Britton:

You know, I don't like this job. It's the only one I can find here in this foul state. In my home state of Wisconsin, nobody has jobs like this, because nobody rents anything. Where you are from—not Columbus, I assume—people probably don't rent anything, either. I know you are a decent person, Leslie. I could tell when we talked the other day. These days, it's too hard to hang on in the city. We're all too broke here. That's why we have to rent. And I understand that you don't have the money to make your payment. I really do. Me, I'm late on my bills all the time. People like me call me at home and pester me. And I feel bad about it. And it makes me as angry as you probably are with me. I am not a mean person, Leslie. I am honest. Tomorrow, I will come back alone and knock, and I promise you I will not take the television. I just want to talk. Maybe, if we're lucky, we can get along. Do you think?

I believe I mean this.

A little sadly, because I know she is inside—freckled and gorgeous and refusing to speak to me—I wedge the nastygram in her doorjamb and walk slowly back to the van, wind and mist in my face. It will be winter soon. I can feel it.

The drizzle has become a steady rain, wind angling the falling sheets, and the Cleveland Avenue tarmac is a solid black, not its usual gray. Water makes the road look new. I'm driving south, bored and heading for the store to get another customer list from Steve Lawson. In the rain I cannot see police helicopters. People wearing no raincoats walk on the sidewalks, and they congregate at the bus stops as they would any day. On WVKO James Brown sings "Cut the Cake" and I tap my fingers on the steering wheel. The windshield wipers beat time with the rhythm section.

When I pull up to United Dairy Farmers on Cleveland and North Broadway, I see Dewy's van and park alongside it, letting our side-panel Winkys get a good look at each other.

Inside the store, Dewy schmoozes with the big cash-register woman: "You think I can't, girl? I make barbecue chops that make you praise God I'm a cook." He talks with his mouth wide open, showing his perfect teeth.

"I've had this man's chops," I say, bumping Dewy. "He's an ace in the kitchen, for sure."

"What up, Cheese?" Happy to see me, all smiles, Dewy winks.

I leave him with the cashier and fix myself a Bhagwan, adding powdered creamer today, making it rich. When I pay, Dewy says to the woman, "You make sure to stop in the store now." She grins and brushes him away with a hand waving like she's directing a marching band.

Without speaking we walk out into the rain and climb into my van, Dewy taking the king seat.

Dewy says, "You look like shit, Cheese."

I check myself in the rearview mirror and notice he's right: big bags under my eyes, like I've been punched. "Fucked-up times after you left yesterday, man. The way life is with Margaret, I'd almost rather be at work all the time."

"My guy Cheese is falling apart," Dewy says.

I tell him the whole story, Margaret's car getting stolen, her period finally coming, how pissed she was I came home with beer on my breath, everything. I'm not ashamed of the frenzy that is my home life, at least not around Dewy, who finds it humorous. When I reach certain parts of the story, Dewy laughs and says, "She dogging you. She really dogging you."

He slaps me roughly on my shoulder, surprising me a bit, and says, "Drive, my prince."

"What about your van?"

"You think someone gonna steal that piece of tin with Winky all over it? Nobody would be that stupid. Might as well stand in front of the motherfucking cops and pull out a gun. Everybody knows whose van that is."

So I drive the way Dewy points me, south to Hudson and Cleveland, where Dewy says, "Stop here."

I ease in along the curb, rain falling steadily on the van top and making a noise like distant drummers, and when the van stops Dewy does not move. He looks out his window, shaking his head. We've parked in front of a barbershop full of old black men reading newspapers and talking.

"How much money you got?" he says.

"Three bucks," I say, which is the truth.

"Well, it'll be my treat then."

He inspects his palms for a moment, wiggling his fingers. Then he claps his hands, points south and says, "Take us to the Green Tavern, Cheese."

What I'm thinking here is Dewy's going to get us some dope, because he's talked sometimes about the superior quality of urban weed. I've always told him that if the time came I'd be glad to burn a joint with him. Since coming to Columbus, what with Margaret on piss-test probation, I've been dry. And the thought of a thick doobie right now seems comforting, a way to shit-can the dirge and constant looking back that has become my life. While I drive the eight blocks to the Green Tavern, pictures of thick buds go through my mind, tight and resinous. If I had dope, I could cope with anything. Imagine seeing Margaret if I had a buzz on. She would be entertaining, much more than television. Each repo stop would be a comedy. Stoned, I would be languid and fearless at the customer's door. There is a reason for dope in the world, and right now I am it.

At the Green Tavern I stop along the curb, open my door to go with Dewy.

"Stay," he says and clears his throat. "Give me five minutes."

The universe of dope is constant everywhere. I have played this scene in Wisconsin a hundred times: The buddy goes in, takes too long, probably has a beer inside, throws darts, bullshits with whoever is peddling the stuff. So if Dewy's long in there, I won't be irritated, because in the end he'll come out holding. I believe this. And I'm paid by the week. Cars pass the tavern, which, as its name implies, is a shade of lime green. The building is one story and square. Next to the tavern is a beauty parlor full of women, who stand in the window and smoke and slap their knees. Rain falls. The van roof pings evenly.

Then the tavern door opens and Dewy appears with two black women, both short with short angular and greased-down hair. The three run to the van, and Dewy lets the women in through the cargo door. I smell the women, a mix of cigarettes and incense and hard liquor. I am smiling, figuring on that first taste of dope, and the women freeze and gawk at me.

"Cheese, this is Kaylee and Chareesa." Chareesa is the larger of the two, has a broad flat nose and a smooth face, wide and dark, which is crumpled up and frowning at me. Her fingers are long and rough-looking with each fake nail painted a different color.

With my dialect intentionally thick, I say, "Pleased as hell to meet you."

"You didn't say nothing about a white man," says Kaylee.

Dewy laughs a laugh I've never heard from him before, what I suppose is an inside black social laugh, and he says, "The Cheese is cool. My guy here is from Wisconsin."

Kaylee is thin, tiny-wristed and bony all over. Her skin is oddly light, her face sad and narrow. She wears huge silver hoop earrings.

"I won't do him," she says, and doesn't look at me.

"I see," Dewy says. "We may need a little negotiating money."

Chareesa says, "Say something else, Mr. Wisconsin Cheese."

"What do you want me to say?" I keep my voice backwoods thick.

"Whatever you want."

"I wish a guy knew what the fuck's going on here," I blurt out, staccato with the consonants.

Chareesa lets off a low belly laugh, reaches to my arm and lightly touches me. Her skin is much softer than it appears. "I'll take him. He talks cute. But it'll be ten extra bucks. Just on the principle of the thing."

"How you gonna play me?" Dewy says in a light-hearted way. "Cheese, you owe me. Next time, you paying."

And I nod, slowly understanding what's about to happen. Dewy reaches into his wallet, produces twenty bucks for Kaylee, thirty for Chareesa, then motions to Kaylee, and he leaves the van with her. I watch them walking swiftly around the corner of the tavern, and I continue staring in that direction after they've disappeared.

"Well," says Chareesa, startling me. "Let's get to it."

In her eyes I see something friendly and at the same time remote, a liquid brownness. She smiles, gestures me toward her with her index finger, on which her nail is painted green. I feel suddenly awkward, as on a first date.

"Who are you?" I say.

"You'll know better soon," she says, and pulls me by the hand to the back of the van and lays me down on some blankets we use to wrap furniture. Winky says, *Never deliver scratched merchandise.* Gently and expertly, she unzips my coveralls, pulls them down to my knees and does the same, so fluidly, with my jockey shorts. I shudder with nerves I've forgotten I have.

"Lord," she says, and laughs deep and low again. "You got red hair."

"Yes." This is all I can say.

"I never stop being amazed," she says, and grips my hand.

"Me neither." She begins her business, her mouth on me and moving, and my mind momentarily remembers Margaret saying the same thing to me once, a joke about my hidden hair, and I remember hearing it from other women, too. I am a freak. But I do not look down. On the van ceiling I see some dents, ticks in the paint. The rain is a drumroll. My eyes shut now, and my inner constant movie shows me only flowing colors, greens and purples. I can smell her, something spicy and store-bought, the wildwood cherry incense odor of houses in the hood. Everything is motion and water falling, and her hair in my hands is bristle wire. I feel liquid, and I am finding a woman named Chareesa, whose name is a smile to say, whose skin and mouth are these new raining days of winter coming on and the death of Wisconsin in me and the end of a woman named Margaret, who I am supposed to love but never will. And I let it all go.

Chareesa rises from me, wiping her mouth. "Well, this much is the truth: It tastes the same, black or white."

I wag my head, reach out for her hand.

"That's all you get, Mr. Wisconsin Cheese," she says, and will not take my hand. "But next time I'll give you the regular price."

In an instant then, she opens the cargo door and disappears, the door slamming shut behind her. All is calm, silent without silence. I pull up my shorts and my coveralls, return to the driver's seat, and light up a cigarette. *Dewy*, I am thinking, *I am alive now. You have delivered me.*

And I wait for him, whatever bothered me about the universe erased, no thoughts of home or of Margaret or of anything. I watch the rain hitting the asphalt, little splashes like bombs hitting the earth.

Through the storefront glass, I watch the rain becoming mist again, the afternoon sky lightening some. A breeze fans the parking-lot puddles. On cars, drops of water collect, gray jewels, and people stand in the lot, and they look at the sky, pointing to it. Me, I clean fingerprints off the door glass with Windex and paper towels, doing a half-assed job, wiping back and forth with no pressure. I don't give a shit how the glass looks. Suckers will rent if the windows were made of brick.

In my mind-movie, I keep trying to re-create this morning and the van and Chareesa and the rain. However hard I concentrate on her, I forget exactly how she looked, the way her head moved when she talked, the precise way she held me in her mouth. When a woman walks past the window, and it's always a black woman here, I look her over carefully—see the thickness about the face, the chalky hands, the multicolored fingernail polish, the skin that looks rough to me but that I now know isn't—and I get the urge to walk outside and ask for a date. I'm seeing myself sleeping with women from all corners of the planet, and I believe each woman would be better than the one before. All I need is a good buddy with a wad of bills and the charity to fork out ten extra for the white guy. I repicture Margaret, too, doing everything from holding my penis to throwing a sugar bowl at me, and I wonder why it is that I love her, when I could love any woman in more or less that same way, which is touch sometimes and holler most times. We fall in love to have someone to hate. I wipe at the glass, occasionally spritzing more Windex on it. I try remembering every woman I've known, ever talked to. I try deciding why I didn't end up with any of them instead of Margaret.

The store is tomblike today: late in the month and customers won't come in unless we've harangued them into paying up. Steve Lawson sits in an easy chair in front of the TV wall, watching fifteen screens full of *Days of Our Lives*. He holds a cordless rental phone in his lap. In the back room Dewy calls cards, as we say, which means he's phoning delinquents and telling them they'd better stop in the store with a payment. Once in a while he raises his voice, says, "Don't play me like that, Miss Green." Or "You just can't keep this shit without paying. I didn't say we *giving* you the stereo." His voice always has a joking quality to it, a lilt that comes from grinning and speaking, which is how Dewy talks when he's got a customer cornered and he thinks he will win the collection war. On Mondays Dewy makes many such calls, because most Crown Rental accounts are due Friday. Usually, 20 percent of the customers don't make their payment on time. By week's end, the company rules read, only 2.5 percent of the customers are allowed past due from the previous week. This percentage is known as card close. Rural Crown Rentals, in Ohio towns like Springfield or Chillicothe or Newark, close at 2.5 percent every week. The best this store's ever done is 5.3 percent, long before I got here. In training, where I had to memorize this stuff, I had to sign a contract, promising I'd bring card close down. Not to worry; this store loses no money. On a slow day, we sometimes take in four grand. On the first of the month, when the welfare checks come out, we might take in twelve grand. Winky says, *I always smile when a new month begins.*

"Lund," Steve Lawson shouts. "You have a phone call. It's your woman."

Just like that, I begin to shake, figuring Margaret has somehow discovered what I did this morning with Chareesa. My arms and hands, I notice, have Chareesa's faint scent on them, that cherry smell. And I can only imagine the smells I carry on my lower, happier parts: lipstick, booze, cigarettes. Really, Margaret couldn't know about Chareesa, but if I say anything unusual, or pick the wrong tone of voice, she'll catch me. That's Margaret for you, always suspecting something. So my mind switches into the fibbing mode I used back in my days of regular cheating on Sara. Whatever Margaret will accuse me of doing, I'll either deny it or redirect. Trouble is, Sara wasn't as quick on the uptake as Margaret. I will keep Margaret talking about herself, what she does best.

Dewy sits at the back-room desk, thumbing through the past-due customer list, grinning and wobbling his head. He's not on the phone.

I say, "Take a break, Dew?"

"You look like one guilty motherfucker, Cheese." He stands, bows, and sweeps his hands toward the phone. "Don't let her dog you out." Then he saunters out to the display floor, humming to himself.

I sit cautiously down, certain I'm going to catch a load of manure, and light a cigarette as if before my execution.

"Would you like me to pick you up at work tonight?" Margaret's voice is cheery for some reason, softer than usual. I rub my hand through my hair, over my forehead and face, trying to maintain calm.

I say, "Did you find your car?"

"I picked one up," she says. "Someone in women's studies was selling a Volvo. One look at it, and I decided it was the car for me. It's green."

I accidentally do the best possible thing here, which is to let out a protracted sigh.

"Yes," Margaret says. "Thank God."

We discuss for a while the purchase, something like a lend-lease deal she worked: two thousand up front and monthly payments. "That way," she says, "my dear Gunnar Lund can contribute to the car and perhaps drive it to work off and on. You can reimburse me for the down payment when you're in better circumstances."

On the desk Dewy has written 1-800-FUCK-YOU, and I focus on that, his letters neatly drawn, rather than Margaret's low and weirdly pleasant voice.

"It will make things so much simpler," she says, "if we can own a car together."

"You're right," I say. "You're right."

For another minute we talk—me in a nervous way and hiding it—about what time she should come. I have to give her directions to Crown Rental, because she has no idea where it is. When I'm explaining the way here, I smell Chareesa faintly rising up from my crotch.

The moon pokes through the scattering clouds, and I drive north three miles to BancOhio on Cleveland Avenue. The asphalt is an early-night dull blue. A thick and lumpy object is wedged under my rump, making me shift my weight around in the driver's seat. This object is a red zippered bag that now holds $3,752.24 in cash. This much, stacked in one spot, feels like a split log of knotty pine. Winky says, *Sorry, I cannot honor your check.* Every night I make the bank drop, and every night I want to throw the bag out the van window, because sitting on it hurts, and Dewy once told me I had to sit on the bag. I do what Dewy says.

It is 7:45 P.M., and the streets are, by this road's standards, quiet, only a few cars flowing along the asphalt river, only an intermittent soul standing at a street corner. The hood always quiets down after nightfall. Even the Green Tavern looks dead. A guess: Chareesa probably isn't in there now. Dewy once told me that black folks at 7:45 are just getting ready to start the night, that the hood runs on BT—black time—which means the party starts a little later and goes a little longer. From what I can see in the darkness, the other vehicles moving around me carry white people following Cleveland Avenue to downtown or to the university or north with me toward Westerville. Headlights shine and slow down and move forward, and the white drivers look straight ahead. I know they just want to make it through the hood alive. All day I feel much the same way.

With each shift of my bottom, each stupid contortion to make myself comfortable driving, I say, "$3,752.24, I could buy myself out of a world of shit with that kind of money." Every night I say this over and over, changing the amount to match the daily bag, like a rosary. I have nothing, really, of my own, no bank account, no checks to write, no car, no coffeepot, no decent clothes. I own the same ten pair of underwear I had when I was eighteen. The same goes with pants and shoes and socks. When I wear out a pair of shitkickers or jeans, I scrape up enough to buy another. But Margaret's got a closet full of shoes. For her whole life she has been able to produce $3,752.24 with a goddam blink. Hell, when she got busted she dropped six grand on her lawyer within the hour she got handcuffed. She dropped two grand on a new car just today. And if she didn't have the hard cash, I'll bet anyone would lend it to her. Someday, when her dad croaks, she'll be worth two million, maybe three, and when she gets that mother lode, if I can make it with her that long, I'll probably still be stuck working a job like this. The money, she always reminds me, will always be hers and hers alone. She says I should find my own way to make a pile: start my own business, like her father did, or I could go to tech school and learn a *real* trade that *really* pays. At times she talks about traveling to Europe—as all college students I've ever known do—and she describes her trips with the dead certainty that she'll go alone. *When I go to London. When I visit the ruins of Athens. When I walk the remote roads of the Pyrenees.* If I ask her why she wants to go without me, she'll say a woman needs time alone, or that I want to be with her to exert control over her. "It's because I love you," I might say, concerning tagging along. "Then let me do what I want," is what she'll respond.

Right now, if I had, say, $3,752.24, I could take a vacation of my own, not to Europe or someplace warm and dry, but I might go back home for deer hunting. With that money I could buy me a new Remington, some new blaze-orange hunting togs, and I could sit among the trees in style. I could walk into the tavern and drink top shelf. I could do whatever I wanted, and I know it wouldn't last, but having the money to spend, if only for that little while, would tide me. And I could go back to my regular life again, knowing, for one small moment, I was rich.

In the BancOhio parking lot are four cars, all newer models, Japanese-looking, and next to the business depository chute three white men stand in front of the instant-cash machine. The men glance about skittishly, shuffling their feet, making sure (I can tell by the way they stare at me and the van) I'm white, too. Like every day, I look beyond the parking lot for thieving types, even though I know if they are there, I'd be dead meat before I could see them coming. Across the street is a small plaza—another Arab-run grocery, a bottle shop, a tiny pizza place—and a few black folks mill around in its parking lot. I watch the glow of lit cigarettes moving in circles or sudden lines.

Like every day, I calculate my walk, seventy-five steps, and I tuck the bank bag in my coveralls. When I close the van door, I breathe deeply, the air tasting of today's rain and the promise of Ohio winter. I stare at the ground and walk tall and in an indifferent way, whistling to myself.

What if some gun-toters want the bag? They can have it. Crown Rental can afford the loss. I figure how easy it would be, if nobody was around, to ditch the bag somewhere and say I was mugged. Just like that, I could have all that cash. Nobody would figure it out. A white guy gets hit up with a bank bag, an easy story, and I could inject a bit more money into everything I do. When Margaret would bitch about money, hell, I'd have some tucked away. A little dough here and there, I could milk all this money out for months. Or I could make my way home to Wisconsin, buy all my buddies drinks and be the king for a week or two.

A man in the line, a short balding guy with a button-down shirt and a big dark tie, says, "Hello." And I hear the West Virginia in his voice, the music of Leslie Britton. I glance up and nod, not recognizing him, not seeing anything like Leslie in his face. When I pass him, I smell peanut butter.

With the Crown Rental bank key, the only Crown Rental item that does not feature a picture of Winky, I open the deposit door and vaguely hold the bag halfway in the slot, knowing again I'm letting all that money go, which I do, loosening my grip on the bag. It slides down a metal chute without making a noise. We give away fortunes that easily.

South again, the night bluish white and darkening, I drive toward the store. The streetlights illuminate the road poorly, as always, and the side streets off Cleveland are so dark they seem not to exist at all. Here and there people walk, girls, women, old men. I look at them closely, gesturing with their hands as they do, seeing if one of the women might be Chareesa. I start thinking about this whole hood-world, what people I know now, what I do each day here. I begin to wonder about love and me falling in it. If I loved Margaret, which most of the time I believe I do, I surely wouldn't have let Dewy buy me Chareesa this morning. Even more, I keep trying to re-create her, the look of her eyes, the feel of her skin and mouth, the sound of her voice. And I believe I now love her, whoever she is. She is Chareesa. She is Leslie Britton, her freckled legs. She is Margaret and Dorothea Dixon and Sara Weber and every woman I've ever loved, and I will always be unfaithful to all of them.

7

I believe I am a green man, coveralls hiding my greenness. People are watching me driving a van down a street, clean yards and trimmed hedges of lilac. This is Wisconsin again, yard-ornamented and in mid-May bloom. I'm not sure who I'm supposed to see. On the dashboard I have taped a list of people, friends, all of them, some bar buddies, some women I've slept with: John Aubart, Mark Jorgeson, Eileen Olson, Stacey Jenkins, and on and on, and I drive. Green men get paid to keep moving. Here is the house, brick and tall, two cypress trees astride its porch, and I'm slowing the van down but not stopping, not picking this house to knock. Here is the house, square lumberjack house, plastic pinwheel flowers set up in rows all over the yard. Here is the crumbling curb where I stand. I have green hands. I see my reflection in the van window, my face bearded still, skin tinted under yellow hair, and it is spring, and I am a Martian. Noise from the other houses, one by one the front doors open. People emerge, appear from garages, sheds, from Airstream trailers parked on cinder blocks. All these people are white, and I can tell they watch my hands and face. No one looks into my eyes. They make no mouth sounds but breathing, but smacking of lips. Sara stands among them and looks at me without recognizing me. They circle me, maybe fifty people. I know them. Even Old Man Peterson, president of Peterson Products, my boss for eight years, stands in the circle, holding a green infant. No one points. No one turns away from me. I have green hands. Beyond the circle, Winky watches me, both eyes open, the line of his smile splitting to show perfect white teeth. I say, "You do remember me. You really do remember me."

The light in our bedroom is pale, only a streetlight shining through the window, and Margaret, head in her hands, sits at the foot of the bed. Her back is bare, and I notice its luster, gray as it is in the dimness. At the base of her spine is the darkened splotch of bruise that I assume she received when we battled on the stairs Sunday. I blink several times, forcing myself awake again. She's awakened me several times already this night. My lids keep sagging shut, but I know I must stay conscious and listen. See, her period, which began Sunday, stopped yesterday morning, when it should not have stopped. She didn't even bleed, she's been saying, for a full twenty-four hours. In fact, her bleeding might not have been bleeding at all, merely a discharge associated with being pregnant. Or maybe it could be stress, she's been saying, that's stopped her up. Or it could be the car getting stolen. It could be that her daddy called her tonight at nine forty-five. He bought her that Taurus for her college graduation. What would he say if he saw her in a Volvo? Since the call, she's been talking of killing herself.

"I can't take collapsing any further," she says, her voice fainter than I've ever heard. "I can't tell him *why* I just bought another car."

I slowly prop myself up with a pillow, squinting and fingering the sleep from my eyes. "Maybe we can make up some bullshit."

"Goddammit, no—he'd know right away." She snaps to her feet and faces me, naked. She's gained some weight these last few weeks, stomach slouching out a bit. Her breasts do seem to have swelled up larger than they were, and I stare at them in the scant light. *The body that got me into this shit*, is what I'm thinking, nothing more.

"Jesus," she dully sighs, and sits down again with her back to me. "No matter what, you'll always think about fucking me."

"I wasn't," I say.

"It doesn't matter really. I have to fix this some way. What you're thinking has no effect." This dog we have walked between us a thousand times tonight.

The clock face now reads 5:37 A.M., a few minutes before my regular alarm time. I finger the switch and disengage the coming buzzer, concocting something Margaret might want me to say.

"What would you like me to do?" This is my best shot, too tired for anything better.

She turns to me, and I make goddam sure to look her solidly in the eye, no body glances. "What are your plans," she says, quite gravely, "if I'm pregnant?"

I merely breathe in long and slowly and try to exhale so she can hear something like acknowledgment of the issue.

"So you want me to keep it?"

"I think you should see a doctor and make certain you're pregnant first."

"The one kid I've got's hard enough on me. And where are you coming up with the money to support a new baby? Kids aren't cheap, thank you very much."

"You're not listening."

"I spend my whole life getting slapped around by circumstance."

"Everything will work out in one way or another."

"I'm going to be forced into taking action. I know it," she says, looks at me, into my eyes, but I feel she's not seeing me at all. Her head and arms quake.

I rise from the bed, open a dresser drawer, fumble out a pair of jockey shorts. My eyes feel scratchy, and my fingers are sluggish.

"I wouldn't be suffering like this if I was dead," she says. "Would I?"

Be goofy crosses my mind, and I remove a sock from the drawer, stuff it in my mouth, shake my head and growl like a dog. This trick used to work in my days with Sara. Always those mornings when Sara was angry with my drinking too much—or never coming home for dinner, never wanting to do anything with her—something stupid snapped Sara into a good mood. I prance clumsily to Margaret, continuing my growl.

"Fuck you," she bellows, and rips the sock from my mouth, giving me a sharp pain in my lower teeth, a sudden sting and ache like I've just gotten punched, which she then does. She slugs me square on my lower chin, straightening me, and I stumble a bit backward, hand to my mouth. In front of me now, she pushes me as hard as she can, and I don't move backward. She begins flailing at me, slaps my arms and ears, and her blows come with surprising speed, though they don't hurt much. I merely cover up and take it, not moving a bit while her arms perform the windmill of smacking me. With each strike I can feel her soft skin, or I look down at her sex, or her lovely legs, or her small feet grinding into the carpet. When she tires, the blows softening some, I watch her right leg drawing back to kick me in the nuts, the leg moving upward toward me. In one sudden flash, I grab the rising leg near the ankle, step back and lift up, sending her flying to the bed, where she lands with a great thump.

Without pause, she sits up, positions herself at the end of the bed, and speaks to me flatly, as if no struggle has taken place.

"I would advise against laying a hand on me," she says.

"I'm getting that impression," I say.

Still, I find Margaret as beautiful as any woman I've known, that elegance she has in her arms and fingers, her gestures graceful even in rage.

"You probably wish I was dead." She theatrically throws her hands up, falls backward onto the bed, turns her head to one side, lets out a tremendous exhale, the death gasp, and becomes perfectly still. In earlier months, well, this would have been my cue to mount her, and whirling picture-memories of me doing just that pop up in my mind. Her legs splayed like they are, summer returns in my head, the whole dope and bourbon mix of it, sweating and being in love: everything there has been between us that is fading or was never there.

"Margaret," I say, my voice a murmur. "I want you to live. Somehow, things will get better."

"They will," she says. "I'll make everybody happy."

The Columbus haze hangs in the Tuesday sky, one more day driving, house stop after house stop, asphalt passing underneath the van like a rug pulled from below my feet. The dashboard clock reads 9:37, and I have been having a first-rate Crown Rental morning. Already I've repoed two televisions and a microwave. They sit wrapped in blankets in the back of the van, trinkets from street battle. In my pocket I hold nearly four hundred dollars, money from payments I've taken this morning. Even without Dewy I'm invincible at the customer's door today. He will be proud of me, no doubt. This is the best series of stops I've had since I've worked here. And, success that I've been, it won't matter if I cut Leslie some slack, which is why I've driven to see her, because I want more from her than her TV.

Leslie Britton's RX-7 is clean inside, no fast-food bags strewn about, no dirt on the floor mats. A set of miniature metal bells hangs from the rearview mirror. I don't know why I'm looking into her car. For certain she senses me outside, knows that the grim repo conversation between us is about to take place. I picture her watching me through a crack in her venetian blinds, anger rising in her, or maybe she will believe what I wrote to her yesterday, that she's safe with me, and I merely have driven out here to North Columbus to chat. But if I stand here a while, and she watches me, she might trust at least that I've come without Dewy Bishop. He never waits this long to enter the repo fray. In front of her door, sparrows peck at the ground. The air feels cool. I have had a good day in the field so far.

As I stride to her door and the sparrows scatter, I have memories of my first high school date, which amounted to walking a homely girl named Wendy Oberton to the Friday-night basketball game. I recall what it was then, the surging of nerves, the inner twinge of knowing what to say and in what order, the hope of holding her hand, and I feel it all now, as yesterday with Chareesa. I convince myself I've been cloddish with women over the years. I should have no nerves. Surely on that first date, now nearly fifteen years ago, I wasn't imagining the whole buckboard heaving and loathing that a woman might mean now. Then a date meant some girl simply agreeing to hang out, and I try to imagine if that was a better, more painless thing.

A small envelope rests against the bottom of the

doorjamb. It has, in green ink, the words *Wisconsin Person* written on it. This makes me happy for some reason—I feel the whole nerve surge of the nastygram I left her yesterday having done its job—and I open the envelope to find another envelope, this one from Ohio Bell, crumpled inside. These words appear on the back:

> Sir, if you are really a truthful person and if you do not have the aura of a lizard, you will prove it to me by going out into the lawn, sitting down on the ground and sticking out your tongue. If you do this, I might could agree to talk with you.

I look in her window for signs of curtain-ruffling or blinds moving, and I listen for her. I rub my eyes, heaving out an extended sigh. I stand back to examine the building more carefully. She is concealing herself well. Up and down the row of apartment doors, there is no movement, silence all around; the only noise I hear is the constant rumble of cars and trucks on Dublin Road a half mile to the south. The sparrows have settled at the far end of the building, and they move about like tiny old ladies at an ice cream social.

"Miss Britton," I say loudly, my voice higher-pitched than usual. "This is ridiculous."

From the haze above, I hear the noise of a far-off jet. But no slight motion comes from Leslie's apartment. It could be she's not in there at all. Nonetheless, my mind generates a gaggle of pictures of her, all of which are inaccurate, I think, because I keep forgetting exactly what Leslie looked like the two times I've seen her. If I can talk with her—our eyes maybe linking one more time—I will remember her better. And how many stupid things have I done in my day? What could it hurt to do what she asks? So I pick out a spot on the grass, looking around first for a car that might drive by and see me, and I sit, feeling the cool wetness left from yesterday's rain. I stick out my tongue, point it toward her front window. For effect, I put my thumbs in my ears and wiggle my fingers, the old playground gesture that meant, before any of us on the swing-set circuit figured it out, *Fuck you*. Nothing happens, but I continue fanning the air with my fingers.

Then her door does open, neither fast nor slow, and she appears, carrying two coffee cups. She wears a light blue nylon anorak, sleeves pulled up to expose her forearms, and khaki army pants. She is barefoot, long thin plain-looking toes. Her straight hair is a tad greasy today.

"Damn, you Crown Rental people will do about anything, I figure," she says with that singsongy rise and fall of her speech that Far Northerners always associate with the South, the honky-tonk in her voice strong. Her green eyes give off happiness, not the irritation I saw the other day, and I notice she has freckles on her nose.

I make the motion to stand and formally greet her, grunting while shifting my weight.

"Sit, sit, let's talk right here," she says, hands me a warm coffee cup, and I accept, peering at the liquid inside, which does not smell at all like coffee.

When she sits, she sits cross-legged and facing me, her knees not a foot from mine. "Well, don't just look at the cup. Take a sip. My own mix, that is."

The taste is like pine needles and cinnamon. The liquid stings the inside of my lower lip, and I tongue after the pain, feeling a little lumpy cut, probably received this morning. I have a brief gray recollection of this early-morning's fracas: Margaret's arms doing a windmill on me. Leslie does not look like Margaret, less kempt. Leslie is smiling at me, and her teeth, a bit crooked, are yellowed.

"Well," Leslie says, drawing it out. "What do you think?"

"I'm glad you decided to talk with me," I say.

She points to the mug in my hand, giggles in her gravelish way. Down in the mug pieces of green and orange stuff float. I say, "It tastes very unique."

She says, "You drink that every day and you'll center yourself. You've been a hard boozer, haven't you?"

Nobody back home would ever say *boozer*. "How can you tell?"

"Your eyes are a daggone mess." She reaches her hands to my face, which makes me draw back from her—like I'm a retriever on a veterinarian's table—till she reassures me with a smile and a slow-motion nod. Her fingers touch my cheekbones and work their way up to my lower lids, and she pulls them down, distorting my vision. Her fingers feel horned and rough. She makes a few mumbling noises, pulling my lids in differ-ent directions, and feeling awkward about her so close to me, I try to look heavenward and examine the perma-haze. My upper lids flutter.

After she releases me and settles back, she says, "You're very unhealthy. I believe you are filled with unhappiness."

Though she's right, I try to deflect her. I don't want her to think I'm anything but in control of myself, a repo man who's giving her a break. I sit up as straight as I can and avoid looking her in the eye. "We're all unhappy."

"I'm not unhappy," she says. "But I used to be."

She swigs deeply from her mug, a drop dribbling down her chin and onto her anorak. She wipes it off with the butt of her free hand, making a few circular motions with it on her upper chest.

She says, "How old do you think I am?"

Her rumply hair and the way she carries herself seem to me that she's not older than me. In a certain oddly giggling way, she seems like she's fourteen.

"Twenty-five," I venture, giving her the younger benefit of the doubt.

"See how little you know. I'm thirty-eight."

Before I can respond, she says, "Let me check out your hands."

She takes both, turns them palm-up, and stares hard into them. The roughness of her hands, I decide, is the only indication of her age. She begins examining my left hand, tracing imaginary lines from my fingertips to the veins on my wrist, tickling me a bit.

She allows a reflective grunt and sets my hands back into my lap. I see a vein on her neck pulsing slowly.

"I have seen much about you, buddy. You haven't always been a good man, but you've always wanted to be. Your life is falling apart."

"You ain't just shitting me on that," I say in factory talk. I look into my hand now, see where my industrial calluses are fading. Only three months ago my hands were sandpaper, and I swear I could accidentally cut myself at Peterson Products, and I wouldn't feel it. These days, the toughness is gone, who I used to be is gone, turned into a twenty-eight-year-old man sitting Indian-style on some wet grass, believing a thirty-eight-year-old woman, who looks fourteen, who knows who I am from my hands, the softening palms I have. She holds my face now so I will look at her, her eyes as green as a meadow in springtime, and she is not smiling.

"But I can heal you, my friend," she says, and she lightly shakes my head. Her nose is a foot away from mine. "I can see you love me, and that's what I need to make you well."

The pressure of her hands on my cheeks has compressed my lips, making my voice munchkinlike. "My name is Gunnar Lund."

"That's what your tag says." She pulls my head to her and kisses me on the forehead, releases me. "I think you should come and see me tonight, after you get off work."

I calculate what it might mean to come see her, not the least of my concerns having to do with just how I'll get to her apartment, or what Margaret would say if I came home late into the night. Unknown things—how nice Leslie seems, how beautiful, how fucked up she knows I am, how I somehow believe she could save me, if that's what it is, from who I really am, which is a guy looking for a Replacement Margaret—make me figure I should do whatever Leslie wants, much as, this last summer, I decided to do whatever Margaret wanted.

"I don't have a car," I say, and I rise to my feet, knowing our visit is ending.

"Take the bus to Dublin and Cleveland. I'll fetch you at eight-thirty."

I help her to her feet and move to give her a hug, but she brushes me off.

"Let's take our time," she says, then gathers the coffee mugs and walks to her apartment door.

I merely nod, say, "Eight-thirty it is." To which she returns the nod and closes the door behind her. I watch the door and listen. Already, I am forgetting the outline of her face.

8

Noon, dull sky and traffic moving, Dewy Bishop sucks the bones of his third Church's chicken breast, licks his fingers and grumbles. We are parked in the Church's lot. Our view is of the blood-pulse of the Cleveland-and-Fifth intersection. Cars and trucks of all sorts pass by. Dewy's morning alone has been shitty, fifteen house calls and fifteen nastygrams, and no one even fluttered the curtains for him, no trapped rabbits today. Winky says, *Persistence settles accounts.*

"It ain't right, Cheese, when you outsnagging the master," he says under his breath, and he belches. "You learn good."

I flush. It always means a lot when I've pleased him. And maybe in my deep-down mind I don't care whether I'm expert at my job, but a man, a decent man, never wishes to be a fuck-up with his work buddies. A guy can fuck off at work, I figure, from time to time; if you're too much the company man, nobody will like you. But men want to keep their jobs, want their work buddies to make them seem worth the company's money, which Dewy has decided I've just done for him.

"You do know what the fuck you're doing, Dewy," I say.

He rips open a Handi Wipe package with his black sausage fingers, and he cleans off each, using a motion like he's trying to screw each finger from its socket.

"We're delivery boys, is what we is," says Dewy. "Gone to college to hang out in a van with the mother-fucking Cheese."

Between us we hold now a short silence—the same as whenever our educations come up—and I know we're both thinking about Steve Lawson, store manager, who never drives the hood, a guy who barely poked out of high school from Delaware, Ohio, not exactly the country's most demanding school district.

"Beats the hell out of welfare anyhow," I say, the same thing as ever.

"Making that money for the power lunch, my brother."

With much effort, Dewy extracts from underneath his seat his prize repo weapon, the megaphone, and he holds it low, presses the trigger. The electronic squelch of the speaker brings a broad-teeth smile to him.

"Let's fuck with people," he says, and points south.

Exactly as he says this, I turn the ignition and pull a

Marlboro from my shirt pocket, mouth it with a grimace, imagining myself a tough-shit movie guy. And I
drive us west on Fifth to Joyce Avenue, then turn south
toward the Livingston Avenue hood, where Crown
Rental will no longer deliver, because four months ago
in that sector an account manager, name of Toby
Smithers, took a .44 slug in the left calf when he tried to
repo a daybed. Toby's on workmen's comp now, probably won't come back to Crown Rental, and he's talking
about a lawsuit, or so the story goes. But Dewy says the
real reason the company won't deliver to the Livingston
Avenue hood anymore is because too many accounts
there were going uncollected.

This afternoon's plan is to make some big hits, shock
tactics with the worst deadbeats, among which will not
be Leslie Britton, because I've convinced Dewy I'm
working, as he would say, the inside dog on her.
Schmooze creates results, in Dewy's way of thinking. If
you romance the customers, they'll make their payments
on time. But in the Livingston hood, we have to use
attack methods, deception, which today will involve stopping first at the home of Donna Jackson, six months past
due on a three-piece living room set and a framed four-
by-six-foot picture, no shit, of Ludwig van Beethoven.

On the drive down Joyce we pass a big cemetery—
nameless, as far as I can tell—that looks regularly used,
fresh flowers on the graves, lots of fresh graves, but
huge weed clumps make up the lawn. The fence surrounding the cemetery is covered with ratty vines.
Three black men eat their lunch on a backhoe parked

some forty yards inside the fence. A hump of earth is next to them, a testimony to their morning labors.

Dewy says, "That's what you and me ought to do, Cheese. We'd make hitting gravediggers." He clicks the van radio to WVKO Lunchtime Classics. An Al Jarreau tune plays, one I've never heard. Dewy nods his head back and forth with the music.

The Livingston hood is big, maybe sixteen square blocks, and it covers the area from I-70 to the projects near the airport bypass. In this hood the houses are all large, sometimes three stories, older homes, pressed together in the city way, which means there's ten feet between them. Nearly each one has an enormous porch littered with brown grocery sacks and empty bottles. On some street corners, small old-time corner stores do a business that, these days, amounts daylong to selling forty-ouncers of malt liquor and packs of Kool 100s. The streets are narrow, tough for two vehicles to pass each other, and the alleys are cracked concrete, green city Dumpsters every thirty yards. This is Columbus's drive-by country.

Donna Jackson, it turns out, lives smack in the middle of it all, on a short cross street called Mercy Avenue. On Dewy's command, I pull the van to a halt a block away from her house. People are everywhere and in large numbers. When they walk the sidewalk past the van, they slow down and double-take at me, and even more at Dewy, who my guess tells me looks out of place in a Crown Rental van with a whiter-than-white guy at the wheel.

"I don't like this shit," I say, looking directly forward, trying to stay calm. "I've never been in this part of town before."

"Cheese, you chickenshit."

Two black men, tall and smoking cigarettes and wearing black Starter jackets, Raiders hats on sideways, stand at the corner fifty feet from the van. Another man, in a yellow rain slicker, approaches them. The three talk, a matter of angular arm movements, flat hands cutting the air like cleavers. One of the Starter jackets produces a Glad bag filled with yellowish cubes of crack, reaches in, and fingers out what appears to be four pieces. Money exchanges hands, and the rain-slicker man walks off. The two dealers stay in place, oblivious to Dewy and me. They don't even look at each other.

"Man, I just want to get the fuck out of here," I say. I'm shaking from the wrists, sweating, thinking about coming all the way to Ohio just to get blasted dead in an alley.

"Look, Gunnar." Dewy has never called me by my name before. "We make this snag, and we look real good. Now, don't be a beandick pussy."

He thumbs through the *Graphic Street Guide to the City of Columbus*, finds a page, and holds it up near his eyes. Sweat beads have formed on his beaver-nap forehead, revealing what's really up in Dewy's mind. Anything can happen to us in this hood, and he knows it. He shifts his eyes from the map to the alley entrance not far up from us, and he grunts.

"Give me one of them smokes, Cheese." And I

remove two from my shirt pocket, handing one to him and lighting it for him. He points to the alley. "Let's take this bitch down."

I drive up the alley at a creep, worried about thugs appearing from behind the Dumpsters, guns in hand. Neither Dewy nor I make a sound. There is crunching underneath the van tires, and remote thudding noises from rapmobiles cruising the area.

"Slow up," Dewy whispers and extinguishes his cigarette forcefully in the ashtray. "Look at me, brother."

His eyes have no sparkle at the moment. They are brown giant pupils, and they aren't kidding now. "Now you do exactly what I say. Don't say one motherfucking word, and you won't get hurt."

"Nothing," I say, slowly moving my head from side to side.

Dewy draws out the plan on a nastygram pad. He will go to the front of the building with the megaphone, and I will crouch under the back stoop. After he starts shouting through the megaphone, he says, she'll be breaking out the back door within thirty seconds. At that point, when she, or whoever, steps through the door, I'm to walk right in, find the merchandise, and start dragging it out. He'll do the arguing.

"All you got to do is stuff that shit through the door, Cheese. Once it's out in the yard we'll both load it in the van no problem. Just don't open your big Wisconsin mouth. I don't give a shit how much you want to start apologizing for taking they shit."

He grabs me roughly by the forearm. "You dig?"

We both quietly exit the van and sneak up on Miss Jackson's house. A patch of brown grass grows on a portion of the lawn, but dirt is everywhere, and plastic children's toys—red hammers, little bright green houses, headless dolls—appear here and there like pockmarks on a face. The stoop is wooden, six steps high, painted an absurd light blue. Weeds, now dying because of fall, surround it. The house itself is a full three stories, off-white, chipped, and dirty, looking like it would fare better torn down or burned. The windows on the upper floors are cracked or patched with sheet plastic and cardboard. From the edge of the roof, old vines tumble, but the vines look more like sprawling moss than ivy. The power and phone lines hang loose and are covered with what might be silt. When I stuff myself among the foliage under the stoop, I breathe in something sour, a milk-and-diaper smell.

I wait for the snag to start, think of ambushing deer, driving them from the thicket. Whatever could have been fear in me changes to excitement, the whole anticipation of winning back merchandise for Crown Rental. I decide that how I feel now—which is I feel nothing and at the same time remember when I *have* felt something—is the new way I should live my life. I should quit giving a shit, and the first way to do that would be to leave Margaret, straight up, tell her to fuck off, and I could find a way to get back to Wisconsin somehow, or maybe I could move in with Leslie for a time. Maybe I'll never go back to the land of cheese and snow. Maybe I'll spend the rest of my days crouching here in the slums of

Columbus, waiting to take someone's couch away. The thing is, if I've got the nuts to make this kind of snag, I can leave Margaret, take whatever irritation she'll pitch at me, and I won't be bothered a bit. *Fuck her*, I'm thinking. *Just fuck her.*

The megaphone: "WE'RE IN FRONT OF YOUR HOUSE, MISS JACKSON. WE KNOW YOU'RE HOLDING STOLEN PROPERTY. PLEASE COME OUT AT ONCE AND SURRENDER."

I tense, prepare to pounce through the open door.

"YOU HAVE TEN SECONDS TO COME OUT, MISS JACKSON."

Sure enough, the door above me opens, just slightly at first, and the sound of a woman breathing heavily follows, and these hushed words: "Motherfucking cops." Then the steps creak and through the cracks I see beat-up loafers and thick brown ankles. When her entire body—short, wide, in a bright orange oversized T-shirt—is visible through the cracks, I make my move. I grab a step, swing my body through the weeds, and snap erect. The back door is open. The woman turns to me, her mouth dropping open, her face wide and moonish. I stare into the yellows of her eyes, and I frown, then mount the stoop and walk in the door. Behind me, I hear her say, "Honky Crown Rental motherfucker." And Dewy's voice, at maximum rant, follows. "The game's over, Miss Jackson."

The room I've entered is an unlit kitchen. In the sink are heaps of plates and dented aluminum pots. On the stove are two cast-iron skillets half full with what looks like cold sloppy joes, reddish fat congealed near the top. But the kitchen smells like rotting carp guts and cheap incense. A narrow hallway is beyond the kitchen, unlit too, and I walk quickly down the corridor, heading toward the sound of a television, gauging the hallway width as I go, making certain I can lug the furniture through. Wallpaper is fraying off the wall, and chunks of plaster dot the floor.

When I reach the end of the hall, I'm in the living room, and in front of a tiny blaring television stand three girls, maybe six years old, all wearing grubby shorts and T-shirts. Each has her hair done in corn-rows. They cluster together, looking silently at me with their hands to their faces. I breathe hard, widening my eyes, glancing about the room. What I need to snag is right here: the couch, the loveseat, the easy chair, the four-by-six-foot framed picture of Ludwig van Beethoven, which hangs over a wide crack in the plaster walls.

"You the devil," screams one of the girls, and they all begin to cry, not mournfully, but a frightened wail.

"I'm just the Rental King," I say, and they do not stop crying.

Biggest object first, is Dewy's snag rule, so I move the couch, picking up one end and dragging it down the hall. The couch is not weighty, made as it is from only the cheapest number-two pine, and I don't concern myself with scuffing the floors and scraping the walls. The house is fucked up anyway. In the kitchen I stand the couch up on one end, wiggle it through the door, and let it drop down the stairs, where Dewy catches it on the fall and drags it out into the yard. He's in a shouting match with Miss Jackson.

"You done played me too long," he's saying. "It's either we take our stuff now or we take you to jail for theft. Then you lose them kids."

"You kiss my beautiful ass," she says.

The loveseat and easy chair are effortless drags, lighter yet, and I have them both stuffed out the back door in a minute flat.

"You should be ashamed of yourself," she says.

"Business is business, Miss Jackson. You know that."

"You definitely burn in hell."

"We burn together," says Dewy Bishop. "Thief."

When I return for the picture, the room appears larger than before, as all nearly empty rooms will. Where the furniture stood, pieces of paper, socks, diapers, and cigarette wrappers cover the wooden floor. The three girls haven't moved, crying still in front of the loud television. Before I take the picture from the wall, I face them one more time, thinking about calming them, maybe sticking my tongue out, making a funny face. The girl on the right's eyes open very wide, and she extends a finger at the picture.

"You him," she says, stops crying.

The picture is the standard-issue portrait of Beethoven: too much hair and it's a mess, the classic beetle-brow frowning, the mouth pursed and holding the world in. By God, this little girl is right. I do look a bit like the old deaf master, and in the midst of the snag,

I find the similarity funny, and I chuckle. I step over to the girl and kneel in front of her.

"That's right, young lady. I'm a relative of the man on that picture," I say, and move my hand to pat her on the head, at which time she hacks a loogey directly into my left eye.

"Dumb honky motherfucker," she says, and runs off, followed by the others.

I pick a dirty sock up off the floor and wipe the spit and snot from my eye. "You ain't just a shitting," I groan through my teeth.

I am not pissed, nor will I say anything about this to Dewy, because he told me to keep my mouth shut, and I didn't. I got what I had coming.

Outside, with Beethoven in my hands, I look at Dewy, waiting for instructions. He ticks his head in the direction of the van.

"My guy Cheese does my dirty work," he says to Miss Jackson. "Why you thinking I'm the biscuithead? Blame it on him."

"You both heading to hell."

I lug everything to the back of the van and stuff it in, placing the picture on top.

This done, I hop in the driver's seat and light up a smoke. I am hot with exertion, broken out in a strong sweat. An alley squirrel chews a piece of bread in front of the van. Twenty yards beyond the squirrel, a lone black bum supports himself on a shopping cart full of aluminum cans. He looks at the piece of bread with longing.

It's 2:35 P.M., sun shining on Columbus. The afternoon air for once tastes clean, the sky a watery blue, and the Cheese drives alone. The asphalt looks bleached and pale. On the sidewalks paper bags tumble and drift about. I am a repo man who does his job well. Put me in some shrubs or on a ratty porch or in the urine-stinking hallways of the Windsor Terrace projects and I'll pounce when my cue comes. I'll take anybody's shit away.

With no hurry or nerves, I pass south on High Street to make another snag, this one not for Winky or Dewy Bishop but for me. This trip is to repo merchandise I call my own things: my bicycle, my underwear, my socks, a couple of shirts. This trip is to tell Margaret I can't stand her anymore.

At each stoplight in the university district I get caught at the red, watch students file past on the crosswalks, each content-looking in their way, knapsacks slung on one shoulder or briefcase in hand. All along this stretch of High Street the students walk, maybe a thousand, maybe more, and mostly they are white or Asian, and their strides are studious and measured and sure. The hood is only two miles to the east, and none of these folks know it. If they did, they would look about when they walk, scan the passing cars for a drive-by.

I believe I'm becoming expert at leaving women. This will be my second leaving in half a year. But I don't feel bad now, no sadness, no loss. All I want is to grab my stuff and get the hell out.

The day I left Sara was a cloudy day, early June, Sunday. The spring lilac bloom at our farmhouse was finally ending, the flowers hanging on the hedge like withered grapes, their dense perfume a memory of May and a grim trip to Minneapolis. In the yard our old golden retriever sat at the edge of her chain, nipping at flies and sniffing the air for the rain that would start later in the day. There had been thunderstorms passing through McCutcheon each afternoon. It was late morning.

Margaret had left town for the week, vacationing with Fred somewhere in the West: South Dakota, Colorado, somewhere out there. The idea was to leave Sara while Margaret was gone. This way, Margaret could maintain her integrity in the matter, keep anyone in McCutcheon from thinking she was stealing another woman's man. Women, in Margaret's way of thinking, should not harm each other. I was not to tell Sara the real reason I wanted out. Personal problems, or some such bullshit, was to be the excuse. Margaret and I had actually rehearsed the scene several times. She had grilled me like a politician before a debate.

Sara and I sat on the farmhouse screen porch, which we had worked together fixing up for the same Memorial Day party where I fell for Margaret. This porch was our new life together, the pregnancy forgotten, our wedding a couple months away. And I remember, while we labored, us kidding around and planning happy times. Our friends would love to come visit, and our future seemed a promise of barbecues and Frisbee and evenings listening to bugs ticking against the screen. We had painted the wooden porch beams white, stapled in new screening, scrubbed the cement floor, planted marigolds around it. The lawn chairs were new, so was the white plastic table between us. I remember I was hungover, had the aftertaste of bourbon in the back of my throat, and my joints ached. And the yard and woods beyond the porch looked soggy, almost as if steam would rise from greenery. The air tasted of compost.

"I really do like this porch," Sara said, the first words between us in two days. "It's peaceful."

The night before, we had been to a birthday party for a guy named Paternoster, a skinny guy whose wife had left him for another woman. Sara and I had known

Paternoster for years, even had attended his wedding six years before. But we had arrived at his birthday party separately. Most all our friends were at the party, even Paternoster's ex-wife, and everyone drank hard. I had avoided Sara the whole time, leaving after two hours to go to the Liquid Forest Bar, where I drank double bourbons and frosted schooners of Leinenkugel's, stoking up the courage to dump Sara. At some point that night, I told the bartender, "Tomorrow, I'm dropping the goddam bomb." He knew what I meant. Everyone in the bar knew what I was up to. In a small-town tavern— roughly the same thirty drunks each day—there's nothing that goes unnoticed.

"Gunnar," Sara said. She rubbed her hands over the arms of her new plastic chair. "I can't take this. Tell me what's wrong."

I heard in her voice eight years of living together, the uplift in her tone, the way she seemed forever a little girl, laughing at the simplest things. I had figured her to be stupid, maybe because I could so easily make her laugh, but the way she looked at me then and began to sob, her eyes squinting that deep Germanic blue, struck me somehow. I realized right then that I had misjudged the depth in her. This was *her* life we were talking about, too.

"Well," I said, trying not to say much. "We've got a problem all right." I was afraid to weep at such a moment, afraid to let her know how much I suspected I would miss her.

I watched the yard, the dog licking its paw.

Chickadees clustered in the lilac hedge, beeping as they do. I could smell the fresh paint Sara and I had smeared on the porch wood. And I could smell Sara's morning smell, which was astringent, some fluid she rubbed each day into her face. Eight years living with her, and I never knew what the substance was, only that sourish odor, which at that moment reminded me of medicinal waiting rooms and men staring absently forward.

"You want to back out of this wedding," she said. "I can understand that."

This wedding. That's how she always talked about it. *This* guest list. *This* invitation design. *This* minister we must see six weeks straight. *This* outfit that will roast the pig for us.

Her voice sounded garbled, like a piece of meat had lodged in her throat. "Maybe we can set this back a couple months. Maybe it wouldn't be so hard for you if we got married in November instead."

I quivered through my shoulders, my skull, not able to say what it was I wanted to say. I should have told her the truth. Still, I never tell anybody the truth. There we were, so long mated that I didn't think either of us had expected one day we wouldn't sit together like this anymore, tranquil and permanent. That's how it is when you live with somebody: The person with you is as ever-present and predictable as breathing or blood pumping.

"Marriage is not something we should ever do," I said. And I stood up, walked into the house, locked myself in the bathroom and cried a long time, running water to hide the sound. When Sara knocked at the door, I cried even harder, my throat sore with weeping and cigarettes and bourbon from the night before. I cried for more than an hour, which wasn't nearly enough. I should never have stopped crying.

So in the end I must have loved Sara, not in the smooth-arm and perfect-legs way I think about Margaret, but in the way that I suppose real love should be, which is all the stuff we're told of need and longing for someone's company. This is why, when I think about it now, I know I probably didn't really want to leave her. It was a chickenshit thing to do, all for a better piece of ass. I never did tell Sara that I'd started up with Margaret. There was never that moment when I stood up, as I must do now, and said, "I want to live with another woman. I want to go because she's more entertaining than you."

On his apartment-building porch, the Cheese stands alone. He is full of courage and indifference. Above me is Margaret—I sense her up there—and I can see my bike locked atop the stairway outside our apartment. I feel remarkably flat. This is just another repo, simple and straight ahead. I've parked the van off Hubbard, so Margaret can't see me from upstairs.

Through the dropping leaves, the sun filters to the street, makes this neighborhood beautiful, the big brick Victorian houses so clean, ivy dribbling down the building sides, the flower beds in late-fall bloom. Everything is stately here, and I take in the scenery carefully, looking up and down this building or that—the odd window ornament, the porticos, the dormers, the turrets—memorizing it all as best I can, because this will be the last time I see it. But I'm not particularly saddened. This beauty is merely something, when I get back to Wisconsin, I can talk about at the bar.

The L-shaped porch has been swept clean. An old green spittoon sets on the railing, full of sand and cigarette butts, and three lawn chairs are lined up on the planking in a perfect row. I open the entranceway door, drawing a bead on my bicycle, and creep up the stairs, cringing each time the staircase creaks under my weight. When I reach the top, I grit my teeth and gently unlock the bike, careful not to jingle my keys. I can hear Margaret inside, boisterously talking on the phone. "The world would be better off if we took all the men and set them afire," is what I catch through the door, her voice deep and laughing in the way she will around people she wants to impress. I suspect it's some schoolmate of hers on the line.

When I go to stuff the padlock in my pocket, it catches on my coveralls, slips from my hand, and bounces down the steps: eight leaden thuds. In the silence that follows, I freeze, cowering, waiting for Margaret to burst through the door. But I hear nothing from inside. The lock looks like a stone at the bottom of the steps, a big slingshot pebble. I grasp the bike by the frame and carefully lift it, shifting my weight, testing how much creaking my trip down the steps will make. I hold my breath.

I hear Margaret's voice again: "You bet, gasoline all over those pigs." I exhale, awash with temporary relief, and begin descending, going slowly and stepping lightly. I do not shoulder the bike for fear of the noise. On my back and neck I can feel that itch of sweat starting up in earnest. The bike makes pinging noises as I move.

Outside, I pick up the pace and grin. I've retrieved my most valuable possession. At a near run I wheel the bike to the van and load it through the cargo door. I keep glancing up into the windows, seeing if anyone is watching me sneak-thief my own bicycle.

A short-haired dumpy woman in a beige business dress passes me on the sidewalk and looks me in the eye, says nothing.

I nod and say, "We can only hope these nice days last all winter."

The woman keeps walking.

This trip up the stairs I make no effort to conceal myself. I hammer my feet into the steps. Rule number 426: Winky says, *Be proud of the work you do for me*. With almost a casual sweep of my hand, I open the door and enter the apartment, erasing expression from my face. In the kitchen, Margaret stands next to the stove, one hand holding her cordless phone, the other a cigarette, which she waves in small circles. She looks at me, her mouth forming an O, and points the cigarette toward me. I can't tell if she's surprised, although, since we moved to Ohio, I've never been in the apartment at this time of day. Her glasses strike me now as too big for her head, her face jowly. Her skin appears somewhat ashen.

She listens to the phone, nodding her head, mumbling agreement. Knowing she's absorbed with somebody else relaxes me. If I'm quick, I can perform this snag and be gone before she's off the phone.

From the top shelf of the bedroom closet I rustle out my old knapsack. Margaret has made me keep the knapsack in a plastic garbage bag, because it stinks so much of Peterson Products, all PVC fumes and hydraulic oil. I toss the plastic bag on the floor. The knapsack is blue and smudged with grease prints. I see in my mind the Peterson Products' factory floor, eight blow-molding machines in a row, the smooth poured-concrete floor, the rusty Baker forklift I used to drive around in the warehouse. I remember workers standing by each machine and putting bottles into boxes. At the bottom of the knapsack is a six-millimeter Allen wrench and some plastic grit.

I open the dresser, remove only what I believe I'll need to survive: a handful of socks, jockey shorts. I take three plain gray T-shirts, too, a pair of sweatpants, and my bicycle shorts, stuffing everything in till the pack cannot be zipped shut.

"What's all this?" Margaret's voice is stern, the voice she uses when she's pissed off at Fred. Hands to hips, she stands in the bedroom doorway, blocking my path. I watch her shoulders flexing slightly with her breath.

"You're off the phone," I say. The veins in my wrist constrict.

"You can do better than that," she says. "What in hell are you doing?"

I reach my hand into the knapsack, stuffing the contents in tighter.

"Grabbing some of my things," I say, and I stare at my stuffing hand.

"That's bullshit."

"It's the truth. I need some of my things."

She takes a step closer to me, dropping her hands, her face appearing to convulse. Her skin has a rubbery look to it. "What do you expect me to think here? You think I'm letting you just run away?"

"I don't think anything."

"This is all so typical," she says, stepping within a foot of me. "Pack up and go. And I'm stuck here with the kid."

"I'm not Fred's goddam father." I say this weakly, because I feel sorry for Fred, marooned as he is here in Columbus with his mother.

Her palms thwack into my chest and she leans into me, pushing me with everything she's got. This time, she succeeds in knocking me back a few steps. I cling to the knapsack.

"Just settle the fuck down for once," I say, and grit my teeth so hard my mouth opens.

"I will not settle the fuck down! You have *raped* me, both physically and financially." Her voice has that hush to it again. She takes an open-handed swing at my head and I duck, avoiding the slap. "That's what it is. I have let you walk into my life and *rape* me."

She swipes at me again, way off the mark, the smell of cigarettes following the breeze of her hand. "I should press charges."

"Let me the fuck go," I say, and I shove her aside. I don't believe I've pushed her very hard but she slams into the dresser and starts wailing. I face her and back out the bedroom door, waiting for some object to fly at me. I swing my eyes from her to behind me, calculating when to make my run for the stairs and to freedom. She matches my steps, both of us moving tentatively, wary of each other as in a street fight.

"Don't leave me," she says with some of the anger gone from her voice. "I can't take you leaving me."

In her eyes, which redden and bulge behind her glasses, I see a hundred conversations between us, the promises we made to each other. Her face is flushed, the same face I fell in love with.

"It's what has to be done," I say. "And you know it."

At this, a noise comes from the bottom of the apartment stairs, the thumping of Fred arriving home from school. Margaret's face slackens, and I sweep the knapsack behind me, hiding it from him. Margaret mouths to me the words *don't go*. Both of us turn toward the doorway. I hear Fred whimpering as he nears.

When he appears in the door, Fred begins to bawl. His nose is bleeding slightly, and it looks like someone punched him in the right eye. The purplish start of a shiner is there, covered with his tears.

Margaret drops to her knees, tenderly places her hands on his shoulders. He cries even harder.

"What happened, honey?" When she's worried about Fred, it's the only time I believe she is genuine. They have the same noses, turned up and split into a bulb, and I decide that this moment will be the last I remember of them. I go through the doorway and tiptoe down the stairs. I hear Fred crying behind me.

After I start the van, I light a cigarette and hoot and holler like I might with Dewy when we drive away from a snag. The Victorian houses are regal in the sun.

10

Things linger, things unsaid. Someone accuses you of something, you get in a scrap, and you always figure, later on, you didn't say what you meant. I took my stuff today, made my clean break from Margaret, and all I can think is that I should have been meaner, should have told her that the only thing I love about her is the feel of her, and all those evenings, now a million miles and years off, we spent happy under the Northern Lights. I want to tell her it's her goddam fault I'm stuck in the hood, nobody else's, and all her money and all her daddy's money could never repay me for this daylong tension of barging in houses and of people always watching me, luminous in the van, the white blue-eyed rabbit of darker Columbus. Back home, people liked me, called me on the phone, talked to me at the grocery

store or at the bar. Here they hate me without excep-
tion, and when I knock they cry and shout and threaten
to scramble my brains with spinning lead.

Right now it's five-thirty or so, and Dewy and I are on
the corner of Livingston and Seventeenth, waiting in line
for a fish sandwich and a slice of sweet-potato pie at Moby
Dick's Fresh Fish. I'm panicking here. The seven workers
behind the tall counter and lined along the deep fryers are
black. The six people in line with us are black. The three
people standing in front of the fresh-fish cooler—which
consists of a heap of ice, a line of gutted ocean perch and
carp and one anemic-looking walleye—are black, not facing the fish but looking at me. The workers are looking at
me. Two young blacks standing outside the window are
looking at me. If the WVKO on Moby Dick's stereo were
to stop, I'd run for the van. I would.

"You got *some* nuts," Dewy says in his repo laughing
voice, "up and leaving your woman like that. Bet she's
having a hissy about now."

I don't speak. The man in line behind me jostles me
slightly, maybe by accident, with a flabby elbow. I don't
turn. Over the counter there's a big sign that says,
PROUD TO SERVE THE COMMUNITY FOR 15 YEARS. A little fluorescent Pepsi sign is next to it, the sort of sign
that hangs on Wisconsin bait-shop walls, which lists
Moby Dick's menu and prices. When I look around, I
avoid meeting anyone's eyes.

"Don't worry about him," Dewy says, when it's our
turn to order. "This man with me's an exchange student
from Wisconsin."

The woman cuts an angry glance at me, shaking her head.

"Say *water* for her, Cheese."

I say, "I'd like a glass of *water*" in my thickest back-woods Wisconsin, and I fake a wide teeth-showing smile.

The woman's face loosens up, her pupil-eyes widening, and she lets out a laugh.

"Don't that beat all," she says. "You the first exchange student ever come to Moby Dick's."

Dewy, happy with himself and his smooth bullshit, orders the sandwiches and pays for them, his treat, because he's so impressed with the courage I showed shitcanning Margaret. We move to the other end of the counter to wait.

"So how you coming up with that kind of nerve?" Dewy says. In the last hour, he's asked this over and over.

"She's out of her goddam mind, Dewy." I'm wishing I'd have said that to her face. "The drastic move was the only way."

A man in line, an older gentleman in a raggedy gray work shirt, grins when I talk, cocks his head toward me.

"And you really think Miss Britton'll take you in?"

"What's the difference?" I say. I'm thinking in a few hours I'll know for sure if she will.

"I worry my guy Cheese be fucking up."

"You don't think I'm going back home to that witch, Dewbert? She'd be way out of hand at this point. She'd spontaneously combust."

On my shoulder I feel his big mitt, squeezing. "Maybe you should chill for a couple days at my crib, think it out before you move on in with a customer."

"Maybe I love Miss Britton, Bud."

"Damn, you white people are all crazy," he says, his voiced raised a bit. Heads all over the store nod in agreement.

Another woman, laughing at me, too, places our orders on the counter: two clamshell Styrofoam boxes. Dewy and I walk outside, hop in the van, and we chow down. The sandwich is a three-piece ocean perch with hot sauce and peppers, and everything Dewy's told me about fish in the hood is true. It's a great sandwich.

Livingston Avenue, like Cleveland Avenue, is a major Columbus artery. The only difference is no white people drive this street, or this part of it. White folks leaving downtown can bypass this area, taking I-70 east to Bexley or Pickerington, land of the whitest of the white, according to Dewy. I've never been out that way. The cars passing along the street here are either beater-ass ancient Oldsmobiles or metallic and bowlegged gangster vehicles. Just now a gangster special passes: a Jeep Cherokee, painted a shiny gold and modified to ride low, gold hubs on the bowlegs.

"That's the height of it all, Bud," I say. "Goddam four-wheel-drive truck made into a lowrider. The boys back home would laugh at that shit."

"You stuck in the hood, my brother," Dewy says. "You sure ain't going back to Wisconsin now. Not for a good while. I suggest you get used to the place."

More cars pass. Across the street is a pawnshop, a short Arab man pulling shut the steel thief gates, closing up for the day. The Arabs flat-out leave the hood at six. Come dark, gangsters will shoot them here. A week ago in this neighborhood, an Arab shopkeeper got blasted in the face with a shotgun, after he'd chased a ten-year-old shoplifting boy down a Livingston alley. The boy blew his head clean off, or so I heard on WVKO, which reported the incident without regret. So it is in the hood.

Dewy holds his piece of sweet-potato pie in hands, looking it over like he might a precious stone. "You ready to make one nasty snag now," he says, and he bites the slice in half, chuckles while he chews. "You crazy, Cheese, but I like you."

As always, the compliment flushes me.

"The feeling's mutual, my friend," I say. And I mean this. I chomp my slice of pie just like he does, laughing with him, a peculiar laugh that gives me goose bumps and relief at the same time. But my belly laugh is not really for Dewy, for having one person in town I can trust, or having mustered the solid brass nuts it took to leave Margaret. I am remembering a note Sara had someone deliver to me after she'd discovered I was moving to Columbus with Margaret. *You will suffer in the city*, she wrote. *You will sleep behind dumpsters and get beat up and robbed and you will wish you stayed with me then.* Sara had that right. I will suffer. I have suffered. But what's the difference? I've got a job, a good buddy to drive around with. I've got a woman in North Columbus who I believe I can make love me. I've got a woman on Cleveland Avenue who will love me for thirty bucks. I have a bicycle, some clean underwear, a gutful of ocean perch and sweet-potato pie, a pack of Marlboros and a Zippo. I am scared at the moment, this is true—two boys over the street are pointing and scowling at me—and in my tavern-and-billiards days back home I can never recall being frightened like I am now. The worst that could happen to a guy back home was maybe (and this was rare) getting swatted upside the head with a pool cue. But when I watch this endless movement of people passing the van, some laughing, some frowning, or kicking paper garbage around like soccer balls, when I see these people do what they must do every day—which is nothing more than living out their lives in the place they're stuck—I figure if they can take living here, if they can adjust to the guns and heli-copters, I can, too. It's a matter of manufacturing some courage within myself. Maybe I'm a pussy for leaving Margaret. Maybe I should have stayed with her, taken her horseshit and hollering at me, or laid down the law, or told her she'd better shape herself up. But it's too late to try again. It would be stupid to try again.

Dewy burps and wipes his hands, points toward a helicopter circling a few blocks off Livingston, says, "Drive there, my prince." And around the van I can feel night setting in.

What we're about to do now is called the Pizza Box Trick, which means we'll fake a pizza delivery to get the customer to let us in. Winky says, *Sometimes a little deception is necessary*. Our customer goes by the name of Joy Witherspoon; according to the printout, though, her real name is Denita, and her refrigerator payment is past due four months, three weeks. Steve Lawson's note on her suggests that she's a handful. He's written this: *She will try to hit you. Big and dangerous. Use caution with this one.* Joy Witherspoon lives in the cream brick fourplex that Dewy and I—and a sixteen-year-old girl named Annalee Head—are overlooking from behind an alley Dumpster. It's a good stretch to the building, more than a hundred yards. Annalee is tall and bony, wears purple pants and a pink sleeveless T-shirt, has very dark arms, finely muscled, and her lengthy dry-looking fingers are fiddling about with the six dollars Dewy has just given her.

"Y'all want me to knock and tell Miss Witherspoon her pizza's come, and you giving me the money for it?" she says. When she talks she looks mostly at Dewy, but not exactly at *him*, more at his big belly. "Y'all crazy."

"You gonna play me like this," Dewy says, "and I'm paying someone willing."

"No, sir," she says, and scuffs the ground with her sandals. "I'll do it."

"You're brave," I say seriously. I'm leaning on a repo dolly, holding thick straps of webbing in one hand, a cigarette in the other.

She turns to me, nods her head, her purple lips parting to show the bright pink gums, the straight pearly teeth. "You the brave one," she says. "Whitey never hangs around here this time of day."

"Anything for excitement," I say, and wink at her, but I worry inside that we're pulling this stunt too late in the evening.

At the end of the alley is Fourteenth Street, where I see the snap of the streetlight coming on. To the west the haze shines orange over the skyscrapers and the hood-noise grows quieter than it's been all day. The air feels damp, cooling as it does at dusk, and it tastes of Dumpsters and cigarette butts and drain oil dumped on the alley pebbles.

"When we go in," Dewy says to Annalee, "you run and you run till you can't see the building."

"Yes, sir," she says, and stuffs the bills in her back pocket.

"And Cheese, you keep that Wisconsin mouth shut."

I grunt and spit, remembering that hot loogey that eyeballed me this afternoon. "Yes, boss," I say, and I wink at Dewy, too.

We walk to the building in a sort of phalanx, Annalee taking the point, me walking beside Dewy and carrying the dolly rather than rolling it and making noise, though its wheels tinkle a bit with each bounce of my stride. Annalee, I notice, has no ass, nothing wide enough to interest Dewy, but the backs of her arms do have some thickness to them. Her ankles, in this fading light, appear to be part of the grassless ground. She smells like Juicy Fruit gum and the gel that slicks her hair into two crooked pigtails. Dewy doesn't look at her, merely at the door on which she'll knock, or at the picture window adjacent to it. The only noise is our steps and breathing, the tiny dolly-wheel squeak.

In front of the door, Dewy points us into position, me on the hinge side, Annalee in front (he gestures at her to smile like a choir director might), and he takes the other side, crouching low, making himself look like a huge mound of malformed clay. He extends a finger to Annalee and nods for her to knock, which she does, four friendly raps. From inside there's television noise— a cop show, sirens, guns—and I can hear the clinking of plates.

"What the fuck you want?" The harsh woman's voice booming through the door is so loud it seems electronically amplified.

Dewy signals Annalee to knock again, to smile. Weighty footsteps follow, massive feet shuffling.

When the door opens, Annalee fidgets in place, balks momentarily, then snaps erect in a peculiar way. "Your pizza?"

The woman's voice says, "I didn't order a mother-fucking pizza."

Dewy springs to his feet, throwing his arm into the door, and says, "Surprise, Miss Witherspoon. Crown Rental comes calling when you least suspect. Time to give me back my shit."

Annalee drops the pizza box, and I watch her bound off toward the van, swerving and zagging like a flushed deer.

With a thonk, Dewy pushes the door back with his fist, steps into the apartment, and I follow him in, carrying the dolly. In front of Dewy, facing him square, stands Miss Witherspoon, a woman who is nearly his height and weight. She wears dark blue shorts, and each leg, pale for a black woman and ridged with fat, is wider than Annalee's waist. On her feet are sky blue deck shoes, which must be size elevens. Her shirt is a paisley tentish smock, and by rough estimate, she's got twenty-inch arms at the mushy elbow. The face is swollen like a McCutcheon River carp—round, puffy, and pockmarked—and her expression is vague and sluggish, the eyes wide-set and puny, a blob of bad mashed yams. In her thick hand she holds a half-eaten buttermilk biscuit.

"You march the fuck out my house right now," she hollers, and takes a bite from the biscuit, chewing at a fierce pace, her mouth open, revealing the yellow paste of biscuit.

Dewy positions his head not four inches from hers. I notice his right index finger is twitching. "Cheese, take the fridge," he says with some trembling noticeable in his pipes.

I move past him with the dolly, and Miss Witherspoon sees me, her tiny eyes broadening.

"Lord have mercy, there's a white man in the house." A glob of biscuit flies from her mouth and sails over my shoulder. I see on the wall beyond her a junky black velvet portrait of Nelson Mandela, Martin Luther King, and Malcolm X, all stern-faced and saintly. These three constitute the Elvis of the hood. Two skinny boys, maybe Fred's age, are seated in front of the television, drinking Kool-Aid and not bothering to look up from *Rescue 911*. On top of the television rests a toy stuffed rabbit and a ragged New Testament.

"You get the fuck out," she says, and angles a beefy shoulder toward me.

"Fear my guy Cheese, Miss Witherspoon. He's from the Irish Republican Army," says Dewy, the grin of his voice slight but unmistakable. "We win this time. We taking the shit."

"I don't care if he the Green Berets. Get that man out my house." Her voice is deep and rough and shrill all at once.

At this I waffle some—the press of nerves making me want to piss or crap my Crown Rental coveralls— and I don't move, looking at Dewy for instructions.

"The Cheese will leave with the fridge," Dewy says.

I move into the kitchen—this one clean, no dishes in the sink, the counters wiped—and open the refrigerator door. On the shelves are neatly lined-up eggs, pickle and mustard jars, the usual stuff, and a turkey carcass occupies the main shelf. There's some other food in there, too, wrapped in tinfoil, and I begin removing everything, setting each item carefully on the kitchen table to avoid ruining it. Winky says, *Leave the delinquent customer with no hard feelings*. While I work, Dewy and Miss Witherspoon commence screaming at each other.

"Your own fault," Dewy says.

"He touches any more of my shit and he might end up the night in plastic."

"You talk all you want. He's taking the fridge. It's ours."

An elephantlike footstep sound follows, and when I glance into the main room, I see Miss Witherspoon has grabbed Dewy by the throat, pushing him backward. Dewy rips her hands from his neck and she throws a forearm to his face, knocking him to the ground. Then she falls on him. Both bodies let out an enormous grunt.

"Dump the fridge. Dump the fridge," Dewy yells. He strains himself up to a four-point grappling stance, Miss Witherspoon on his back and thumping him with her chubby fists. "Right now! Dump that mother-fucker!"

I reach around the back of the fridge, a sticky feeling back there—settled dust and airborne grease—and tip it face forward, its contents spilling everywhere on the floor. Jars roll. Milk mixes with orange juice and spreads over the linoleum like fresh puke. Eggshells dot the ooze.

"You a dead honky now," shouts Miss Witherspoon.

I panic, shake the fridge hard, two wire shelves falling out and clanging together. I whip the dolly underneath it and fumble with the straps, which I tighten down as best I can, hands quaking, my torso shuddering every time the mastodons boom in the other room.

In a hurry, I begin backing the dollied fridge through the kitchen door and past Dewy and Miss Witherspoon, who Dewy is now sitting on. "You dead," she's saying. "You don't know how dead you is."

The two little boys are on their feet now, watching the struggle silently, but they aren't crying.

Then I'm outside again, and it's a full dark football field to the van. I lug the fridge across the clearing, and the fridge bounces, making a noise louder than tennis shoes in a dryer.

When I'm nearly to the van, Dewy appears in the light of Miss Witherspoon's doorway. I see him in silhouette, arms churning, and he moves in a jagged line as he hits a dead run toward me, cutting and weaving like a fullback.

"Load that thing," he yells, and I yank open the van's back doors, and he helps me heave the fridge, still dollied up, into the cargo bay. He slams the doors shut. "Go, man. Bitch is gonna shoot!"

The driver's side is facing Joy Witherspoon's apartment. For some reason I'm interested in what scared Dewy, and I slow up, pause to look at her apartment door. She stands there all right, eclipsing the light of the doorway, and I watch her raise her elbows as a chicken might to stretch its wings. *Thank God*, I think, *she's not after us.*

An orange flash appears in front of her—a delay—then a close-by sound like cloth tearing, then a sharp sting in my forearms and neck and legs and I hear the metallic concussion of the gun blast. *I've been fucking shot and I'm standing here and I'm not dead and I'm not moving.*

"Cheese, come on," Dewy says, "She coming closer!"

I'm not moving and I've been shot and I'm alive and the pain is like I've been bashed with a shovel.

"Cheese, you gonna get killed!" And this brings me around. I feel my heart thumping and I pile into the driver's seat, fire the ignition—another sound like one quick burst of rain and pants ripping comes from the side panels—and I squeal off down the alley, swerve out onto Fourteenth Street, and drive full bore till we get stopped at the red six blocks up. We are alone at this light, Dewy and I, and my hands are stinging.

"Turn on the dome light, Cheese. Let's see if you okay."

I flick on the interior light and look at my hands, fanning my fingers, making fists. The only blemishes are the freckles that have always been there, but a stinging persists.

"She toting a shotgun, Cheese. Just a little harmless spray. Look, no holes on them coveralls." In the dim light I check myself over and nothing is wrong with me, only a nagging tingling, and from deep down within me I experience relief like I've never felt.

"I'm alive," I say, and knock Dewy in the shoulder. "I'm really fucking alive."

We laugh, then hoot, and I kill the dome light and drive again at an easy pace.

Dewy says, "Now *that* was a woman."

"No shit," I say. "First-rate."

The streets are dark and radiant, with taillights

blurring in front of the van. I am becoming invincible. I can feel it.

"That Miss Witherspoon," Dewy says, "is one spectacular woman."

"One of the finest," I say.

Her sting on my hands and legs is fading.

I am a bindle stiff, sweating and pedaling. In my knapsack ride all my belongings: some underwear, two T-shirts, my Crown Rental coveralls, fifty-six bucks, Dewy's phone number, and a German-made six-millimeter Allen wrench covered in Wisconsin factory dust. I'm rolling the Cleveland Avenue sidewalk north toward Leslie Britton, huffing, trying to smear away the constant pictures in my head. One moment I'm seeing Margaret, one moment the brief orange muzzle flash of a shotgun, one moment Chareesa, the top of her head bobbing. If I pump my legs hard, I can't sustain more than four solid strokes. I coast along the concrete, my bike jolting me when it rolls over cracks and potholes. When I drop over a curb, I wince at the handlebar shock and I flash through my last six months and through today, everything in me becoming a blender of memory. Overhead, clouds have covered the moon.

At a well-lit intersection maybe a half mile from where I'm supposed to meet Leslie, I stop to check my wristwatch: fifteen minutes till she'll be there. I make a fist with my left hand, and it looks like a map of Ohio. I open the hand, press the fingers together, and extend the thumb: Wisconsin. This section of Cleveland Avenue is spacious, development signs posted, and no one walks the sidewalks. Once, I suppose, this was farmland. Now tall grass stretches into the distance. A ways off, the lights of a condominium complex loom over the grass like fireflies. The city around this spot hums with faint noises from the power lines, and diesels from the freeway whine. Four miles south, sirens blare in the hood. I recognize the siren sound, an echo and a cry. I pedal again, spinning my legs with no pressure.

The corner of Cleveland and Dublin has a BP filling station on the southwest, a Dairy Mart on the northwest. At this point Dublin Road is officially known as Route 161, a divided state highway that stretches to the eastern and rural sections of Ohio. In the afternoons traffic is brisk on 161, commuters, trucks, humvees from the Ohio National Guard. But now the highway is quiet, and the night air holds a chill I can feel in the bike sweat drying on my forehead and arms.

I lean my bike against the gray brick BP storefront, sit elbows-to-knees on the raised concrete entryway. Behind me there's a display stack of Pennzoil, some cross-piled rock-salt bags, and a display of windshield-wiper fluid. On the eastbound lanes of 161, headlights appear and pass, and I concentrate on each car, looking for Leslie's RX-7. It is now 8:25, and she should be here soon. With each new approaching car, I make my face into a grin, ready myself to stand and greet her. I want her to examine my palms again or talk to me in her West Virginia barroom gravel. When she gets here, I want her hug to be sturdy and full of tears and I want to hold her and mean it, running my hands through her hair, letting her know I'll be faithful and earnest. When I picture her face, I mouth the words *I love you*, which is the only way I can tell her how much I think she's saved me from Margaret. I want to tell Leslie everything that I couldn't tell Margaret four months ago.

A few days after I left Sara, Margaret drove me through the countryside surrounding McCutcheon. A steady rain was beating the pavement. We didn't say much. We sped past stands of birch trees, and they blurred in the rain into a long white fence. From time to time, Margaret would say, "You really did it." And I would nod and reach for her hand, veined and tanned, which immediately she would remove and use to rub her forehead. I remember thinking for a while that I had blown it, leaving Sara for Margaret. But Margaret smelled like campfires. She looked better than I'd reconstructed her while she was away, windblown and rumpled and flushed. I wanted to touch her bare thigh, smudged as it was with vacation ash.

Eventually she pulled off onto a fire lane and drove

us maybe two hundred yards into a grove of tall sumac, the leaves bright red in the rain.

"You'll have to make me some guarantees," she said.

From her sock she removed a shiny cigarette case, thumbed it open, revealing six large joints that were so perfectly rolled they looked like cigarettes. She lit one and drew deeply.

"Whatever you ask I'm willing to do," I said, feeling my face grow hot with blood.

She exhaled but didn't pass me the joint. "I have a problem trusting you."

"You shouldn't. I'll do anything to make you happy. You know that."

"I'm sure you told Sara the same thing once. And look where you are now."

"True," I said. Condensation formed on the window next to me. I rubbed it away with my elbow, saw beyond it tall grass wobbling in the rain. "But you aren't Sara."

Margaret said, "You promise me monogamy?" She handed me the joint, wet at the end her lips had touched, and I took a long toke.

I said, "I've never been more serious about anything."

"Let's shake on monogamy then," she said. And like realtors we shook hands firmly, her head doing a businesswoman's nod.

We watched the rain strike the car's hood.

"Monogamy it is," I said, and reached for her hand again. She brushed me away.

These days, when I think about that moment, I see

my hand, still grimy with Peterson Products filth, or I see Margaret's hand gripping the steering wheel as if white-knuckling her driver's test. I see smoke clouding in the car and streams of rain flowing down the front window. And I remember, right then, discovering I had made a huge mistake. Here was the woman I'd just dropped my life for, and she wouldn't even hold my hand. Here was a woman who would never trust me. I remember Margaret finishing the joint, then smoking another and another after that. When I would start to say something, she would say, "Skip it." Or "We'll adjust to each other." Or "How will I live in Ohio without dope?" This was the first time I noticed her fidgety movements, the jerk of her hands and arms, the head shake. How could I have missed knowing I would never be happy with her? I sat in that car, hoping for her to smile or say something friendly, and I played it wrong. Maybe she needed, as all people do, reassurances that I would be by her side for the duration, would be loyal and decent to her. But I didn't say I loved her. I didn't tell her she was so beautiful, her legs and arms and fingers so perfect in my mind that I would never be happy with another woman. Hell, Margaret didn't let me say anything at all. So instead of professing the inner sweat-and-beauty truth of my love, I merely shook hands with Margaret, sealing the deal.

So when Leslie Britton arrives, I will tell her I love her right away, which will earn her trust, which will keep her, in the long run, from hating me. For once, I need to start something without fucking it up.

But Leslie Britton is late.

It's 8:37 and the concrete underneath me is cold and my legs are stiffening up. I am growing exhausted with everything not going the way I plan it out. If I could, I'd lie back and sleep myself into thin air.

Finally a gold RX-7 eases into the parking lot. I walk toward it, grinning for all I'm worth, but when the car stops at the pump, a large white man, wearing blue shorts, a jean jacket, and a feed cap, steps out and stares at me.

"What," he says, without rise or fall in his voice.

"Nothing," I say. "I thought you were someone else."

"Well, I'm not someone else, Bud," he says, and I walk away. The man stares at me, shakes his head.

Leslie's apartment is maybe three miles from here, a short ride, and the only thing to do, I decide, is to ride there and knock. She doesn't have a phone, no way to reach her but to show up. So I sling my knapsack over my shoulders, mount the bike, and pedal west, that woman from West Virginia in my heart.

In the darkness Leslie Britton's apartment window seems friendlier than in the day. A warm light shines through her venetian blinds—she's home all right—and without hesitation I knock on her door. I lean on my bike so I appear casual. Sweat runs down my forehead and into my eyes. I hear quiet music from inside.

When she opens the door and the inside light cracks through, I begin mouthing the words *I love you*, but she speaks first.

"What are you doing here?" she says, her voice indistinct and dreamy. "You only see me in the day."

She's wearing the same army pants as this morning, and a plain white T-shirt. With the light shining behind her, I can't clearly see her face and eyes.

"I thought you were going to pick me up at eight-thirty," I say.

She leans against the doorjamb. "Did I say that?"

"I thought you wanted to talk to me."

"I'm just so tired." There's much exhale to her voice, the gravel I'm used to gone. "I've spent a long time today thinking. I wish I could remember what it was about. Lordy, I just can't focus."

"You don't remember saying you'd see me?"

"Well, you're here. I guess I must have said something."

I bow toward her, feign a little clownishness.

"I suppose I should invite you in then," she says. She slowly turns away from me and shuffles barefoot across her carpet. Her ankles are thin and milky.

I raise my voice. "Is it okay if I bring in my bike? Can't afford to have it stolen, you know."

"Do what you need to do," she says, though so soft I'm not sure that's what she says.

Gently I wheel my bike through the doorway and lean it against the wall. The apartment air is thick with sandalwood. Three old-fashioned lamps give the room a faint golden light. Near my bike, a huge fish tank stands on a wooden pedestal. Blue rocks line the bottom of the tank, at the center of which is a skull that releases a steady stream of bubbles. Two snails suck algae on the glass facing me, and a school of neon tetras swim about the skull. On the other side of the room Leslie sits on a brown beanbag, eyes closed, her legs and arms splayed as if she were dead. She has heavy calluses on the balls of her feet. On the wall behind her hang various wooden heads, which look to be from all parts of the tropical world. The entire room, in fact, is lined with heads. Some have long brown hair; some are flat and faceless; some are painted and smiling perfect white teeth. Next to Leslie there's a futon with a black metal cargo trunk on the floor in front of it. Two coffee cups, an ashtray, a pack of Camel Filters and a glazed-clay skull rest on the trunk, her coffee table.

The Crown Rental twenty-seven-inch color console TV is situated beside the fish tank, and a boom box on top of the TV plays some instrumental music, airy and electronic and meditative.

"Do you want me to leave?" I say. Her eyes do not open.

"Have a seat," she says. "I'm fixing to wake up."

Padding lightly on her carpet—all the heads on the wall watching me—I maneuver myself behind the trunk and ease down onto the futon. The wood creaks when I sit.

"I really like your apartment," I say, the best I can do. Across the room an angelfish darts to the tank surface and settles again near the bubbling skull.

"Well," she says and sits up, "since you Crown Rental boys are so interested in coming to see my apartment, you'd best like the insides."

"It's just a job," I say. A basketball-sized voodoo head, with a chicken bone through its broad flat nose, looks at me.

"Now why did I forget to pick you up?" She looks at me briefly, then rubs her hands in her forehead and through her hair. "What *was* I thinking about?"

Her eyes are red, and the skin on her face looks dry. Crow's feet fan out over her upper cheeks. On the base of her neck one wrinkle stands out like a small knife-wound scar.

She reaches across the trunk, slides the glazed skull to me. "Where are my manners? Certainly you'd like a bong."

I examine the skull, turning it about in my hands. Sure enough, it has a carburetor hole on the back side, near the occiput, and a pipe bowl mounted in the gap of the nose.

"Yes, please," I say, maybe too politely. Why can't I come out and tell Leslie I love her?

From a side pocket of her army pants she produces a Glad bag full of dope, a scant eighth ounce, by my guess. "The bong's name is Yorick. I've had him nearly twenty years."

"That's funny," I say. "A buddy of mine back home used to say all bongs should be named Yorick."

"I heard that once, too," she says, and stuffs a bud into the bowl. "Must be how I came to naming him."

I say, "See, things are the same all over."

She hands me a pink Bic lighter, our fingers touching in the exchange.

I set flame to the bowl, and Yorick emits a gurgling sound. I hold in the smoke, focusing on the blueness of the fish tank. My wrist veins constrict. When I exhale, I taste the bong-water sulfur of my life in Wisconsin, of two o'clock in the morning with a few work buddies, sitting in a trailer and smoking and laughing. I blow the smoke downward, where it spreads across the trunk and fades into dust.

"You miss West Virginia?" I say.

She motions for me to take another drag, which I do, sucking hard. "I don't miss anything," she says. "West Virginia, I guess, is just the place of my raising."

I exhale again, and this time I cough, feeling the color in the room modify slightly, the electronic music becoming more poignant, Leslie's eyes growing increasingly friendly. Rising bubbles in the fish tank form one solid column of white. Above the tank a large plastic monkey head grimaces at me. Next to it there's a bearded head, a bald head next to that, a pirate head with a hat next to that. Everywhere I look eyes return my glance.

"What's with all the heads?" I say.

She takes Yorick from me, stuffs in another bud, and lights up, a long muscular draw. While she holds in her hit, she sits up into a meditation posture and closes her eyes, then she steadily releases the smoke through her nostrils and it spreads about her lap. "For each time I sleep with a man, I buy a fake head and tack it up on the wall. Sometimes I make the heads, a little arts-and-crafts project."

I scan the room, try counting them. Perhaps there are seventy heads.

"I have more upstairs, too: in my bedroom, the bathroom, all over the place." She stands effortlessly, takes a seat next to me on the futon. In my dope-vision, her hands appear smooth and nimble and practically glowing. Her sandalwood scent is strong. I picture the other men, the heads she's held in her hands, and I imagine every one of them making that serious face of lovemaking, which is what love is: a serious face.

"You can be another head, if you want. But it doesn't matter much to me."

"But you matter to *me*. Hell, I pedaled all the way out here to see you." My bike is blue-hued next to the fish tank. My knapsack hangs from the handlebars. "You talked to me this morning like I mattered to you. I think you're toying with me."

"You're not so smart as that pretty note you left me, Mr. Wisconsin Cheese Person. I'm telling you I'll sleep with you. That's what you want, right? You aren't here for a daggone palm reading."

She sets her hand on mine, slides it up to my forearm and back to the wrist. Her fingers feel different from earlier today, softer now, oily.

"I don't know why I'm here." This is all I can say. And I wince a little, seeing in my mind's eye the bright orange muzzle flash at Miss Witherspoon's, feeling the individual pellet sting again in my arms and legs.

Leslie's face has a dull shine, her lips thin. Her hair, greasy and straight and long, is tucked behind her ear, and the ear is small and delicate.

"You are beautiful," I say.

"You don't need to use lines on *me*," she says, and lets go of my hand. After she takes another hit from the bong, I notice a trembling in her cheeks as she releases her cloud.

She holds the bong in front of her face, her head absently nodding. Her nose is rounded at the tip, the nostrils tiny. Her face slackens into a grin and her eyelids flutter and her neck flexes. She extends her hand to my face, as she did this morning, and I guide it toward my lips. Her palm is peach-colored, and I feel her resisting somewhat, so I release the hand.

"Maybe we should take our time here," I say in a whisper.

"What's the difference?" She takes my hand again, turns it palm-up, and runs her index finger lightly over the creases. "You like fucking. You think about it all the time. It's what men do."

"You're probably right," I say, but it bothers me a little to say it aloud.

"I could care less about fucking," she says. "I'll go through with it, sure enough. Don't do anything for me, though. It's afterwards, when I'm lying there in the quiet and dark, when the man can't possibly want anything from me anymore—that's when I like having him around."

She lets my hands go and sashays to the fish tank. She makes circles on the glass with her index finger.

"Why are you telling me this shit?" I say.

"You need to know it, buddy. You're a nice enough man. If I'm up front about who I am, you won't get hurt."

She stares at her tropical fish, and I stare at her, at the heads on the wall—this one made of coconut, this one of papier-mâché—and I can suddenly see her in the same scenes I've lived now for years: the hollering, the windmill arms striking me, the full-blown hate of being in love, which is how it always is. The flashes keep coming—Sara, Margaret, other women I've touched over the years. Today, I have left my second woman in one year, and just like before, I'm doing it for a ludicrous reason, because I believe some new woman will deliver me from sadness. Good gravy: I should know better by now.

"Come on, Wisconsin man," Leslie says, and tugs me to my feet. "I believe it's time we go upstairs."

"Maybe it's not the best idea," I say.

She cups a hand to my cheek. "Don't worry about being a gentleman. Going upstairs with me don't mean we're getting married."

"I don't want to be just another head."

"Well," she says, "then I won't make one for you." She pulls me to her and kisses me. Her lips have a sandpapery texture. "But you do have a head worth remembering."

And she leads me across the room, up the staircase—so many heads along the ascent I feel like this is a public performance.

In her lamplit room she turns to me and removes her shirt, slides off her army pants. The whole of her body is milk, and her breasts are mere rises over her visible ribs. She leans back, runs her hands through her hair. There's a memory in her movement to me, the feel of her soft back in my hands, her hair against my face, the quiet scurry of lovemaking in its first stage—and I ease her down on her bed, kiss her neck in the way I've always kissed necks, my eyes open to see the creased spots and blemished places, and to see below the bristling hairs of her womanhood: all the things I wish to remember, later, when this moment between us has been reduced to still pictures. Now she lightly pushes me away, rolls to her side and reaches for the lamp on her nightstand. I follow her outstretched arm with my eyes, and I see above her hand four heads, not a foot above the bedstead. The second head in line is a black man with a wide smile and a beaver-nap haircut. This head has painted eyes with a lilty glint. And before Leslie switches off the light, I recognize whose head that is: It's Dewy! It's that grinning and guffawing manner of his captured on a carved coconut.

Leslie turns off the light, puts her hand on my shoulder, and I flop away from her, trying to get a fix on that coconut through the darkness.

"Is that Dewy Bishop up there?" I say, and get on my knees and grab for the head.

Leslie pulls me back from the wall, giving me a friendly wrestling tug. She says, "I guess you were bound to figure it out. You betcha. That's fat Dewy Bishop all right."

The Crown Rental back room is spotless in the early morning, 7:05 A.M. All the repoed fridges are in a line, broken washer parts neatly arranged in cardboard cartons, air conditioners boxed and stacked in a pile. The stock is orderly, dusted, the floor mopped to a linoleum glow. This back room is respectable. A guy could conduct himself professionally in this room. But minutes ago I stood here, stinking from the long ride down from Leslie's, and I did a bum's job of freshening for work. At the utility sink, I sponged the bike-sweat from me, scrubbed my pits with a fridge-cleaning rag, and washed my hair with bar soap, rinsing my head under the spigot and drying off with brown paper towels. I donned my coveralls, which I've worn now three days straight. They smell sour and flatulent. I tucked away my bike and knapsack in the storage room.

In my eyes the scratchiness persists, the lingering effects of Leslie's West Virginia dope, and I had little sleep last night, lying in bed next to Leslie, her hair draped over my forearm. I spent the night thinking of her mucking around and doing the rib-tickle with Dewy Bishop. I counted artificial heads on the walls around me, and I thought about loyalty and what it means when two buddies, over a time, end up sleeping with the same woman. Winky says, *Your first concern is maintaining the reputation of the company.*

Like generals, Dewy and I stand over the back-room desk and look at past-due printouts, planning the day's repo stops. Dewy thumbs certain printout sheets, making fists, thumping the desk, saying, "They shit will be ours." Last night Dewy bought a new fake gold bracelet at Schottenstein's, a thick link chain, studded with fake diamonds. My guess: The bracelet set him back ten bucks. While we talk, he tugs at the chain with his index finger.

"I'm the best-looking repo man in town." Dewy runs his hands over his black acetate shirtsleeves, takes a pull on his gold tie as if it's a cow udder, and puffs out his chest. "Today, the Bishop be snagging that merchandise in style."

I manage a meager smile, my insides upset with Dewy because he didn't tell me about Leslie.

Dewy gives me a stern glance and says, "You all right? You don't look so good today."

"I'm fine, man," I say. "Anxious to get out on the streets, is all." This is bullshit and Dewy knows it. He snorts and mumbles something under his breath. After he stuffs a fresh nastygram pad into his repo bag, he begins a chuckle but then frowns, his big cheeks tightening.

Then the phone rings, startling me because I know it's Margaret.

Dewy casually picks up the receiver, adopting his wide, customer-meeting smile. "Thank you for making Crown Rental your choice." We always answer the phone that way. And before he finishes the shtick, naming himself and announcing Winky's special of the week—a daybed for $11.95 weekly, eighteen months rent-to-own—his eyes widen and his head tips forward.

"You take it up with him," he says, runs his index finger across his throat, the old slit motion, and he hands me the phone.

I bring the receiver to my ear, Margaret's voice cracking through at full boom.

"Really cute, Gunnar. I think this whole thing is really cute." Her voice rises at the end of each word. When she speaks I feel my intestines going haywire with tension and guilt.

"I did what I had to do," I say, which is all I want to say.

"So you have some new piece of meat lined up," she says. "Is that what this is? You found someone you can *rape* without obligation?"

"That's not what it is," I say. "And you know it." But

I picture Leslie, her fine greasy hair draped over my arm, the heads hung on her bedroom wall.

"Well, you can count on repercussions. I will not let you get away with this."

She keeps talking at a controlled holler, and I take the receiver away from my ear. I shrug at Dewy, who makes the throat-slit motion again and points at the phone, shaking his finger and baring his teeth.

"Look, Margaret. Try to control yourself." I wink at Dewy, and he gives me the thumbs-up.

"It cost me a fortune to lug you here," she says. "So when things get complicated you want to run and hide. Goddam you. You owe me more respect than that."

"But all you ever do is say how miserable I make you," I say.

"You don't know how miserable I'm going to make *you*," she says. "Just watch me."

Near the utility sink, Dewy tippy-toes like a ballerina, makes dainty gestures with his arms, and whistles "My Favorite Things." He picks up a dust rag and waves it at me, bats his eyes like a flirting southern belle. I can't help but let out a laugh, throaty and quick and loud, which stops Margaret. The line goes soundless.

Then Margaret says, "You think women are a joke. You think you can knock me up and leave me and nothing's going to happen to you."

Dewy flips a mop upside down, strokes its fibers as he might hair. He coos.

"I'm not jacking you around, Margaret. I can't take your abuse anymore."

"So that's what it is. You think you're getting the worse end of this."

"I didn't say that."

"I'll bet you're telling your work buddies I'm a bitch."

"Once in a while," I say, "I tell people the truth."

"You will pay," she says, and hangs up, though I hear the double-click of her missing, the thump of her receiver hitting the floor, and I hear her yelling something when she fumbles to pick it up. Then the line falls silent. I squeeze my eyelids together so hard that I see purple stars, and I feel a pint-size dope-shudder and remember Leslie's sandalwood odor and Leslie's voice, so matter-of-fact, so calm and without hate.

When I put the phone down, Dewy says, "My guy Cheese is a classic. His woman is having a hissy and he talks to her like a customer."

I gather up the repo bag and the stack of past-due printouts. "Let's snag some shit, Dewy."

"My guy Cheese is figuring the business out," Dewy says.

Thirteen fifty Kenwood is a two-story prefab, gray with white trim, chipped paint, and torn screen windows, a rickety faded red board fence surrounding the yard. This is the home of Janelle Starks, a full year past due on a living room suite, and this house is only six blocks from the store. It's a miracle she's kept the stuff this long. But Miss Starks has eluded the Crown Rental collection efforts for the following reason: *Big Vicious Dog.*

The printout says that fifteen unsuccessful attempts have been made on the living room suite, and Dewy's face, grinning and confident, tells me that today will be the last attempt. From the van and through the gaps in the fence, I have a clear view of the yard itself, spotty grass like every yard here, and there's no sign of the mutt. Overhead, the thin Ohio haze begins to give way to the morning sun, another beautiful day.

"Must be a Rocky in there," Dewy says. "Mother-fuckers will sneak up on you."

A Rocky is a Rottweiler, more or less the standard guard dog in the hood. They are enormous dogs, some-times 150 pounds or more—solid black with brown trim—which look like a cross between a Doberman and a Newfoundland. I've heard that these dogs are often friendly and playful and all that doggy-do, but whenever I've seen one loose in an open alley I've been nearly inspired to shit my pants. A Rottweiler's head is as big as a watermelon, the voice deep and bombastic. A Rottweiler is quick on its feet, like a cat. Dewy says they can break boards with their jaws.

I carefully scan the yard, looking for a chain or dog turds or any sign of digging and general big-dog destruction. I see an empty plastic milk jug and a wad of peach wrapping paper.

"Maybe she doesn't have the dog anymore," I say.

"Why don't you walk through that fence gate and see," says Dewy.

"He's not barking yet," I say, "if he's even in there."

Dewy cups his hand to his ear, his head cocked, and

I picture his likeness on Leslie's wall, the big grin carved into that coconut, the eyes so like his, a happy and scheming brown.

"Dogs barking all over the hood," Dewy says, "because the big dogs from Crown Rental have come to play."

"I hear *that*," I say, which is what I figure he expects me to say, and we both chuckle. Dewy then makes a bass drum and high-hat sound, buzzing and clicking his lips, and he executes a couple of angular dance moves with his arms.

"How well you know Leslie?" I say. I couldn't wait any longer.

"Knocked on her door a few times, Cheese." He keeps buzzing and arm-dancing in the passenger's seat. "Didn't know her good enough to snag her shit."

"I saw your head last night, right above her bed."

With his fists he nails down the drumbeat on the dash and windshield, still performing his imaginary tune. "So you found me out. The Bishop of Back Rent will sometimes get bored with his daily chocolate. Sometimes that vanilla pudding is just the thing."

"Why didn't you tell me you fucked her, man?" I feel a sourness beginning, a constriction deep in my gut, which is part pissed off, part admiration for Dewy keeping his mouth shut for so long. If things were the other way around, I'd have told him straightaway.

"The Bishop always looks out for his pupils," Dewy says. "I saw the way you looked at her, Cheese. You wanted her, and I just kept out your face. Now you happier. I can tell by the way you working. A little pussy will make a man concentrate better at his job. And my guy Cheese is knowing what he's doing these days."

As with any compliment, this sends a flush into my face, and I look away from Dewy to hide how I feel. Winky says, *Do not let the customer know what you're thinking*. Up this street, I see little glints in the asphalt, like ground glass shining in the morning sun, and I think about telling Dewy the truth, which is that getting laid has nothing to with what him and I do here in this van, in this hood. Work, as it's always been for me—from every day of eight years at Peterson Products to my first job stocking the frozen-food aisle at Piggly Wiggly, long ago, when I was sixteen—is about friends and doing your best not to disappoint them. Nobody at work wants to be a piece of crap.

But I don't say anything about it. I rub a thumb over my beard. I say, "I appreciate what you've done for me, Bud."

He quits shucking around, turns to me and gives me a serious face. "You okay, for a biscuithead. I'll keep you straight."

He extends a hand to me, and we shake hands in the arm-wrestling way, and for this pleasant moment we both smile and nod.

I say, "Now let's take back our shit." I open the van door and step out. When I slam the door shut, Dewy's door slams at the same time, one unified crunch of Crown Rental steel. We stand at the fence gate, peering into the yard.

Still, there is no indication of dog, no paw prints, no gnawed pot-roast bones. With its spotty grass and pebbled dirt, this is just one more yard, one more stretch of turf in the way of our merchandise. Near the east side of the fence some cinder blocks are placed side by side, a piece of industrial grating stretched between them, the barbecue pit of Miss Janelle Starks. Farther up the fence two dented aluminum garbage cans stand together like sentinels. I see no movement in the house windows, and above the mail slot a sign reads HOME SWEET HOME, which is no doubt just what this is, a pleasant little place for a cookout.

Dewy says, "I'm thinking we should walk right in, do the friendly knock, and barge for the furniture." But he doesn't unlatch the gate. His eyes are scanning the house and the hidden spaces at the far end of the fence.

"Looks dogless to me," I say, and I gently elbow Dewy in his side.

He stands to like a soldier for inspection, exhales through his teeth, and says, "Let's do this." He opens the gate and I follow him in. It's ten steps to the front door, and we make them quiet and sure. Before knocking, Dewy glances at me and winks.

His four knocks are soft, but by the fourth the tremendous barking begins, along with the house-shaking sound of a gigantic dog bounding to the door. Dewy takes a step back, his head snapping from right to left. "Cheese, I told you. The dog is the real thing."

Behind the door window there is darkness, but the curtains move and the dog barks and snarls, pawing the wood. I can clearly hear his claws clicking on a wood floor. Then the curtains part, just slightly, and there's the dog, a Rocky all right, all teeth and slobber and gray gums, and the dog freezes there, looking at us.

"Miss Janelle Starks," Dewy shouts, and the dog goes wild again, barking rapid-fire. The door shakes. "Come on out of there."

The muzzle is moving, a controlled quiver between barks, which have the quality of an amplified tuba. Flecks of brown crud line the canine teeth. Snot and slobber smear the glass and gradually obscure my view.

"She ain't here, Dewy," I say. "Let's blow out of here."

"Bag," Dewy says, and with one hand he taps the glass in front of the foaming muzzle. With the other he gestures for the nastygram pad, and I give it to him. The door shakes, a few flecks of paint dropping from the doorjamb. "Dog thinks he's tough behind that glass."

Dewy scribbles a few words on the nastygram pad, tears off the sheet, stuffs it in a crack on the wobbling door. Winky says, *Crown Rental is not intimidated by dogs.* Then Dewy beats the door eight times with his fists. The dog goes wild. Underneath me, I can feel the dog's shifting and lunging weight. I'm reminded of dogs, back home, that chased me when I rode my bicycle through the countryside. Once, north of Window Falls, a pair of German shepherds caught me near the top of a big hill. I set my bike down, kneeled, and said, "Please don't." And they sniffed my head and walked away. But those were country dogs, expert, no doubt, at chasing deer and fetching tennis balls. Maybe this Rottweiler, at heart, is a friendly dog, the kind to fetch beers from the fridge and set his head happily on his master's feet, but I doubt it. He snarls in the glass, snout quivering. We are not dealing with Lassie here.

In one monstrous rip, the dog tears the curtain away from the door window, slams his paws up into the glass, and I get a clear view of him: probably five feet tall up on his hind legs, the head as wide as a steering wheel, ears pinned back, the open mouth big enough to stuff a football in. Behind him there's a staircase, the railing painted green, and next to the staircase stands a spinet piano with some sheet music open on its music stand, and some framed portraits lined along the top: no doubt the happy Starks relation. Above the piano hangs a large framed portrait of J. S. Bach, the full torso shot, the double-chinned master holding a curled piece of parchment in his left hand, a quill pen in the other.

"Look at that piano," I say. "I never thought I'd see one in the hood. It's goddam middle-class, is what it is."

Dewy continues beating the door, agitating the dog. "We got all sorts of shit in the hood, Cheese Biscuit. Even pianos." Then Dewy presses his face to the glass, opens his mouth into a snarl of his own, and the dog and Dewy are muzzle to muzzle. "How's he gonna play me?"

Everything is the dog barking and the door rattling and Dewy's fist pounding, and I think my life has come to this: a job where I torment dogs, where each house is one more person whose day I'll make worse, a job, when the day's done, that leaves me nothing to look forward to. On the door glass the dog-slobber has become a thick liquid sheet, and Dewy is smiling, unafraid. And I am standing, my eyes on Dewy and the dog, laughing along with Dewy because he's laughing, and probably I am doing what I do best in the world, which is watching it happen and feeling nothing about it.

Just like that, the barking stops, and there is silence, save for a lone jet passing way overhead. Dewy peers in the window, his eyes scanning. The morning air feels cool and calm.

I say, "I guess all dogs get tired."

Dewy turns away from the door and sighs. "Too bad—I was enjoying myself. Nothing like fucking with a mean-ass dog."

As we begin sauntering back to the van, a huge cymbal-crash of glass sounds from behind us, followed by a yelp. The Rocky has leaped through the window glass. But he's not on the attack. The dog lies on his side, motionless on the concrete stoop. Without thinking, I rush to the dog, which is surrounded by broken glass like a chocolate egg in an Easter basket, and the dog breathes. His eyes roll. Yet he doesn't appear to be severely cut.

"Now that's the shit," Dewy says. "Big dog done fucked himself up."

I drop to my heels, look over the dog carefully. The fur's in good shape, a fine healthy gloss, and the paws bleed, but only a few drops. From the dog's nose, a thin line of blood and snot extends down to the concrete, forming a discolored puddle the size of a flattened beer can. The breathing is regular, and I listen for something gurgling, something that might tell me he's done for.

"I think he's okay," I say, and break into the sort of smile men only give when they feel relief for dogs. "Probably knocked himself out. I think we should leave a note and explain what happened."

"Don't be a pussy, Cheese. Motherfucking dog tear you up off if he got the chance." Dewy toes the dog's throat with his size-fourteen repo boots. "I think we should put him out his misery."

In slow rolls, the dog's eyes move in half-circles, a drunken and watery spin. His jaw is open and slack, the teeth harmless now, and close to his head I smell his dog-food-and-table-scrap breath, sweet and grainy. On his ear are three straight-line slices, which dribble dots of blood.

"He's not bad off," I say. "This is a big dog. He'll be fine. That's how it is with dogs. They recover quick." I place my hand to the dog's side, feel the heavy musculature rising and falling. The fur is soft and fine. "It's hard to believe jumping through that window knocked him out."

"I say we kill him." Dewy kicks the dog in the throat, and I feel the force of his foot through the dog's side. "Make a statement to the bitch. Miss Starks been getting away with this shit too long."

"It's not the dog's fault," I say. "He's just being a dog."

Dewy rears his leg back to kick again. "So you can leave your woman and you too much of a pussy to take this pooch out." With a meat-thud, he kicks. "You wanna be tough, you gotta be tough all the way."

The dog lets out a long breath, fanning the widening puddle of blood below his nose. His eyes roll and moisten. I finger the dog's tag so I can read it: *My name is Sebastian. 1350 Kenwood Avenue. Please bring me home.* On my knuckles I feel the soft folds of his neck skin.

"I'm not doing it," I say, and stand up, square myself to Dewy.

"When have I steered you wrong," he says. "Tell me once when I didn't do you right." The lilt and joke have disappeared from his eyes. "I'm telling you, boost this mutt proper, and we won't have any trouble settling this account."

"We kill their dog and we'll never get the furniture," I say, my voice cracking feebly.

"My experience is talking here." Dewy places his foot on Sebastian's side, shifts his body so he presses down hard. The dog does not make a sound. "Sometimes you have to lay it down, set the terms, and the customer will listen then."

I feel sun on my back, a comfort, and the beginning of sweat. Maybe Dewy's right. If I were a tough-shit—if people thought I really were a tough-shit—then maybe everything else in my life wouldn't be going wrong. I could say, *I killed your goddam dog because it's what he deserved. Don't ever fuck with me.* For a long moment I envision Margaret, that warm and happy afternoon we spent picnicking on the banks of the McCutcheon River. I should have told her then—*don't ever fuck with me*—and we could have come here to the flatlands of Ohio and she wouldn't spend all our time together telling me I'm a disappointment, because she would understand that I'm a guy who won't tolerate being in love with a woman who hates him.

"Boost the mutt, Cheese." Like a father, Dewy puts both hands on my shoulders, a slight smile crossing his lips. "It'll take loads from your mind."

And without thinking any further, I scan the yard, now pale in the sun, and my eyes rest on the barbecue pit, the cinder blocks supporting the grate. Five strides and I'm removing the grate, leaning it against the fence, soot and chicken grease on my fingers, and I pick up the closest block, weighty and slick, with my right hand, carry it like a briefcase at my side. I face Dewy and he nods, mumbles something rising in pitch, the go-ahead, and he looks away. In one movement I hoist the block with both hands and raise it over my head: a hockey player holding the Stanley Cup. Sebastian breathes, continues rolling his eyes. I stare at his head—let it become Margaret's head, let it become my years at Peterson Products, let it become Sara and the vacuum hose that sucked out our child—and the blood puddle ripples under Sebastian's nose. With all my strength I smash the block down, where it strikes Sebastian's head dead-center, making a sound like gravel crunching under car tires.

Nothing happens, no sudden jerk, no dramatic last

whine. The breathing merely stops. I feel soot in my fingers and rub them against my coveralls. Off in the distance, I hear the brake-squeak of a city bus and the sound of children playing, the remote thumping of the police helicopter circling the hood. And below me lies Sebastian, absolutely still, the cinder block balanced over his head, broken glass around him like grave flowers.

"There it is," I say.

Dewy says, "There it is."

And we walk together to the van, leave the fence gate open. When I turn the ignition, I see the black dog, inert on the stoop. The cinder block is his headstone.

13

It is ten-thirty, the morning beautiful, pale blue and breezy, and we drive for the sake of driving. We criss-cross Cleveland Avenue north of the store, occasionally getting within a block but always staying out of sight of Steve Lawson, who no doubt stands at the window, rubbing his chin, watching for us. Mornings are always slow in the store. In twenty-five minutes Rally's will open for business, and Dewy's got a hankering for a beef sandwich and fries. Sometimes we slow down in front of certain houses, homes of Crown Rental deadbeats, and Dewy has me gun the engine to let them know we're always out here, lurking in the alleys and side streets. Rule number 226: Winky says, *Establish your territory and control it.* But we don't stop and pound on any doors. No nastygrams till Dewy's had his lunch. When we pass women, walking in groups or in pairs pushing strollers, Dewy grunts, grabs his crotch, reaches to the steering wheel and honks. He is hungry and happy, and the dog has not bothered him. He hasn't mentioned the dog since we drove away. But I haven't stopped thinking about it. I smoke cigarettes, flick ashes out the window, and replay the dropping block, flex my arms to feel the muscles that did the killing. I hear the crunch. I remember Sebastian's barking. When Margaret enters my mind, or Leslie or Sara, the thought transforms into Sebastian, the crud on his canine teeth, his paws pressing up against the window glass. Sure, he was a mean dog. He slobbered. He pinned his ears back. If he had the chance, he would have chomped a two-pound roast from my thigh. Sebastian's only responsibility in life was to defend that house. We banged the door and riled him up; was he supposed to wag his tail and lick our hands? Jesus! The dog was being a dog, and for no good reason I killed him. But in the end, Dewy was right about one thing: Since I dropped that cinder block, I've forgotten the hate and slap of Margaret. What guilt I feel over any other rotten thing I've ever done has started to slip away. I am a white man and a leaver of women, true. And nobody I know is nominating me for Man of This Goddam Year. But I am a killer of dogs, which, at the moment, seems unforgivable.

I say, "We went too far this time."

"You make too much of things," Dewy says.

We are crossing Cleveland on North Broadway, the third vehicle in a line of seven, and I make a big deal out of lighting another cigarette, groaning and mumbling when I take my first drag. "Some things," I say, "are worth dwelling on."

"See what it is: You can leave your woman and smile, but you boost a pooch and you all fucked up about it." Dewy waves his cupped hand out his open window. I can hear the wind rushing over his arm.

"I'm fucked up about a lot of things," I say, and I give the van a little extra gas.

The day has become gorgeous, sun everywhere, and each car we pass shines, whether it's a rusty Delta 88 or a gangster Mercedes with gold hubs and trim. On the sidewalks, people congregate at the bus stops and in front of the tiny Arab groceries, and in the empty parking lots of boarded-up gas stations people have parked old vans and set up shop selling paisley T-shirts of Malcolm X and black X hats and purple flowers and beads. Dance music booms from the tenements and from the rapmobiles, and the hood has the feel of opening day at the county fair.

Dewy directs me to pull into a church lot, which I do, the van nose bouncing when we cross the gutter. I park at the edge of the lot, near a bus-stop bench where three old men sit fumbling with their hats. The sign on the church reads JESUS MOVES THE MOUNTAINS HOME. The church itself must have been a small grocery store once, one story and flat-roofed, and its brick walls look freshly whitewashed. The double doors are stained oak.

In a semicircle in front of the church stand seven men moving in choreographed dance steps—a shuffle one way, switch, shuffle the other—and they are singing an up-tempo tune, clapping their hands on the offbeats.

I don't mind testifying to the joy
God and the Holy Ghost give us.
Jesus lives within us. He feels us.
Relieves us.

And Dewy and I step out of the van, lean against the grill and listen. The singers watch us and smile, taking turns in front of the semicircle, soloing, swaying and dipping. Dewy taps his huge feet, and the urge to clap along overcomes me. I pound my freckled hands together with the music. Soon Dewy claps, too, and we sing with the small choir, though quietly, hitting the chorus over and again: *Jesus lives within us. He feels us. Relieves us.* From time to time, Dewy and I look at each other and grin. I feel heat clicking from the van engine, and this parking lot seems a happy place. In the air I smell charcoal fires, barbecue, and festivity, and the breeze from the east is light. For this moment we dance, sing. We do not think about dead dogs and furniture.

The three old men on the bus-stop bench turn to the small choir and nod their heads in rhythm. The music is beautiful and sad, and the seven singers fold their arms abruptly and stop singing.

Dewy says, "Thank you, my brothers."

To which, in near unison, the choir says, "Praise be with you." But all of them look serious, not a one of them looking pleased about the music they just made.

Then Dewy points back to the van, walks to the passenger door and opens it.

Before I take my seat to drive, I tip my head and wave at the choir. Nods and knowing glances are what I get in return. One of the singers counts off a slow four, and the choir begins singing a swing tune in elaborate harmony.

> If we ever have needed the Lord before,
> We sure do need Him now.

I turn the ignition and drive again. Dewy hums the gospel tune, riffling his big fingers on his knees. "That brighten you up, Cheese?"

I swing back out on Cleveland Avenue, head north toward Rally's.

"Yes," I say. And I wonder how it is that people can fill these streets on a weekday.

When I pull us into the Northern Lights Shopping Center lot and point us toward Rally's, Dewy throws up his hands. "Cheese, how much money you got?"

I ease the van to a stop, feeling my wallet in my coveralls. "Some." In my head I recite the figure: fifty-six bucks. The Northern Lights Shopping Center is an eight-acre stretch of asphalt with weeds growing through the cracks, which is surrounded by a Kroger's, a Super X, a state liquor store, and three dozen tiny shops. The place is a dump, but I've always been fond of its name because it's the kind of name that would be on a dump like this back home.

"You got enough cash for some entertainment," he says, and he blows a kiss at the windshield.

"Don't you want a sandwich?" I say.

"Pussy's always better on an empty stomach," he says, and rubs his gut like the Buddha.

Fifty yards to the left of the van, a group of young gang toughs walk. They all wear Raiders jackets and jeans, even though it's eighty degrees. Farther off, people file in and out of Kroger's. Everyone is taking their time today, a sluggish hot day in the fall.

"You never ease up, do you?" I say, and reach for another cigarette. It's the last in the pack, bent and ratty, but I stuff it in my mouth, crumple the empty pack and toss it out the window. When I touch the Zippo flame to the cigarette I notice I'm not tasting anything.

Dewy says, "It'll all be for fun. This afternoon, we'll make a bunch of hits. Some pussy, some lunch, that sounds about right to me."

I picture Chareesa, who hasn't crossed my mind in a while, the wiry soft feel of her hair in my hands, and a trickle of sweat starts in the small of my back.

"The Green Tavern?" I say.

"You should be driving there before you speaking the name," Dewy says, and he pops me in the shoulder. "Sometimes I wonder if you ever gonna learn."

So I get back on Cleveland and drive south past the side streets and moving cars and people walking, everything bleached out under the blue sky, and I fix a memory-bead on Chareesa, her cherry incense smell, the fingernails painted each a different color. This time, I'm thinking, I'll insist on the regular price for my relief, because that's what she promised me. Here and there along Cleveland groups of people gather, some to hear the Gospel, others to talk or drink or smoke. The big wooden porches are filled with people today, some of them pointing as we pass, and when I see a hood dog, chained at the edge of a porch, my throat tightens up and I think of blood puddles and the early sun at my back—a brief sharp crunch and the silent space that followed.

Six women stand in the beauty parlor next to the Green Tavern, three with folded arms, two pointing at Dewy and me, one shaking her head. Their mouths grimace and move fast. Behind them are large hair dryers that look like spaceships looming in the shop window. The women watch us exiting the van and walking to the tavern door.

Without making it obvious I'm looking at them, I say, "What's up with them?"

Dewy gives me a fake grin. "They talking about your dick, Cheese."

"Maybe I should let you go in the bar alone," I say. And in front of the steel tavern door I stop and shuffle a few steps backward.

"You really afraid of niggers, aren't you, Cheese?" Dewy pronounces *niggers* in a sarcastic way, drawn out and singsong, and his eyes close to slits. "Sometimes I believe that's what you thinking, quaking all the time and shit. You got as much chance of getting fucked up here as me, my brother, whether you a damn white rabbit or not."

"Look at those goddam women." I nod upwards with my nose, indicating the beauty-parlor window. "You think they're pointing at *you*, for Chrissakes."

Dewy grips the door handle with one hand, grabs my shirtsleeves with the other. "Be used to it, Cheese. Eventually the hood will know who you are and people will quit looking at you funny." He tugs me toward him, and he's much stronger than I am. I flop into his side, our guts touching.

"Dewy," I say. "What's with you today, man?" He is frowning at me, then his face softens and he lets me go. He runs his hand lightly over his beaver nap, exhales long and heavy.

"Work's getting to me, Gunnar." When he calls me Gunnar, that's as earnest as he gets. "I don't mean to be chumping you around. Maybe if you and me'd be pimping a line of girls or something, we'd be getting along better." He blows a kiss at the beauty parlor.

I place my hand on his shoulder, feel the thick muscle. "We're buds, Dewbert. I think we're getting along just decent."

Dewy steps away from the tavern door, circling around me but not looking at me. He looks at the sky and the asphalt, which, a few days ago, I watched, wet with rain. "See, everywhere we go you gonna be the white guy. And that's cool with me. But it adds me another stress to the job, covering your white ass."

I begin circling, too. I imagine the women in the beauty shop think we're getting ready to box. "Not much we can do about it, Dewy."

"I know," he says, and stops moving. "What can be done is what *you* can do. You gotta quit flipping on me about the white-boy thing. Just hold your head proud and blend in. You dig?"

I glance down at my forearms, paler than pale, thin white hairs everywhere, and I compare them with Dewy's forearms, which are thick and reddish brown. "I'll try, man. It's something I can't help noticing, is all."

"But inside, Cheese, you cool. If you act what's underneath your rabbit fur, people in the hood will give you respect." Dewy steps to the steel tavern door again, grabs the handle, and smiles at me. "Now let's get a drink and some pussy. What do you say?"

"I'm with you," I say. And I think that each day makes me progressively more numb. But drinks at near midday, dice and shooting the bull, that's the Wisconsin way. Hood or no, I will enjoy this, even if, only three blocks from here, Sebastian lies dead on a concrete stoop, late-October city bluebottle flies resting on his breathless nose. I will raise my glass for that dead dog.

When Dewy opens the tavern door, I see pitch black and neon, and I follow him in, my eyes filling with purples and false shadows, my lids relaxing from the squint of the sun. I don't look around until Dewy motions me to take a stool, and we both sit down, adjusting our stools in unison, both of us familiar with the protocol of barrooms. I take in the sugar-and-malt smell of beer. The bar itself is fifty feet long and made of oak. A brass foot rail lines its bottom. The back of the bar is oak, too, and mirrored—looks to me like an expensive setup, an antique worth haggling over. Only twenty bottles make up the booze selection, most of it cheap stuff—lime vodka, no-name gin, Christian Brothers brandy—and I notice there's no schnapps, like I used to see in any bar back home. A half-full bottle of Rebel Yell whiskey sits on the top shelf, and it strikes me odd to see Rebel Yell here in a hood tavern. When I set my hands on the bar, the wood feels smooth and clean, the sign of a well-kept gin mill. I don't see any beer taps. In the mirror Dewy and I are Mr. Bones and Mr. Jones, me in my Crown Rental coveralls and pale like an egg, he in his black acetate shirt and thin gold tie. And I watch myself trying to look inconspicuous, a friendly backwoods smile on my face, my eyes blue and using the mirror to scan the rest of the tavern. At the end of the bar, two pool tables look like empty duck boats, cigarette fog wisping over them in the scarce light from the beer signs. Next to the pool tables stands the jukebox, pink-lit like any juke anywhere, and Aretha Franklin plays, soft and steady. I hear people talking, but I make it a point not to look at anyone. I strain my ears for Chareesa's voice, which, hard as I try to replay our Monday moment together, I don't clearly recall.

After an unusual wait where Dewy and I say nothing to each other, the barkeep appears in front of us. She is short and thick, has mahogany skin, and does not smile.

She places her hands on the bar. Her fingers are stubby and have gnawed nails.

I watch Dewy in the mirror. He gives her his best wide and charming grin.

"Get us a couple of Red Bulls," he says, and thuds a ten spot on the bar wood. "Nice and cold."

Her lips smack into a sneer, and she stares each of us in the eye, shaking her head. "Y'all been bad today. I can tell by looking at you."

Dewy waves the ten spot in her face. "We been good enough for you to take our money."

She reaches for the bill, and Dewy pulls it back beyond her extended fingers. Her arms drop to her sides, chunky under a tight pink T-shirt, and she glares at Dewy, then removes two twenty-two-ounce bottles of Red Bull from the metal cooler underneath the bar. When she twists off the tops and sets the bottles down on the bar, she does it roughly, and each bottle foams.

"Y'all drink deep," she says. "Dog killers are always thirsty." Then she makes her lips into an O and says, "Woof, woof."

In the mirror I watch myself snap into perfect posture and reach into my shirt pocket for cigarettes, a panicky wince crossing my face when I realize I don't have any smokes. Dewy shows no expression at all, doesn't change the way he's sitting, which is leaned over on the bar like a longshoreman with his beer.

"I don't know what the fuck you talking about," Dewy says, raises his bottle and bubbles a long swig.

The bartender says, "Don't even think about denying it. Everyone knows y'all killed Janelle Starks' Rocky." And she gestures down the bar. Sure enough, the eight black drunks lining the bar are watching us, smoking cigarettes, nodding gravely or flat-out scowling at us. Some women are gathered at a booth near the pool tables, and they don't look at us at all. A certain way one of these women has of easing her head from side to side makes me think it might be Chareesa.

"My guy Cheese and me do many things," Dewy says. "But dog killing ain't one of them."

I take a long pull from the Red Bull, taste the molasses-thick malt liquor, feel the coldness running along my gullet and settling in my belly. I watch myself raise the bottle again, a halfhearted motion but a practiced one, perfected after years of sitting in taverns, and I do my best to appear stern and unfeeling, which is the way all the best drunks appear at the bar; although when people stare at me, my inner nerves touch off pictures of the dog, that instant I held the cinder block high and could have stopped myself. My mirror image is, I believe, different from who I am—dog killer, woman leaver, chickenshit, man with fifty-six bucks, nowhere to stay, and no cigarettes—and I see my mirror self as somebody tough, eager to throw fists over an insult, or break bottles over somebody's head. Next to Dewy, whose beaver-nap hair and smooth face make him look cultured and scrubbed, I am a yellow-haired and unshaven brawler, grease marks on my coveralls, smudges on my fingers.

"Woman," I say to the bartender, "sell me a pack of

Marlboros." I scratch a few times at my whiskers, staring at myself. "It's tough to drink beer with no smokes."

Out of her vision, at knee level, Dewy raps me with his fist, a sharpness passing through my lower thigh, and he politely grins at the bartender. "My guy forgets his manners sometimes."

She looks at me, a lip-curl of disapproval, and says, "I suspect nothing less from either one of y'all." Then she waddles down the length of the bar to fetch me my cigarettes.

Dewy and I converse through the mirror, him smiling and inspecting his twiddling thumbs. "Cheese," he whispers, head moving in time with the jukebox, "I thought you was about to quit that stupid shit. Can't you see we got a situation here?"

"No shit," I say, mimicking Dewy, my head moving in time with his, my smile nearly as big. "We fucked it up this time."

"But with the dog it was *me* fucked it up," Dewy says, still happy-looking. "All my doing. I was playing with you, just to see if you'd do it."

"It's done now," I say.

"It's beginning, my brother. I'm telling you, we in the deep shit today." And when the bartender returns with my smokes Dewy's smile and bow is so cordial a guy could sweeten Limburger with it. "Thank you so much," he says, and he pays for the smokes. Then the bartender bumbles away.

Three hard raps on the bar to pack the cigarettes, then I tear the cellophane and stuff a smoke in my mouth, light up, watching my movements in the mirror, where I imagine myself a cowboy, exhaling through my nostrils. I take another hard swig from my big bottle of beer, now feeling the beginnings of booze working into my system, a dullness arising at my earlobes first, then downward to the nose, warmth then spreading about my face.

"Dewy," I say, still quiet, maintaining my cool. "Pussy's probably out the question, eh?"

He knocks me on the shoulder. I watch myself not recoiling, and in the mirror we catch each other's eyes and both smile. "We having ourselves a day all right," he says.

I turn to his ear, over which flows a line of brown nap tonic discharging from his sweating head, and I say, "And all's I wanted was Chareesa's regular price."

We chuckle and take unison belts from our bottles, dipping our heads with the jukebox rhythm and blues, and the bar air is cold and filled with feathery clots of moving smoke, purples and pinks becoming stronger now, my eyes adjusting to the midday darkness. I blow smoke rings and stick my finger through them. Dewy's shoulders loosen, his body taking on the beat of the tune. We are happy drunks here.

Quickly then, my bottle gets knocked over—a thick glass ashtray slides in front of me and drops over the inner edge of the bar. Beer spills everywhere. Someone has thrown an ashtray at us, missing, fortunately, our heads, and I feel the beer seeping into my coveralls. As sudden as it happens, both of us are standing, facing the back of the bar. Standing in front of the juke is a tiny woman, gray and thin in the bar light, and she wears a flowered sundress, exposing her shoulders, which appear jagged and knotted up like a stick of pulp fire-wood.

"You two motherfuckers," she screams, and I can't make out her mouth moving. "You killed my dog."

"Holy small world, Batman," Dewy says, and raises his hands in front of him like a cop stopping traffic. "Miss, I believe you got the wrong men."

I say, "We're just delivery boys, Miss Starks."

"Shut up, Cheese," Dewy says, elbowing me.

"There's the motherfucking proof," the woman says. "You know who I am." She reaches for something, jerks her body forward, and I get a glimpse of a pool cue sailing toward me like a javelin. I duck, throw out my hand, and catch the cue midair, twirl it a half turn, and bump it butt end to the floor.

Dewy guffaws, speaks under his breath. "Damn, my guy's trained in Wisconsin kung fu."

"Lucky grab," I say, and the next object flying toward us appears to be a beer bottle. It zips past my head, a drop of fluid touching my cheek, and it crashes into the wall behind us. As in the movies, the jukebox falls silent.

"I'm gonna kill y'all," Miss Starks says, and she picks up a chair. The women in the far booth now stand behind her, shouting encouragement: "Whoop they ass, girl." "Make the bad boys pay." In the scant light I see Chareesa among these women, all huge teeth and grimacing, and the soft outline of her mouth says, "Scumbag motherfuckers." Winky says, *The customer will turn on you without warning*. Dewy and I are on the backpedal, matching steps with the advancing Miss Starks, who waves about the chair with great speed—a feat, considering her diminutive arms.

When she gets within swinging distance, Dewy yells, "Break 'em off some, Cheese. Let's move." We both pile into the steel door simultaneously. Dewy, bigger and stronger, forces through first, the brilliant sun blinding me, and I trip and fall, palms first, into the parking-lot asphalt. I hear Dewy's feet ahead of me. "Get up, man," he hollers.

My eyes settle on a frayed condom wrapper that sits near my head. *Guaranteed to bring her a smile*, it says. I hear my breath, feel the hot tar below me, and that's when the pain shudders through my back. Three direct hits from the chair, hard and biting, and I make a squeaky sound like a crying child, then roll over, getting a good view up Miss Starks's dress—white panties, a few dark curls of hair, a smudge of voodoo butter in the center of the cloth—and this time I catch the chair leg before it strikes. With some powers I don't know I have, I jerk to my feet and toss the chair to my right, throwing Miss Starks along with it, and she rolls a few times, flops like a beached fish. I hit a run for the van, jump in, fire it up, and drive out into the Cleveland Avenue traffic, screeching the tires and barely missing a rusty blue Ford Pinto, which blares its horn, but I drive too fast to hear it for long.

At the third light up, I stop at the red and twist about, the chair blows throbbing throughout my back. The inside of the van is baking hot in the sun. My view of four teenage girls milling at the intersection is blurred with the heat. Each move I make tightens the muscles, bringing groans up from my torso, but I can move the full range. I don't believe Miss Starks has broken any of my ribs.

Dewy rolls down his window, grunting, and he wipes his brow with a gold handkerchief. "It'll be weeks before this shit subsides. You know we marked men now."

I stretch my elbows back, little needles all over my spine. "You're the boss, Dewy. You figure a way out of it."

"Let's get us a sandwich." But there's no laugh to his voice. "I suspect then we better go back to the store and tell Steve we fucked up."

The light changes. I follow the stream of traffic north, sweating and hurting and tired, and I start thinking about the worst thing that could happen to me now, which would be to lose my job over a dog.

We have a gutful of Rally's roast beef, me and Dewy, and the beer on our breath has become horseradish sauce and hot peppers and fries dunked in ketchup. We are sober repo men pulling our van into the Crown Rental lot. We are not fuck-ups. For the hour since we escaped Miss Starks and the mob at The Green Tavern, that's what we've been telling ourselves: *We are not fuck-ups.* But it doesn't matter how hard we convince ourselves we're decent men; two City of Columbus squad cars are parked in front of the storefront glass, both of them sparkling in the one o'clock sunshine, their chase lights refracting red diamonds into three giant Winkys. These Winkys say, *Thank you for making Crown Rental your choice.*

Dewy says, "Deny everything, man. Anybody could have killed that damn mutt."

"Not one word from me," I say, and roll my eyes. "Hell, it wasn't my idea in the first place."

"I mean it, Cheese. We're talking losing our gig here."

"I know," I say, which I do.

I slow the van to a stop, thinking of handcuffs and dog-abuse charges and unemployment. I think of that dog, how he breathed, the thick muscles in his side, and I think that moment I smashed the cinder block down was when I cashed in whatever good life I might have left here. With a steady gig I can afford, at least, to carry on with Leslie Britton a while longer, spending my nights wrapped in sandalwood and dope. With a steady gig I can save enough money to get home. But the gig's gone now. We'll get our pink slips today, and nobody in this country will hire a man who once killed a dog on the job.

When I step out of the van and make the slow walk to the storefront, I stare at my feet, my shitkickers fraying a bit at the toes. The sun is so direct the asphalt looks white. The lot is filled with people sauntering and talking, as always, and nobody pays attention to the squads; the cops here are constant, regular as breathing. Next to me, Dewy cusses quietly and mumbles. He jingles quarters in his pockets.

Through the glass doors, I see at the back counter four white cops talking with Steve Lawson. The group looks solemn, folded hands and bowed heads. I open the door for Dewy, and before he walks in he says, "I been in worse shit before, Cheese. I'll get us out of this."

"I hope so. You got us the fuck into this," I whisper back, and I follow him, matching his steady lumbering gait. The two of us zag through the furniture maze.

The store air conditioning is on at a blast, a chill wind from the ceiling; it's so cold compared to the outside heat that I shiver, which gives me pains along my back, the chair-thumps hurting me yet. That injury to my back is proof I killed the dog, a thought that tightens me up more. I look carefully at the display merchandise—a black vinyl pit group, three console TVs, two rows of eight Crosely washers and dryers, five fake palm trees, one row of white refrigerators, six microwaves on a factory-made rack—and I inspect the Crown Rental all-weather carpeting, seeing little stains and flaws, things that should, on slow days, be scrubbed. I see marks on the carpet Dewy made, just three days ago, shuffling his feet to the Gospel. And on the walls high and low, on each piece of merchandise, each table lamp and reclining chair, I see Winkys, some as big as a wading pool, some small, like drink coasters, and on each Winky I see, like never before, rips in the paper, fingerprints, dents and mushed edges. Mornings, we dust these Winkys. Evenings, we make sure they're hung neatly. All day we scrutinize them, keep them smiling perfectly for the folks who come in the store and stand among them. We keep this store spotless and yellow-tagged, but everything here, underneath, is in ruins. And this, I tell myself, is what I'll remember, years later, when I'm back in Wisconsin and telling stories to my buddies at the Liquid Forest Bar. *It was all made to look better than what it really was*, I might say, *just like the bitch I moved there with.*

Dewy and I halt at the counter, both of us snapping erect, heels together, as if for military inspection.

The four cops are men, all with buzz cuts, and by my guess none of them is older than twenty-four. They are honed men, muscles standing out on their forearms, and they are thin, have chiseled faces, not a sign of whisker growth. Veins bulge on their necks. They all look like triathletes, which, in the city, I guess they would need to be, tough on the foot chase, expert reflexes on the draw and shoot. Their name tags introduce them: McConnell, Dietz, Williams, and Gambino. Only their names set them apart, as far as I can tell, and I'm sure these fellows don't take their breaks at Winchell's Doughnuts. They probably do lunch in some out-of-the-way parking lot, sip bottled water, chomp on a nice crisp Washington apple, do some paperwork; and before they return to work, I'll bet they check their pulse rates. When I look at these guys I wonder whatever happened to fat cops.

The cop named Gambino steps up to me, moves his head within a yard of mine. His eyes are deep-set in the sockets, gray and lusterless, demonstrating the slapstick humor of a fresh-cleaned brook trout. "You must be Gunnar Lund," he says. His voice is oddly high, girlish almost, but he speaks in monotone.

"That would be me," I say, and the words come out in a high voice, too. I concentrate on holding my expression solid, but my mind races through lies about the dog and how it was not me who killed it.

Gambino's eyes drop to my chest for a moment, and I watch him considering my name tag. I can smell his cologne, which reminds me, for some reason, of the Episcopal church I attended as a child, that smell in the vestry of lingering incense and candle wax and flypaper strips. "I'm afraid," he says, "you'll have to come with us, Mr. Lund."

I cup my hand into my chin, meet his eyes indifferently, and rub my beard. "What's the charge?" I say, and try not to grin, because for reasons I don't understand, I've always grinned when I'm lying.

"You're not under arrest," he says. He holds my stare, not a twitch anywhere on his face, and I have the urge to call him a fish. "But you have to come with us right now. I'll explain the problem on the way."

Steve Lawson says, "Lund, I'll keep you on the time clock. Everything's okay. They'll bring you back to work in a bit." And he gives me a nervous smile, revealing his misshapen teeth. Lawson fiddles with his wedding ring, which is large and pewter, the kind of ring only white trash ever buy. He wears a pressed white shirt, tapered along the chicken-sandwich bulge of his midriff, and his thin tie is dark blue.

I look into my hands, a few grease smudges leftover from early this morning, and I wonder, if I tell Officer Gambino straight out I killed the dog, could we settle this matter here? Gambino could write me a ticket, holler at me, and I could take my licks without him driving me around in the squad, making a public show of me. I remember what my hands looked like holding a spanner wrench or a brass hammer—tough hands then, mapped with small industrial cuts—and I squeeze them into fists momentarily, then drop them to my sides.

Dewy clears his throat, but Officer Gambino doesn't look at him. Then in a remarkably polite voice, Dewy says, "I think you should tell Gunnar what he's done wrong before you take him."

Still locked in on my eyes, Gambino says, "Mr. Lund is needed at home. That's all we can say right now."

"You got the right to know what it is, Cheese," says Dewy, and I sense him glaring at the cops.

"What *have* I done?" I say. "You can't just take and haul me away without giving me a reason."

A slight tic furrows Gambino's eyebrows, and his expression changes, loosens up so he appears to me now like a regular guy, like any poor slob doing his job. "Your girlfriend's going off, Bud. We had to take her kid from her this morning." His head cocks, muscles tightening in his hollowed jaw. "We'll need your help settling the situation. She's asking for you."

In a hundred separate pictures, I replay the arguments Margaret and I have had these last few days. I see her falling backward on the stairs when we struggled over my bicycle. I see her thumping against the wall when I shoved her out of the way. I see her hand, soft and wild, windmilling the side of my head. I see her lips mouthing the word *rape*. And there's no question she's bringing charges against me. The cops will take me to face her, and she will point at me, scoff and accuse and cry, and that will be the end to that: Gunnar Lund, convicted of abusing a frail Ohio State University scholar, and, no doubt, her ten-year-old boy. This is the logical move for her to make; she can't stand being outdone by a man. I up and left her, and my punishment will be shame beyond anything I've ever imagined, jail terms, work release, newspaper articles; she might send the story to the *McCutcheon Daily News*, for all I know. That way, Margaret will have beaten me, proved herself the stronger of us two, and she will walk the university halls telling stories of the monster who lived with her. That way, she can battle oppression as one who has suffered through hateful love and torture, that misery she so admires about the masses.

"I'll come willingly," I say, which is the only thing to do. The innocent come when they are called.

Then Gambino breaks his eye lock with me, turns to Lawson, nods, and thanks him. But Gambino does not look at Dewy, who lifts his hand limply to his forehead, gives him a half-assed salute. Gambino moves past me and Dietz follows him, then I fall in, with the other two cops in the rear, and as we walk through the store I contemplate their uniforms, pressed shirts and clean pants, shoes polished daily. I think how I must look in the middle of them, a big sloppy man in blue coveralls and under guard. I imagine myself in shackles, and I move with the shuffle of the condemned.

Dewy shouts, "Be cool, Cheese."

I twist around to see him, chair-hurt yet in my back, and I say, "I can't be anything else."

Outside, the air is hot and thick and full of noise and

city smells. The hubbub of traffic moving and people talking with one another gives me a jolt, and I stop so fast that Officers McConnell and Williams bump into me, their arms hard and unfriendly.

Gambino says, "Come on, Mr. Lund. We gotta get moving here." Then he grasps me by the elbow and tugs me to one of the squads, where Dietz is waiting with the back door open. When I step in, every muscle in my back stinging, ribs feeling badly bruised now, Gambino pushes my head down, just like on TV, so I don't bang it on the roof. Then Dietz and Gambino hop in the front, slamming their doors in unison—a good team, I think, just like me and Dewy—and Dietz drives, zipping the squad through the parking lot and onto the southbound lane of Cleveland Avenue.

Between me and the officers is a stout aluminum grate, dented in a few places, no doubt from violent struggles, the nature of which, these days, I can well imagine. Each officer's head looks the same, the haircut a perfect line above the collar, and the only thing different between the two is a tiny brown mole a quarter inch above Gambino's collar. A Remington Wingmaster points up between them, short-barreled and no good for bird hunting, which I decide to tell them.

"I bet you guys don't shoot much grouse with that twelve-gauge," I say. "That stubby barrel just don't cut it in the brush."

"We only use the riot gun in emergencies," Gambino says in his humorless voice. "Weapons like this are not meant for sport."

His mole looks like a mutant tiny wood tick, and if the grate were not in the way, I would reach out and flick it with my index finger.

"So what do you guys *really* want me for?" I say, and my voice is as sincere as I can make it.

With no pause, no neck flex to think it out, Gambino says, "Your friend Margaret's in a bad way. She's asked that we bring you to her." He adjusts his hat with steady and clean fingers. "That's all I can tell you."

On the cop radio the dispatcher talks in numbers I don't recognize, squelching on and off, the hiss and crackle of maintaining the law. I listen for my name, or Margaret's, wait to know the specific crime I can call my very own. Officer Gambino, I decide, is holding something back. Whatever's going on, I have a hard time picturing Margaret politely asking the cops anything, let alone asking for me. Margaret hates cops, as is to be expected; those who've sold the weed avoid the pigs. For her to sic them on me, I must have pushed her last button. When I up and left her, I must have pissed her enough so that she would risk anything to see me in trouble.

The squad travels at an even pace with the traffic around us, and I watch the buildings we pass, rickety and chipped, the folks on the porches drinking beer and smoking cigarettes or sitting alone staring blankly forward. It's funny, I think, that I never watch these buildings all that closely, because it's always me doing the driving, and what I see of the hood is forever at a quick glimpse, one stuttering image after another: the broken tricycle here, the shabby fence there, the picture windows boarded up or the high broken gutters and tattered brown shingles. The buildings themselves are big, once new and sturdy and each unique in its way, maybe something unusual about the dormers or the chimneys, but now they are left to fade and crumble and be replaced by uniform rows of government projects, or by nothing at all. These buildings are the wastelands I look at each day. These are my stands of birch and forests of jack pine, my rocky rivers and lakes full of fish. These buildings are what I know of love and what's happened since I have fallen in it.

We turn left at Cleveland and Fifth, the Church's Chicken on the northeast corner doing a big late-lunch business, and the squad moves toward High Street, gliding. I scratch my beard and watch the pedestrians gradually change from black to white. When there's a bump in the road my back tightens into three knots, three punishments for killing a dog. Soon, each pedestrian wears a knapsack and walks in the long brisk strides of a white Big Ten student eager to hit the books.

Then we enter Victorian Village. Here's an outdoor espresso shop: Around the cast-iron tables sit the white punkers—some smoking, some talking, some reading newspapers or thick paperbacks. Here are Audis, Hondas, brand-new Fords along the street. Then we head south on Neil, coasting the last few blocks to the apartment building I told myself, just yesterday, I would never see again. Leaves drift down from the oaks, and each moving car sends up a cloud of them.

When we near the apartment, I see flashing lights

everywhere ahead of us, squad cars, an ambulance, a fire truck, people rushing about carrying cameras or medical equipment. The street's blocked off with black-and-white sawhorses. In front of the crowd, a lady cop with a thin sad face and a yellow ponytail directs us to stop in front of the blockade.

Officer Dietz lurches the squad to a halt smack in the middle of the street, and he jumps out, as does Gambino, the two of them waving their arms in short right angles, like jugglers.

Gambino opens my door for me, an abrupt snatching of the thing, and he says, "Move quick. There's not much time."

I stand up, gingerly stepping out onto the asphalt, my back all dog-penance and agony, and I groan long and low. I raise my hands and say, "Why are you people hustling now?"

Gambino doesn't answer but points toward the apartment building, around which is gathered a crowd of policemen and photographers, news crews and passersby. A police helicopter hovers overhead, its rotors loud this close, and it occurs to me that after all this time wondering about helicopters, I will finally see what the helicopter sees. Everywhere people are walking quickly, some running, and an occasional collective gasp rises from the crowd. Officer Gambino tugs me through, forearms and elbows bumping me as we go, each jolt sending needles along my ribs, and he's shouting, "Here he is." And "Get out of the way." He's shouting, "We've got him right here."

After twenty yards blocking through the crowd, we reach an open space, a circle maybe seventy square feet, surrounded by police, and in the middle of the circle sits Margaret, legs splayed in front of her, her short hair nearly blond in the sun. She sits, hunched over slightly, on the sidewalk. In her lap she holds a three-gallon plastic can of gasoline. In her right hand she holds the gold Zippo I gave her the week before we moved to Ohio. She wears one of my red flannel shirts, floppy on her but hanging close, and a pair of my bib overalls. The clothes glisten, and I can smell gasoline from where I stand. The afternoon breeze puffs through Margaret's hair, the only part of her that's dry.

Gambino pushes me toward her. "Stop her," he says, and the noise of the crowd lulls to a chatter.

I clasp my hands in front of me and shuffle a few steps toward Margaret, who looks in my direction but doesn't seem to register my presence. Her eyes are steady and reddened.

"I'm here," I say, loudly, so she can hear it.

In slow motion she cocks her head to me and nods three times. "You shouldn't have had them take Fred from me." Her voice is deep and ghostly flat.

The crowd mumbles, and I hear a few cameras clicking, autowinders spinning.

I let my hands fall to my side. "I didn't do anything to Fred."

"Goddam you didn't," she says, still no rise or fall in her voice. "They came this morning and they took him away."

"Who took him away?"

With considerable effort she hefts the gasoline can and dumps some over her shoulders, and another gasp comes from the crowd. The gasoline seeps into the flannel shirt, a Christmas present, oddly enough, I received from my father three years ago. From somewhere in this assembly I hear a woman crying.

"How does it feel," Margaret says, "to separate a child from his mother?"

"I swear, Margaret, if someone took Fred, I didn't have anything to do with it."

She lifts her left hand, which, wet as it is, looks beautiful in the sunshine, and she points at me. "Nobody else but you would call the police and have them take Fred."

"I wouldn't do that to you," I say, "and you know it."

"You think really hard about it. After this is over, you will remember calling."

With a flourish, she waves the Zippo about her face. Screams come from the crowd, cameras clicking at factory speed. Margaret chuckles, her body shuddering underneath the soaked shirt and bib overalls, and she hums to herself. Some quality of her voice reminds me of better times, conversing quietly over a beer, or telling stories on the banks of the McCutcheon River. I take another step forward. My nostrils fill with gasoline fumes.

"Why don't you ease up?" I say. "You're being ridiculous here." And her face contorts, eyes widening, her cheekbones thin and soft.

"This is to show you." She hefts the big red can once more and splashes herself on the shoulders and chest, and I think it's carefully, to keep her face and hair presentable and dignified. "You owe me more than what you've given me."

"I'm sorry," I say, though I'm not sure I am. "I shouldn't have left you, I guess."

"I guess! Is that the best you can do?"

All noise from the crowd ceases. Even the cameras stop. But the helicopter is loud overhead, thumping, thrashing the wind down. I wish I could talk to Margaret quietly, use some voice of an older and happier time between us. Her neck is smooth—the chin and lips I remember touching. I remember her mouth fixed in a smile.

"I love you," I say. "You and me just don't get along. A simple thing like that, you just can't miss."

A calm runs over Margaret's face, a relaxing in her cheeks. "You do still love me," she says.

Hours of us in each other's arms, evenings under the Northern Lights—I remember it all, and I love this woman.

"Yes," I say.

She lets out a long stream of air. "Good." And we lock eyes, Margaret's huge, brown, fluid as ever, her forehead not touched with one bead of sweat.

"How do you feel?" I say in a forgotten voice.

"It itches." Her right hand presents the Zippo, pops open its lid. There is a distant scratch of flint, and her eyes close.

The sound is muffled, like a great sigh, and a burst of heat follows. I leap back and raise my arms, looking through them for Margaret, who does not move and does not make a sound. I see orange and purple, the heat waves distorting my view of three firemen circling with extinguishers to the mass of flame. Screams are everywhere. Feet are stamping the asphalt, people running away. Cameras click behind me, autowinders. Shouts come from close by and far off. Now another great hoof, this one much louder, and an enormous mushroom of fire blasts to the heavens. A hard shock pushes me backward, like someone invisible diving from the explosion and slamming into me. My knees buckle and I fall backward, each muscle in my back giving me so much pain I can't get up, can't even sit up. My face feels suddenly sunburned. All I see, hovering way overhead, is the police helicopter, a column of black smoke rising toward it, its rotors beating the smoke down, keeping Margaret from her place in the firmament.

Close above me now stand two firemen in oxygen masks, and they grab my arms and drag me away from the fire. I yell to them, "Look at that helicopter. Look at him up there watching us." And they keep dragging me along the asphalt. Then the firemen lift me into sitting position, the small of my back wedged into the curb. Fire has spread around Margaret, a pond of burning gasoline, and her body has tipped over on its side. Around the pond of flames, firemen shoot extinguishers, but it's clear they cannot save Margaret.

I lean back, lift myself over the curb, and I lie still, watch smoke climb toward the helicopter. It hovers there, two lights blinking on its underbelly.

Now I have seen what the helicopter sees, which is the end of love and a woman burning.

15

This is why a man's minutes are years. I know the body under the sheet. She is Ann Margaret Hathaway, and she is dead. I know the stairway to the apartment behind her, the creak of the steps, the angle it takes to stuff a couch in the upstairs door. Each chair inside, each towel, each fork, knife, and ladle—even the road they traveled to get here—I know. I know the way she smiles, her lip curled, head cocked, her nose split into a bulb at the turned-up tip. I know the bar where she peddled dope after her college classes. I know her son, of the night he was born, how she named him after Frederick the Great. I know the nature of her divorce, ink and paper and a story about an ashtray smacking her and a six-pack of Leinenkugel's Bock dumped on her head. I know the way, on good nights months ago, she would buck her pelvis underneath mine. These are years, still pictures coming to me rapid-fire—the Liquid Forest Bar, the pine trees in McCutcheon, a handshake we made like realtors, a brawl we had on our apartment-building stairs—and I see these years with the minutes passing.

I stand now on the curb, fumbling with a cigarette, shying away from the gleam of my Zippo. On the street around me the crowd has dispersed some. People mill in groups, murmuring; others trudge away to resume their lives, what they've seen here a topic for conversation, nothing more. The cameras are quiet now. When a shout rises from the crowd, I swallow hard and hold myself rigid, doing my best to remain dignified in front of these strangers. But I am not dignified: I wear dirty coveralls and have filthy hands. My throat aches from swallowing. My nose runs and my eyes feel puffy from forcing myself not to cry, which is what I should do now: let it all go. Throughout the crowd, eyes are staring at me, knowing eyes, because it was me, after all, who stood before Margaret in her last minute. I can well imagine what these people think of me, the man they believe, no doubt, whose fault this violent death was, and this is the way Margaret wanted it. In a minute, she could fix on me the blame for her thirty-three miserable years.

Overhead, high thin clouds gradually obscure the sun, haze returning, graying Columbus again, and the afternoon breeze cools my face. The helicopter is gone now, thumped away to overlook some other disaster, some other falling-apart of love.

Five police officers have cordoned off a small area around Margaret with yellow tape. The tape twists and flutters, as does the sheet over Margaret, little rufflings of lives I remember. When I look at the sheet, I see in my mind the flash, that last instant her eyes could have seen me, and I wonder what it was she felt in her final minute, if the burning was so intense it crushed her nerves at once, or if she was filled with a million pains, each more agonizing than the next, her death a symphony of torment and anger. I think about burns I received through my life, holding a match too long or getting seared by hot plastic at Peterson Products. I remember being burned as the worst of pains, the most sudden, the most intense. I know she suffered in the fire. She must have. But way inside me, in that space that remembers Margaret at her most beautiful and brilliant—arms wrapped about my torso or arms waving to make a point about the failing of the world—I hope she did not suffer. She was a mean woman, sure enough, vicious and unpredictable, maybe because the world of raising a kid and hammering out her own life in the university overwhelmed her. I try recalling her face, maybe her teeth bared in a scream, but I merely see the hush of the flames beginning, the commotion of the crowd, the helicopter overhead. I try to remember feeling anything when those flames began—shock, maybe; sadness, disgrace—and what I see is a mushroom of fire.

Everything is pictures, objects in front of me, memories flipping through my mind like pages in a scrapbook. Everything is a search for where our lives went wrong. Here is a curb and me standing on it, wide-eyed, hands to my sides, shoulders loose with the slump of the guilty. Here, where there should be thickets of tag elder, groves of tall sumac and pine trees cresting the glacial hills, are cops and newspapermen and a body covered with a sheet. There should be a faint taste of snow in the air, not the smell of Dumpsters and exhaust and the lingering greasy smell of burnt Margaret.

I do not belong here any longer.

Tears surge into my eyes, and I clench my fists to suppress them.

I hear a woman's voice speaking my name now, repeating it steadily, her voice fading into my head like ghost words, and I feel a tapping on my shoulder. Next to me stands a short woman in khaki dress pants and a powder blue button-down shirt. Her hair is brown and shoulder length, her skin white as the sheet over Margaret, and this woman has thin lips, vaguely smiling.

"We're not from around here," I say. I point to Margaret's body.

The woman says, "I'm Rita McGee."

"People might think we're from West Virginia or someplace. But listen to me talk. I talk like Wisconsin."

"I know where you're from," the woman says. Her voice is plain Ohio, middle-range and nasal. Behind her, a tall white policeman picks his nose and looks at the sky.

"You're from Columbus. I can hear it," I say. "How could you know anything about me?"

"I'm from child protection," she says. "I know all

about you." Then she folds her arms and tips her head forward, looking up at me with her eyebrows raised.

I scan the crowd, counting cops—at least sixteen—and my forearms break into goose bumps. "I didn't do anything to the boy or to Margaret for that matter," I say.

"Nobody said you did," she says. She keeps trying to seal a stare between us, and I keep glancing away.

"Look," I say. "I can't explain all this." And my back muscles contract, giving me a brief electric spasm. I lean backward and groan.

"Are you injured?" says Miss McGee. Her eyes are gray as clouds, and she wears no makeup. The wind blows a wisp of her hair over her face.

"I'm fine," I say, and grit my teeth.

"You look in quite some pain. Maybe we should get you to a doctor."

"I fell down at work, is all."

Now she looks away from me and over to Margaret's body, the sheet fluttering. Two men are preparing to load the body onto a gurney. Miss McGee purses her lips several times, flares her nostrils, and I can sense her thinking, probably thinking I'm hiding something. When she clasps her hands and faces me, I say, "I mean, I really fell down at work. I'm a repo man, you know. Things get exciting sometimes."

For an uncomfortable moment she checks me out, from my old shitkickers all the way up my coveralls, pausing at the name tag, then she square-up stares me in the eyes. "Those rental outfits are criminal. They really are."

Too much, I'm thinking. Something caustic-tasting rises in my throat, and I feel my eyes going bloodshot with anger.

"Get me a different fucking job then, if you don't approve," I say, my voice cracking at the end, and I squint my eyes shut, swallow hard, trying to keep myself from sobbing. I hear around me silences, footsteps slowing down. An autowinder zips somewhere near.

"Nobody is blaming you for this, Mr. Lund," she says.

My nose fills with snot, and the soreness intensifies way down in my throat. Pictures continue flipping through my mind: McCutcheon, the hood, Margaret, Sara, Leslie, Dewy's head on her wall. I say, "I came here from Wisconsin. I didn't expect all this." I open my eyes and sniffle.

She says, "I'm very sorry." Her voice sounds as genuine as one can be, mild and descending with each word. She touches my shoulder, and I see her hand there, but I can't feel it.

"There it is," I say. Under her sheet, Margaret's feet wobble when the men strap her on the gurney, wheel her to the back of an ambulance, and stuff her unceremoniously in. One of the men shuts the ambulance doors and looks at the asphalt, shaking his head. Beyond the ambulance, the police have finished clearing the main stretch of Neil Avenue. Whistles blow and cars begin passing, mostly heading south and toward the skyscrapers. Some of the drivers gawk over at the scene; others don't look at all, as if there's nothing of interest here—so commonplace police scenes in the city must be to them.

I say under my breath, "The Cheese stands alone now, doesn't he?" I exhale through my nostrils and reach into my coveralls for another cigarette.

Miss McGee says, "I beg your pardon?"

"I'm all alone now, is what I said."

"Well, Fred would like to see you," says Miss McGee, "if that makes you feel any better."

"He didn't see all this shit?" I say, my throat making the words sound tentative. I remember Margaret, when I first arrived here this afternoon, her flat voice accusing me of taking Fred away.

"No. We took him an hour before it happened." Miss McGee runs her tongue over her lower lip, then shuts her mouth tight, purses her lips in a steady rhythm, flexing them like a heartbeat, her cheeks taut, eyes squinting, and she folds her arms. "Fred called the police and told them his mother had hit him."

"It never ends," I say, which is all I can say because now I worry it's my fault. Winky says, *The account manager who doesn't think a situation through is an account manager in trouble.* If I only would have stayed with Margaret, somehow I might have calmed her down and been the focus of her anger, someone besides Fred, and Margaret might be alive now.

I say, "Does Fred know what happened?"

"I'm afraid he does," says Miss McGee. "We have him in a car just around the block, if you'd like to come see him."

I hesitate momentarily, smudging out memories racing through my mind, and I try to fix on Fred, always the kid cowering in the other room, listening, and I think he's heard more about me than a ten-year-old should.

"Is the kid all right?" I say.

"Right now," says Miss McGee, "you're all he's got. We haven't been able to locate his father yet."

And it's that word, *father*, that pulls me together. Somehow I feel my head flushing itself into focus, into some world where I realize I'm a man and certain decent things are expected of me. I nod my head and perform a curlicue motion with my left hand, indicating to Miss McGee I will follow.

Rita McGee's strides are stiff, like city pigeon steps, and she moves quickly, excusing herself when we pass clumps of people. All around me I hear people retelling the story. "Then she held up the lighter." "Could feel the blast from all the way back here." "Her body didn't move an inch when she went up." People see me walking and they give me serious looks, knowing, as I'm sure they do, that it was me standing in front of Margaret when the flames began. These are white people here, dressed in nice clothes, pressed white shirts, shoes free of scuff marks. When I look at them, I think of Dewy, him and I standing in Moby Dick's Fresh Fish, and Dewy said, "You white people are all crazy." And I suspect Dewy was right. A fellow never hears about spectacular suicides in the hood, or crowds gathered to watch them. In the hood, death is straight ahead—a gunshot, a knife—and people go on about their business.

We hustle across Neil, the bounce of each step sending further agonies through my back, and we stride along the cobbles up another block. The houses appear as stately as ever in this neighborhood, vines creeping up the bricks, hanging plants in the ornate dormer windows. I sense people looking down on me from their turrets. Then we turn left and stop in front of a black Chrysler four-door with CITY OF COLUMBUS printed on its sides. Behind the wheel sits a chunky short-haired woman in glasses and a white shirt, too tight about her vast chest. This woman's hands look like stubby bananas on the steering wheel.

The back door of the Chrysler opens, and Fred steps out. He is wearing one of my old factory T-shirts, black with the word BEKUM silk-screened on the front, after the make of bottle-making machine I used to operate. The shirt is a tent on Fred, hangs down to his bare knees, and the whole shirt blows forward in the wind, a sail flapping over his little frame. He's wearing the black high-top sneakers that Margaret bought him a month ago. Margaret had arranged extra chores for Fred, because she thought those shoes were too extravagant; he should learn to pay with sweat for things he could easily live without. It had struck me odd then that Margaret, coming from all that old money, would think such a thing. Now Fred looks so much like Margaret, his eyes fluid and brown, the nose split into a bulb. He has redness around his eyelids from crying, and his left eye is in a full shiner, which I know Margaret didn't give him; that's the shiner he came home with yesterday.

Miss McGee says Fred's name a couple times, using a voice nearly like baby talk. "Is this Gunnar Lund?"

His head does not flinch. He merely fixes his eyes into mine, a stare I return sadly, thinking, as I am, of his mother.

"Look at my goddam name tag, Miss McGee," I say, but I say it with a calm voice. "You think I'm impersonating myself?" Winky says, *My picture is your identification tag.*

The three of us stand in a semicircle: Fred and I squared off as if ready to wrestle, Miss McGee with her arms out like a referee. A single leaf falls in between us.

"Fred," she says. "You need to tell me aloud that this man is Gunnar Lund."

Fred raises his hand, a miniature of his mother's, and cups his chin. "It is," he says, his voice strangely low, like the voice of a young man, even though he's ten. I'm hearing his voice as if for the first time.

Still locked in on Fred's eyes, I say, "Do you think this man and I can have a moment alone?"

And Fred nods.

Miss McGee lets out an officious grunt, and she walks twenty feet away, where she stands with her feet planted wide, her body squared toward us. She's watching, I assume, for any mismove on my part.

I take a stutter-step toward Fred. I don't stop to think: "It's bad" is the first thing out of my mouth.

He continues fixing on my eyes. "Been through worse," he says, and I hear my voice in him. It's the kind of thing I might say to him when I come home from work, my way of brushing aside the awful things that make up my days in the hood.

On a nervous impulse I reach into my coveralls for another cigarette and stuff one in my mouth. When I produce my Zippo, I turn away from Fred to light the smoke, hiding the glint of metal from him.

Fred shifts his eyes to Miss McGee. Little trembles go over his body—neck, hands, knees. He rocks on his heels, and I can tell he's keeping himself from crying. "I did it," he says, his voice weak and near to cracking. "I called the police." Now he looks down at his shoes, which he moves back and forth. Since he got those shoes, he's had the habit of staring at them.

"Why did you call?" I say almost under my breath, because I'm afraid to say the wrong thing. Lord knows, I've said enough bad things in his presence already. I clasp my hands together and squeeze.

"I don't know," he says, still meekly, and he leans up against the car. He makes repeated fists with his hands, thumping himself lightly on the thighs when he does.

"Your mom didn't hit you, though. Did she?"

He scratches his ear, tugs at the lobe. "No."

"I figured as much," I say. "She always saved that stuff for me."

"Mom said you had it coming," Fred blurts out, his voice becoming high-pitched and stronger than before. But as soon as he speaks, he peers downward again, flipping his toes back and forth. The afternoon wind is picking up, carrying with it a chill, and it ruffles his hair.

"I called the police because Mom was getting out of

hand," Fred says, and he faces me, frowning a little. I notice a glob of jelly near the collar of his shirt. His neck and face are grayed with a thin layer of apartment dust. A few fingerprint trails cross his cheeks. I imagine what Margaret must have been like in those last few hours, rampaging around the apartment, making furious calls back home, trying to call me at work, where, as it turns out, I was in the process of killing a dog. Fred probably heard her saying all sorts of things about me, probably how I'd knocked her up, probably how she figured I'd be sleeping right away with another woman who I could use to my advantage and spit out like a peach pit. In Fred's eyes, I can tell he knows these things about me, secrets a man keeps from a ten-year-old boy, and whatever speeches I make to the kid, whatever advice I may give him, it won't really matter, because he knows I haven't been a good man, or an honest one. I have lived these last few months for myself, myself alone, and Fred knows it. Nonetheless, Fred is ten, plays GI Joes, for Chrissakes. I'm the only adult he knows in Columbus. Whether I like it or not, whether Miss McGee likes it or not, I'm going to take the boy.

I take another step toward him, just a quick shuffle. "Did Miss McGee tell you what they were going to do with you?" I say.

"They're trying to find my dad." This perks him up some, brings his eyes to my name tag. "But I told her I wouldn't mind hanging out with you."

"Why'd you say that?"

"I felt like it."

"So you wanna stick with *me* for a while," I say.

He cuts his eyes at me, his face that same moonish structure of Margaret's, and his shiner appears moist. "Things have been worse," he says, and he snaps erect, his hands rigid cleavers at his sides. If this wasn't a puny kid in front of me, I'd swear he's a grown man, toughing out a lousy break.

I step to him and reach out my right hand, balled into a gentle fist, and I move it under his chin to give him the old chin-up tap, but he jerks his head back and bats my hand away. Then he stands perfectly erect again, scowling at me. He will not let me treat him like a kid; that's all there is to it. So I offer my hand to shake instead, hold it extended for a moment till his face slackens a tad and he reaches out and grabs my hand—his hand sticky and harder than his mother's—and we perform one perfunctory shake. He does not smile, nor do I.

Miss McGee stands on the sidewalk, leaves at her feet, wind pressing her khaki pants into her legs. When I glance over at her, she angles her head away, fakes interest in the trees across the street, but she's paying close attention to me. I can feel this. And the way she stands there, her eyes wandering away from mine, makes me decide I've had enough of having my life controlled by other people and spending my days worrying how people will react to whatever I do. I want to be a stand-up guy on my own terms, a grown dependable man willing to do what he's supposed to do, which, right now, means I've got to take this boy under my arm and make sure nothing will happen to him.

I say, "Miss McGee, we're ready for you now."

All concern and professionally serious face, she walks to us in her pigeon steps. I watch the sway of her hips, and my inner movie begins playing scenes of me and Miss McGee.

"It does look like you two had a good talk," she says.

I imagine her skin, so pale, trembling under my freckles. I invent the smell of her neck, a musk of government offices and Xerox machines and rubber bands. I wonder what her thin lips must be like, smiling and pursing at every thrust.

"This man and I are from the same town," I say. "We can understand each other just fine."

Then I look to her eyes, which are gray and milky, and I see in them a woman who has a job that's important to her, a woman whose profession is to make people's lives better, as opposed to me, whose job it is to make lives worse. This is a person a hundred times more respectable than me. For the first time in what seems like years, I make myself forget what it might be like to sleep with a woman I just met.

I say, "I'll be pleased to mind Fred till we can contact his father." I give her a wide backwoods schmoozing smile, and it's clear this works, because she smiles back, gives me a trusting look I get from my customers when I've won them over to making payment.

She says, "Do you want to stay with him, Fred?"

He does not look at her, but he says, "That's fine." And he watches his shoes.

I gesture at Miss McGee with a sweep of my head,

pointing at a wide crack in the sidewalk a few yards off, and she follows me over so we can have a private word.

"By the looks of him," I say. "I don't think much has sunk in."

"Yes," she says in a breath. "Fred says you've known his father since high school."

Lordy, Fred can tell a flat-out lie better than I can. So much for ten-year-old boys acting like kids. "Me and Paul go way back," I say. In truth, I only met his dad once. I think I said a total of six words to the man, whom I despised for having once slept with Margaret on a regular basis. So much for Gunnar Lund and the world of tolerance.

"How about you?" says Miss McGee. "How are you dealing with this?"

And I avoid her eyes, watch a chipmunk crawl up the base of an oak tree a few yards away. "The boy's more important," I say, and the bruised muscles in my back constrict some, making me grit my teeth and wonder if I believe myself. "But I'll tell you this much: It's been hard. Very difficult." The chipmunk scurries to a low branch, chatters a complaint of some sort.

Miss McGee says, "The law in this instance requires that Fred spends the night in foster care." She touches my arm and smiles that schmoozed-customer smile again. "But I see no reason we couldn't send a car by your apartment, say, at eight o'clock, if you'll promise to keep him there with you."

I feel the inner glow of winning at the repo game. I say, "I have no problem with that."

"You can have Fred for a few hours then. I'll call you a half hour before we come to get him." She spins toward Fred, crunches leaves as she walks to him, and says, "Everything will be fine. You can stay with Gunnar until this evening."

Then the three of us start walking, Rita in the lead, Fred and I following side by side. No one speaks. When we turn the corner onto Hubbard, I see that the scene has subdued from the carnival it was a while ago. The ambulance is gone. Traffic moves evenly up and down Neil Avenue, and only four police officers stand around the circle of yellow tape. The crowd has dispersed, no doubt, because Margaret's body has been taken away. The entertainment has vanished. The rushing and scraping sound of moving leaves is everywhere. And in the sky the clouds are darkening. The air has that nitrogen taste of sprinkles beginning.

We approach the intersection at a slow pace, and Fred stops, points to the circle of yellow tape, but he does not say a word. He dips his head down, recognizing, I'm sure, that this is the place where his mother died. I put my hand on his shoulder discreetly, feeling his bony shoulder, and he shrugs me away, grunting just loud enough that Miss McGee gives us a concerned tic of the face. She ushers us across the street, looking for cars for us, like Fred and I both are ten years old, frightened and helpless.

From the apartment-building steps, I see the scorch marks on the sidewalk as clearly as fresh scars, and the grass on the boulevard is black. A stocky man in a blue suit wanders around in the tape enclosure, taking pictures and jotting down notes on a pocket-sized pad. He mumbles aloud, but I can't make out what he's saying. I don't think he notices us watching him. He pauses from time to time to look up at the clouds.

Fred takes the lead up the staircase, two steps at a time, his habit, and Miss McGee follows with choppy strides. I follow her, watching the shift of her ass, which is small and flat, like a man's. The apartment door is open, and when we walk in and cluster in the kitchen, I'm surprised to see that the place is clean. All the dishes are put away, the counters wiped—none of Margaret's papers and mail are on the kitchen table. I had expected to see the apartment in shambles, perhaps my name scribbled in lipstick on the wall, slash marks through it. Instead, what Margaret left behind is an immaculate apartment, the only trace of her a fuzzy tinge in the air of cigarettes and coffee and lemon verbena.

Miss McGee tugs at my sleeve. "I assume you'll be trying to contact Fred's father, too."

And I mumble and nod that I will.

She says, "Fred, you have been very brave this afternoon."

Fred says, "Whatever you say." He sits down at the kitchen table, flopping his legs forward to look at his shoes.

Miss McGee stares at Fred's feet, cocking her head to peer under the table, her lips tightened and cheek muscles flexed.

"Gunnar, here's where I'd like you to contact me, if

you find Fred's father," she says, and produces a business card from her wallet and hands it to me, pointing at the phone number. The card is so plain, the typeface so ordinary, I wish I had one of Dewy's Winky cards with me, just to show her what an effective business card should be.

Miss McGee says, "Till eight o'clock then."

"Of course," I say, and I tip my head in a pleasant way, walk with her to the door and thank her. She walks out, a steady thudding down the staircase, and I hear her shut the entranceway door.

Back in the kitchen, Fred has dropped his feet solidly to the floor, has rested his elbows on the table, supporting his head with his palms. When I sit across the table from him, I groan and stretch out my arms, testing my back. I scan the room, my eyes resting on the Hathaway family portrait on the wall, the group of them smiling in their TRUE LOVE T-shirts. In the photograph Fred's face is stern and disinterested, the only person in the picture without a champagne grin. The real Fred in front of me looks that way, too. He looks away from me. The movement in his eyes follows my hands, which I'm rubbing back and forth now across the table.

"I messed up my back something serious at work today," I say, leaning back and grunting to emphasize the hurt.

Fred's ears move slightly, something he usually does when his attention's been grabbed, and just for a second he catches my eye. "Taking somebody's couch?" he says in the curious voice he might use any normal day I'm telling him a story about Crown Rental.

"A customer whacked me with a chair," I say, and tilt toward him and smile. "I laughed at her."

Now Fred gapes into my eyes; his eyes relent and he chuckles. "Did you get her stuff anyway?"

I replay in my mind the scene on Miss Starks's porch, the dog lying there barely breathing, and I remember the feel of the cinder block when I held it high in the air. And I remember, a couple hours later, in front of the Green Tavern, the thud of the chair on my back, the smudge of voodoo butter between Miss Starks's legs.

"We got our stuff all right," I say. "We always do."

These are the lies I tell Fred about my job. No matter how bad work gets, if I'm telling Fred about it, I describe Dewy and I as perfect repo men, fearless and cunning, men who can dodge bullets and rocks thrown at us and laugh it off it like it's a playground game. If nothing interesting happens on a given day, I'll make something up, do anything to amuse the boy, because it's the only way I can ever figure to get along with him. I want him, I guess, to look up to me and think I'm a good man and a tough one.

Through the open kitchen window the late-afternoon traffic noise is a lull of cars passing over leaves, and the wind blows into the kitchen, filling it with the usual city smell of exhaust. Fred fidgets in his chair, sometimes carefully examining his hands, thumbing his palms and smoothing out the dirt there. I watch him from the corner of my eye, making sure he doesn't think I'm gaping at him. I keep wanting to ask him what Margaret was like before he called the police, what she said, how she looked, what she was doing, or I want to ask why Fred lied to Miss McGee about me knowing his father, but I say nothing, only think of ways to perk the boy up. Little time as I've spent with Fred—or even thought about him, really, because of his mother—I worry I can't keep Fred entertained. And if this boy will be back in Wisconsin soon, I won't be doing him any favors by sitting here with him and waiting for Miss McGee. He needs to see something he'll remember for years: what Columbus has been for me, which is a van driving along the side streets, dirty doorways in the projects, people selling crack on the street corners, minutes of disgrace and laughter and hours with Dewy Bishop, who, finally, is a good man, who I'm sure is smart enough and decent enough to handle Fred now, give Fred his lilty grin and his broad-teeth smile. Dewy's my best friend. Dewy's the only man I know who can help me with the boy. To hell with what Miss McGee says I should do.

I say, "Fred, how'd you like to go hang with me and Dewy?"

Fred says, "I've done worse things." And he keeps staring at his expensive shoes.

This is a setup to snag furniture: six o'clock, night coming on, the evening chill and damp. We're parked in an alley off Kilbourne Street, a big green city Dumpster partly concealing the van, and the printout gives us the name Tonya Leonard, who is six weeks past due on a three-piece living room suite. Steve Lawson's note says, *This one will play you for sympathy, a master of excuses.* For the last hour drizzle has been stopping and starting, dotting the van windshield, outlines of true fall, the way it would be up north, windy and bleak. The alley streetlights give the sky an orange hue, which, despite the drizzle, keeps my mind thinking of fire.

We are three repo men now—Fred, Dewy, myself—and Dewy's been calling Fred the Whiz, after Cheez Whiz. Since Dewy picked us up at four-thirty, all smiles and *how do you do, Whiz*, he hasn't said a word about Margaret. Twice, Dewy's met my eyes seriously, and I have known by the way he crinkled his forehead that he's known what's happened to Margaret; it must have been on the news this afternoon, but we haven't talked about it. Dewy has joked around, made Fred laugh by calling me biscuithead and punching me on the shoulder, the punches producing wild giggles from Fred. I've been doing the driving, as always, nodding and steering where Dewy directs me, and Dewy has captained us through a full tour of the hood. When we've passed crack dealers, Dewy's said, "Whiz, they're doing it. Right there." When we've passed prostitutes, Dewy's said, "These women make a man out of you." All this time Fred's taken in the sights like he might be visiting a zoo, cowering and open-mouthed; when we've slowed at intersections where groups of black folks mingle, Fred's looked at his hands, opening them, fanning the air.

Beyond the Dumpster stands Miss Leonard's house, khaki-colored and the standard HUD square duplex. The upstairs windows are unbroken, and from this angle I see bare bulbs shining in each of the upstairs rooms. Six sparrows sit in a line at the point of the roof, the shingles of which glisten a little in the mist. The alley itself is darkening and quiet, no sign of anybody moving up ahead.

Dewy says, "Whiz, are you man enough to be the lookout on this snag?"

"I'm a man," Fred says, his voice cracking.

"I bet you is," Dewy says and chuckles and elbows me in the arm. "But my guy Cheese shakes in his boots every time we go knocking."

"If Fred's on lookout," I say, "he'll be on lookout locked safe in the van."

"Check around you, Cheese. The place is dead as hell. Nothing'll happen to him." Dewy pounds several drumbeats on the dash.

I wince for a second, thinking that Margaret would destroy me for risking Fred here in the hood. I remember Margaret alive and brooding and ready to swipe me across the face with an open hand. But Fred's mine right now, the two of us lost souls from Wisconsin, and if the boy wants to watch Dewy and I on the job, so be it. Dewy won't let anything happen to Fred, anyhow. And this alley in front of us, this Dumpster, this ratty duplex—this is the kind of thing I'd like Fred to remember when he's grown up; when he's a man back in Wisconsin, Fred will know there's more to the world than pine trees and scrub-oak thickets full of hiding deer.

I say, "Fred, can you stand in the alley while we're in the house?" Fred sits on a repo blanket behind Dewy's king seat, and his body is gray in the dim light, his hands waving about.

"I'll do a good job," he says. I hear Fred rubbing his hands together.

"The Bishop will buy you something to eat when the snag's done, Whiz. Just keep your wits about you." And Dewy contorts himself in his seat, reaches a hand to Fred, and they shake. "You a good man, Whiz."

I sense Fred flushing much the way I do when Dewy hands out a compliment, and Fred stands up and puts his forearm on Dewy's shoulder. When Fred does this, I feel a tiny jealousy rising inside me. Fred barely knows Dewy, and already the kid likes Dewy better than me. I can see it. Since Fred's met Dewy, he's been all goggle eyes, hanging on Dewy's words. This is like Fred meeting his first professional football star. Whatever Dewy says, Fred will agree with. But how could this be any other way? Dewy is always the boss.

"Let's go ahead and take the shit, then," I say gruffly, and step out of the van, shutting the door quietly, when I really should have slammed it, making that crunch of Crown Rental steel that signals the beginning of a successful snag.

Dewy and Fred pile out their side, Fred scrambling with excitement right over Dewy's seat. They walk to the front of the van and stand before me, neither of them looking at me; they both peer at Miss Leonard's house.

"Why don't you just take the kid in the house with you," I say. And I hear a whining quality in my voice, that tinge of greenness over Fred's taking to Dewy. "I'll stand here in the alley and be useless."

Dewy glares up at me, a profound hurt in his eyes, and he puffs out his chest.

"Let's have a word, Cheese." But his voice is soothing, has its typically joking upturn to it. He pats Fred on the shoulder and says, "Whiz, lean yourself on the grill and relax while my guy Cheese and me work out a plan."

I follow Dewy past the Dumpster and a few yards farther to a row of haggard lilac bushes with paper trash jammed in the lower branches.

Dewy says in a soft voice, "Control yourself."

I kick at a pebble, sending it scuttling across the alley. "What do you expect out of me, man? My old lady's dead and here I am with her goddam kid."

"I don't expect nothing out of you, Cheese. But don't be fucking up in front of the Whiz."

"I'm doing my best," I say. "What do you think I'm supposed to do?"

"Make him laugh," Dewy says. "The Whiz, he likes that."

"I know," I say, and reach with my tongue for a tuft of mustache, pull the hair into my mouth and chew.

"What are you going to do with him?" Dewy says, and his voice is so plain and flat it sounds like a broadcaster's.

"I have to get the boy back to his father, no doubt. One way or another, somebody's going to take him home. If I can find a way to deliver the boy myself, I'd feel better about it."

"What's the difference?" Dewy says. "You left the bitch before she offed herself. Why you supposed to pick up her slack now?"

Fred stands where Dewy told him to—in front of the van grill, his hands in his pockets—and I see in Fred all the things in this life I've messed up, and all the things, if I do right by Fred, I can now do better.

"Look at the kid," I say. And Dewy looks over my shoulder, and through his slackening cheeks I can tell he's making eye contact with Fred. "It's not his fault this shit happened, Dewy. It's mine."

"Cheese, you being stupid. Nothing you did made that bitch toast herself." He puts both hands on my shoulders, just like this morning, when he persuaded me to smash Sebastian's skull. "But I admire you for taking the Whiz. I didn't think you had it in you, worrying about somebody aside yourself." Dewy shakes me, smiles at me, and a great grin comes over me, relief and joy, because this is the one thing I've always needed to hear, which is someone telling me I'm a decent man, a man people could look to on the street, tip their hat and say, *This man has honor. I wish we'd all be like him.*

We turn to walk back to Fred, and I say, "I appreciate what you're doing for me, man."

Now headlights appear at the far end of the alley, moving toward us. The car emits a heavy buzz-and-boom sound, the signature of a gangster vehicle, the shark of the hood, and as it nears I see its bowlegged wheels, short and wide, rubber protruding a foot from the car body. When I turn to Fred, I see him standing by the van grill, his eyes dog-red in the headlights, his body seized up.

Dewy says, "Move, Cheese. Hide the Whiz." And Dewy steps out in the middle of the alley, blocking the path of the gangster car. I snatch Fred and pull him around the van. Fred and I crouch like soldiers huddling in a foxhole. I tuck Fred into me, smothering him with my arms. Between my legs rests an empty sixty-four-ounce bottle of Old English 800, its label partially peeled away.

"Just stay still," I whisper to Fred.

I hear the car crunching to a halt, the rap falling silent, then the sound of footsteps and a power window. Under my fingertips I feel Fred's small heart beating wildly, like a bird heart. Fred smells vaguely like cigarettes and Margaret.

Dewy says, "Sorry, fellas. I thought y'all might have been friends of mine from Cleveland."

A screechy voice then: "With wheels like this?"

Dewy says, "Come to think of it, you wheels much smoother. This car's a hitting machine. It's the shit, my brother. For real."

The voice says, "We straight then."

The power window sounds once more, and the car slowly drives off. The rap inside the car resumes, a thudding like cardboard buzzing. The taillights head down the alley, turn to the right, and disappear, and in the distance the music still booms, a dance hall moving from street to street around us. When I stand, I lift Fred to his feet.

"You okay?" I say. I hold him tight about his shoulders, and he lets me.

"I thought it was looking bad," Fred says, and I feel his weight pressing into me.

Now I grab hold of Fred's chin, turn it upwards so we can lock eyes. Fred's chin is rough in my hands, his head bigger than his mother's, but way in there I can't help seeing he's his mother's son, the pupils huge and fluid.

I say, "I'll get you out of this shit. I'll get you back home. I owe it to you to make sure you're all right."

For the smallest instant, Fred nods his head and his eyes seem to me distinctly his own. That trust between man and boy—between men—is more important at the moment than his dead mother, or the ways I treated her badly. Right now, cowering in this alley a long way from home, we are all each other has.

Near us, Dewy says, "Whiz, you listen to what the man says."

At this, Fred squirms loose from my grasp and stands to face Dewy, shifting his small weight from one leg to the other. I remember as a boy I never liked to be touched by an adult, especially around other adults, because it made me look like a kid. For certain, Fred wants to be a man on the job, nothing else.

The three of us gather in a loose circle, all looking over the Dumpster to Miss Leonard's duplex. The mist strengthens, wind blowing the moisture into a light rain, drops forming on Miss Leonard's upstairs windows, obscuring the view of the bare bulbs inside. The bulbs look like moths on a wire screen. From the hood around us there is little noise, a car door slamming way off, a rapmobile now and then, but we might call this silence in the hood, people huddling away from the beginning rain. This is as quiet as the hood ever gets.

"I want to make the repo with you guys," Fred says.

"You're staying right here," I say. "You're the look-out man."

Then Dewy palms each of our shoulders, says, "It won't hurt to bring him to the door. Miss Leonard's safe."

"How do you know that?" I say.

"Trust me, my brother. The Whiz does."

"Well, what the fuck," I say, and Fred lets out a giggle. "Let's bring him on in."

"Say it, Whiz," says Dewy. "A man can always say *fuck* on the job."

So Fred says it. "What the fuck."

When Fred then chuckles, I chuckle, too, as does Dewy, and we three repo men share a moment laughing in the light rain. Fred's is a healthy laugh, relief in his voice. He steps in front of us, does a stutter-step like a dance, his hips wobbling each time he says the word *fuck*, which he does three times, followed by a percussive *shit*. Then Fred turns and points to Miss Leonard's duplex.

"The man's got that work ethic, Cheese," Dewy says. "Let's do the snag."

Like gunfighters, we walk in a row into Miss Leonard's backyard, all taking deliberate steps and taking them together. Fred assumes the middle, his elbows flared, flexing his shoulders, trying to look puffed and muscular. The backyard is big and open and littered with garbage, more so than any backyard I've yet seen in the hood. When we walk, we step over beer bottles and cigarette packs, ripped-open lawn-and-leaf bags, newspapers, half-eaten Dairy Mart sandwiches, paper plates, soggy napkins, Styrofoam cups. Trash crackles under our feet. The smell is sour, like we're wandering through a giant Dumpster, mist wafting the stench about. Only the cool wind keeps the smell tolerable. Beyond the alley there's an open flat area the size of several football fields, and I figure the bulk of the garbage in this yard blows in from over there.

We stand for a time in Miss Leonard's porch light. Her door is steel, covered with dents and Magic Marker graffiti, lengthy scratches marring its gray paint. The graffiti consists of well-drawn pictures of handguns, Rastafarian heads in dreadlocks smoking joints, and three thickly veined penises blowing their wads toward three huge and bug-covered vaginas. On the upper left-hand corner of the door is a picture of an enormous cockroach with a human head. A talk balloon is attached to the cockroach, which says, FUCK YOU AND YOUR REVOLUTION. The handwriting is crisp and neat. My impulse is to grab Fred and turn his head away, but Fred's looking at the door with a big grin. With what the boy's been through today, I'm pleased anything can make him happy.

"Give it five knocks, Whiz," Dewy says.

Fred reaches out his fist tentatively, glances up at Dewy, who points at the door. Fred makes his five hardy thuds, but they're a little weak, I know, for Dewy's taste—we are on the job here—so Dewy pounds the door twice with the meat of his fist. Some footsteps sound from inside, feet descending a staircase.

When the door swings open, widening the shaft of house light, a woman stands there—tall and skinny, wearing faded bib overalls and a pink sleeveless T-shirt that exposes her thick and smooth arms—and her jaw and head drops. She stares down at Fred, who shuffles his feet.

"Are you Miss Tonya Leonard?" I say, making sure I speak first, to impress Fred.

"It's me," she says, but she doesn't take her eyes from the boy. "Y'all recruiting delivery help young, sure enough."

Dewy says, "We come for the furniture, Miss Leonard. You been playing us long enough."

With her right hand she swings the steel door back and forth, maybe three inches each way. The skin on her wrist and upper arm shines in the light, her shoulders rising and falling with her even breath. Her entire body is loose, not one show of fright from her. Still, she stares at Fred. "I ain't been playing anybody. Steve knows I'm paying him soon. Waiting on a refund check, is all."

"How many months more you plan on waiting," I say, my voice raised some.

Then she snaps a look at me. "Y'all can take your shit, and I'll keep my money."

I say, "We'll take it right now then." Winky says, *Always call the customer's bluff.* An instant passes where her face shifts from anger to surprise, the pockmarks in her cheeks appearing to enlarge and make her look like no more than the seventeen-year-old girl she probably is.

"I'm sorry," I say. "But you knew this was coming."

"Business is business, Miss Leonard," Dewy says, and steps in front of her, sweeping with his hand. She stands back from the door, placing both her hands to her face, and we walk in.

Her living room smells of ammonia and baby shit. The three-piece living room suite is arranged on the far wall from the front door. All over the linoleum floor lie newspapers, fast-food wrappers, empty cigarette packs, and chewed-on plastic toddler toys. There are two lights shining in the room, both from ratty lamps, which are situated on either side of the sofa section of the Crown Rental three-piece living room suite. The lamps are supported by cardboard boxes. Behind the sofa a wide crack runs down the wall like a varicose vein. Astride the crack hang the standard hood portraits of Malcolm, Nelson, and Martin, all three stern and gray-faced, looking as if about to take their place at the right hand of God. On the sofa itself three balled-up dingy blankets sit in a row.

When Dewy and I move for the furniture, Fred remains, pale and quivering, next to the door and Miss Leonard. His eyes shift from spot to spot around the room, glancing at me or Dewy or a hunk of garbage on the floor, but mostly resting on Miss Leonard herself, who stands holding the door with one hand; her other hand she has stuffed by the fingertips into her mouth.

Biggest item first, of course. So Dewy maneuvers himself to one end of the couch, as do I, and we move the respective lamps aside at the same time.

Miss Leonard shrieks. "Don't move that! Those are my babies." And she rushes to the couch, picks up one of the blanketed lumps, which emits a gurgling and forced breathing noise. She cradles the lump in her arms, flipping the blanket to expose the face of an infant who appears to be probably a few months old. The child's face is a fine light brown, and its eyelashes are long and striking.

Dewy grunts and looks at me in a confused way, part guffaw and part grimace. His hands are on the couch, ready to hoist the thing. "Miss Leonard," he says, but he's staring at me. "These all yours?"

A pause, another gurgle from the infant she holds, then she says, "They mine all right."

I take a step in front of the couch and finger the gap in each blanket. Sure enough, each blanket contains an infant that looks exactly like the other, the clean light brown face, the meaty eyelashes like you'd see on a grown man. When I stoop to check out each child, I feel little pains in my back, but the pains are fading like memories.

I face Miss Leonard, who gazes steadily down into her bundle, poking it with her index finger. I say, "All *three*?"

Without making contact with my eyes, she says, "You could say I been blessed. And they all healthy boys."

Fred lets out a cautious mumble, a squeak almost like one of the infants, and we all turn to him. "They're called triplets," he says, and clasps his hands together. "Mom told me about that once."

Dewy crinkles his forehead, looking at me. His lips and jowls slacken. "I'll bet she did, Whiz," he says, and he tips his head toward Fred and smiles, a slight wince visible from the side view, a twitch near his big right ear.

The baby in Miss Leonard's arms begins a muted cry, sputtering, and Miss Leonard presses it to her chest, rocks forward and from side to side in a kind of slow dance step. The way she stands there—her bib overalls baggy and soiled in places with chunks of food and spatters of greasy stuff—and the way her thick bare arms close about the child strikes me as the sad and humdrum world of motherhood, of hours holding bottles in an infant's mouth, of endless nights filled with whining children and sleep for a half hour at a stretch. What stroke of fate gave this young woman three children at once I can't guess. But looking about her apartment now, the garbage on the floor, the crack in the wall, I see no evidence of a man, no boots placed by the door or ball cap hanging from a nail. Even if she gets money from the government, she's tending this brood on her own, a task that will wear down the hardiest soul. There's a nobility to the way she handles herself, unflinching in the face of repo men. She's doing the best she can. I see that my job, which has nothing to do with what's conspired to make this woman's life miserable, is strictly to take the little extra money this woman has, collect it, and send it on north to Canton, Ohio, where five white men use it to take vacations in the Caribbean or to spend happy Saturday afternoons in Cleveland, with their children, watching the Indians play ball. And if she doesn't have the money, by God, I've got to take away the only place, besides bare linoleum, that's safe to set her child.

Under Miss Leonard's eyes are dark circles, like punch marks, and at the corners of her mouth a white residue has settled. She is neither smiling nor crying. She merely sways and rocks her child quiet. A year ago, I suppose, she was beautiful and maybe thirty swigs into a forty-ounce of Red Bull malt liquor, and for reasons of trust and longing—or whatever it is that makes us come together and grope one another—she made love with some man, a man she probably thought was beautiful as she. She couldn't have known then she'd end up with three babies at once. She couldn't have known that the crappy furniture she rented out at a cheap price late in her pregnancy would be taken from her a few months later by a big black man from Sandusky and two white folks from Wisconsin. She rented the furniture in good faith. She made love to that man in good faith. I came here to Ohio in good faith. Hell, Margaret brought me here in good faith. This is the nature of the decisions we make. No one does anything with the intention of fucking it up.

Fred totters by the door, his face in concentration, and he says, "Did it hurt, having all those babies in one day?"

No expression crosses her face, no jerk or sag of the lips. She says, "Yes." And she continues rocking her child.

"My mom says it hurt a lot when she had me," says Fred.

"They say it always hurts," Miss Leonard says.

I watch Dewy, whose head shakes slightly when Miss Leonard speaks. He steps to the front of the couch, bends to look each infant in the face. When he peers down he grins and says, "You cool, little man. I'm sorry your mother can't keep this couch."

Then Dewy picks up one bundle gently, hoists it to his shoulder, bobbing his chest forward from his stomach. With a bounce in his step he carries the baby to the far wall, sets the child down on the floor. A tiny wheeze escapes from the bundle. I merely stand and observe Dewy, Miss Leonard, Fred, the children—the room quiet, save for small breathing and the bubbling of saliva on those infant lips—and I know now I can't do this anymore. This job is not a matter of reasonable business between decent folks. If Dewy and I had any decency, we would leave this shitty furniture here. The company won't fold if the account goes uncollected for another day. But we're going to repossess this stuff because we get paid $265 a week, which means we're supposed to take pride in what we do. Dewy reaches down for the other bundle, grunting when he squats to pick it up. With this child in his arm he smirks, and I'm not sure why. Dewy keeps a lock on my eyes while he carries the bundle to the wall and sets it next to the other, and when Dewy stands up again and rubs his hands together, Miss Leonard doesn't flinch or look at Dewy. She stares absently at the child in her arms.

"Cheese," he says. "Let's get it on." With a jerk of his neck he points me to one end of the couch, but I do not move. I stuff my hands in my coveralls and shift my eyes from point to point in the room.

Fred is moving his shoes back and forth again, his face and eyes looking downward, admiring them. He is ten and surely not wise in the world. Short and grubby and wearing my old factory T-shirt like a giant black frock, his slender fingers and olive arms make him, no matter how I try to forget, a miniature Margaret. I'm responsible for this kid now, and after everything I did to his mother, all the fighting and not coming home and driving her crazy (or that's what he must think), what am I telling him about me if I walk out of this apartment with Miss Leonard's furniture now? What kind of man would repo the only furniture a poor mother of triplets has? But Margaret is dead. For the last week, Fred has been stuck at home with her raging, and it's an easy guess Margaret said and did things that no boy, let alone grown man, could suffer through without cracking.

"Cheese," Dewy says, irritation in his voice, a growl and upturn. "You want me to get the Whiz to work for you?"

These words lift Fred's eyes, and he makes a half smile at Dewy, takes a tentative step toward him.

"Fuck it," I say, and I take my place at the opposite end of the couch from Dewy, who exhales through his teeth and glares at me. Then under my breath I say, "I'm not letting the kid take shit we should by rights leave here."

"Let's just get it on," Dewy says, and he hoists his end of the couch.

Winky says, *Never hesitate in front of the customer*.

So I lift my end, which sends little needles through the bruises in my back, but only from bending down; the couch, as all Crown Rental couches, is cheap and light. And I begin the backwards walk to the steel door, stepping carefully with my heels, feeling behind me to keep from falling over. When we lug the couch past Miss Leonard, I don't look at her. I merely sense her presence near, her mother smell, old milk and diapers, her quiet breathing. Everything now is Crown Rental standard procedure. I set my end down near the door. Dewy pushes his end up so we can wiggle the couch through. Outside, rain is falling steadily, wind pushing it at an angle, and we set the couch down on the trashy grass.

When Dewy turns to head back in, I reach for his shoulder to tell him we should return the couch to its spot on the linoleum, but he walks too swiftly for me to get his attention. I follow, watching the flex of his massive shoulders, which fill the door when he passes through.

Inside, Fred stands over the two bundles, Miss Leonard beside him. They are not speaking to each other. They are simply looking at the children.

Dewy points me to the chair, always the repo general, and he picks up the loveseat without emitting a sound. Then he moves his way through the door, saying "Come on" as he goes.

"Miss Leonard," I say, and grasp the chair, the fabric of which feels crusty. "I can't tell you how sorry I am about this."

Her head turns up toward me, but her eyes seem to be looking at a spot on the wall behind me. Her eyes are yellow and slightly bloodshot. She says, "You never be sorry enough." And her voice is muted and calm.

I say, "I really mean it."

She waves one hand in the air. "Leave."

"I didn't want to do this."

"Leave," she says, her voice louder, beginning finally to show some anger.

And I heft the chair, propping the cushion on my knee. Miss Leonard steps to the door and gazes outside at the falling rain.

"Come on, Fred," I say.

I carry the chair past Miss Leonard and through the doorway into the rain. I hear Fred's shuffling feet behind me. The steel door then closes and we stand— Fred, Dewy, and myself—in darkness and among three pieces of furniture growing soggy on this blustery night.

"The couch, Cheese," Dewy says. But I do not see Dewy's mouth say this.

I say, "We're going to hell, Dewy."

For a moment he's silent. All around us raindrops strike plastic wrappers and cups and garbage bags, a noise like a far-off drum corps warming up, wee snare drummers tapping out their sad rudiments. Above Miss Leonard's duplex the streetlights shape the rain into separate orange sheets, wet fire falling on us and on the hood. I feel the water striking my hands.

"I'll give you that, Gunnar," Dewy says. "We going straight down. But it's my living, man. If I did something else, I'd be heading straight to hell, too. No matter what the gig, you take something from somebody."

"This is my last repo, Dewy. It's just not in me to do it anymore."

Still, I can't clearly see Dewy's face, but when he talks now, his voice doesn't sound angry.

"So you going home," he says. "My guy Cheese is heading back where he belongs."

"You understand," I say, and I believe he does.

"Me, I'm not going anywhere." I hear him shifting his weight, stepping into position on one end of the couch. "Columbus is home enough for me."

I assume my position at the couch and lift, start back-shuffling the hundred-yard stretch to the van. Through the tattered and wet couch fibers I feel Dewy's strides, plodding and sure. I feel his hands rising and falling, heaving the light load. For now, we've said what needs to be said. We've both spent our working lives watching people come and go: people you know for a time, then never see again. That's how it is within the workaday world. Nobody stays. I walk backwards, garbage and wet fall grass at my heels, and I see the outline of a big black man in front of me, a ten-year-old white boy stepping slowly at his side. My steps are slow and solid. I am a man who has become used to carrying things backwards.

I drive Dewy, as it should be between us, the boss and his underling, and it is nearly eight o'clock. The street-lights on Cleveland Avenue make the wet street shine, but the rain is letting up, the last few spits dribbling into the windshield. Along the road the ratty houses, crumbled sidewalks, and the withered trees look like a tired wet army at rest. Tomorrow sun might shine over the hood again, and this rubble will breathe with people like it always does. Columbus will remain Columbus. As it happens, this is Dewy's night to lock up the store. Thursday, Steve Lawson's got visitation rights with his two kids; nothing gets in the way of Steve's night with his kids, not even his number-three employee's girl-friend going up in flames. When Steve left the store for home, he told us he didn't want any fuck-ups. That's all he said, what he always says. So five minutes ago Dewy set the security system, shut the lights, pulled the steel gate shut, said, like every day, *another stretch in the hole done.* And, like every Thursday, Dewy's coming with me to make the bank drop. This is my last official Crown Rental task, Dewy knows, but Steve Lawson has no idea I'm about to quit. Maybe if Steve knew, he wouldn't let me drive around with $5,972.29 of Winky's money. The same as any drop, I recite the amount in my head, a chant of sadness and my poverty and my hope it will someday end, and the bank bag is uncomfortable underneath my rear, like a chunk of firewood.

Dewy taps his fingers against his knee, saying nothing. From time to time he exhales heavily through his nostrils. In the back of the van, Fred leans against the spare tire, humming the theme to a Campbell's soup commercial, his feet extended over my bicycle, my old green Miyata, the only possession of mine I want to take back home. The old spokes ping at Fred's heels. Only a few people walk along the sidewalks or mill around, smoking cigarettes and talking. A car occasionally moves by on the southbound lane, the last raindrops like dust in the headlights. On certain porches people gather, pointing out at the ending rain, testing the night.

When I pull into the BancOhio lot the van nose jumps over the gutter bump, and Fred lets out a small squeal. This evening no cars are in the lot, nobody standing in line by the instant teller. The lot resonates with the afterbreath of rain lingering, the asphalt hue purple from the lone fluorescent light mounted on the bank wall. Dewy's profile is green and gray in this light.

"Go on," he says, and hands me the keys for the bag. "If you open it with the key, you won't need to cut it later."

And I don't move. There are seventy-five steps to the deposit chute, a count I've made dozens of times. There is a way of walking those steps, chin up and casual, a way of walking those steps like I'm not carrying the money.

"Open the bag," Dewy says. "And don't tell anybody I told you to."

I can't clearly make out Dewy's eyes, only the crease of his jowls, his faint fatherly smile, and I take the keys, feel them still warm from Dewy's pocket. When I insert the key and click the brass bag lock, I pause for a moment, wondering what Fred thinks is going on, but it doesn't matter now. This money will get him home. Fred will be safe then, these months of sadness in Ohio a memory, and his life will be Wisconsin and wintertime snow and happiness. My hands shake, visions racing through my head of handcuffs and felony charges, all the humiliation I probably deserve. I feel sweat breaking on my neck, and a constriction begins in my throat and stomach. I pull the bag zipper, a muffled sound, like cloth tearing.

I attempt saying *thanks*, but the word comes out garbled, my voice too high, too nervous.

"Now drive on north a few blocks," Dewy says, and he throws up his hands like a priest.

"Maybe we shouldn't," I whisper.

"Just do what I say, Cheese."

So I believe in Dewy. I always have. Three months, I've talked to him every day, laughed with him, and we've been men together. He's showed me his way through the world, and I've followed. And I am alive. I snap the van in reverse, ease back, then lurch onto Cleveland Avenue. The tires hiss over the wet street. Wherever I look—the sidewalks, alleys, bus stops—I see no people and tell myself I must remember no people saw us, saw me with Dewy in this van.

After three blocks, Dewy says, "Pull on over here." And I slow down in front of a northbound bus stop.

"Make sure to get the Whiz fed," Dewy says.

He opens his door, the dome light illuminating his face, tougher than I ever remember it, whiskers and pockmarks making him look for some reason old. His skin is a shade of red ochre.

I clear my throat to make this a farewell as it should be between men, a few words on *so long* and *take care*, but Dewy beats me to the gesture, offers a hand to me, and nods his head. His hand feels big and rough. "You be cool, Cheese," he says.

Just like that, he's out the door and closing it. The last thing I see of him is his wrist, thick and chalky in the dome light. Then the door closes, and I'm driving the van north again, an easy pace over the road, a full tank of gas in the van, no need for fuel till Indianapolis.

Fred's in Dewy's king seat now, buckled up like a responsible citizen, and he's munching Fritos and slurping from the can of pop I bought him at United Dairy Farmers a few minutes ago. We're one mile from the I-70 bypass and the long westward drive home. Here a bit north of Dublin Road the side streets are beginning to dry. The rolling tires are almost soundless. The overhead sky is night gray, a puff of low cloud here and there reaching toward the ground. In Ohio I never see the stars. This is one last stop, one more customer I need to see. This is good-bye to Leslie Britton.

Leslie's street is calm, as ever, four cars lined along the curb in front of her building. Lights are on in her front room, a gold glow in her venetian blinds. When I stop the van I say, "One minute, Fred. That's all this will take." He crunches chips and doesn't respond. I dig into the bank bag and slip out a handful of bills, maybe a third of the money, cram the bag back under the seat.

The grassy walk to her door is a matter of mush under my feet and memory: how, days before this, I sat here like a Buddhist and stuck out my tongue, how she offered me tea and said she could save me from myself; or how I saw her once running across this grass in her sandals, the flip-flop sound of her escaping, and Dewy and I chased her; or how, the first time I saw her—her freckled forearms and skin pale as a snowdrift—I believed Leslie was the woman I was born to love. Now I raise my fist and knock its soft edge on her door—four knocks, the friendly rap—and I know I didn't love her at all. She is a woman who is not Margaret. Chareesa is a woman who is not Margaret. Margaret, in the end, was a woman who was not Sara, and I suppose I could say the same for every woman I've been involved with, which is why I've come here with money. Leslie Britton has served a purpose for me, the same old purpose, sure enough, a female way to forget the life I lead. Leslie has been a diversion to me, and it hasn't mattered who she really is. She could be any woman willing. A few bucks in her pocket, a kind word, this is the only way I can cover my guilt.

Leslie's door opens sluggishly to a crack, the golden light breaking through. I shove my hands in my pockets like some high school kid arriving late for a movie date, trembling, my face flushing hot. Before I see her, she says, "It's you." The gravel in her voice seems to have disappeared. "I wasn't expecting you."

"I've brought something for you," I say.

"Shitfire," she says in full West Virginia now, and she quickly opens the door, steps out, and closes it behind her. "I hope you ain't bringing flowers."

She's wearing a raggedy flannel bathrobe, maybe four sizes too big for her, which extends to her ankles, luminous skin down on the dark stoop, feet small and assured. Her eyes are difficult to see in this nighttime view, but her head tilts downward and sways, a way, I imagine, of checking out my hands. Close as she is to me, I smell her sandalwood odor, her smell of medicinal tea and good hillbilly weed.

"No flowers," I say. I grab her hand with a bit too much force (I feel her tugging away from me), and I stuff the money there. "I've brought you this." When the bills hit her hand, she relaxes.

A few moments pass wherein the only noise is a diesel horn somewhere out on the freeway. Water drips off the apartment building eaves, off the lone shrub by Leslie's door.

"How much is this?" Her voice is sad, a twang in her words, the voice of remote hills and dirt-floor bars.

"More than what you have now," I say. "When Dewy knocks at your door next, why don't you go ahead and pay the man." I place my hands in front of me as if I'm holding a hat.

She fumbles the money into her bathrobe pocket, muttering something that seems embarrassed and confused. She says, "Kind of you, this is. You know, I was sure you wouldn't be back again. I seen you on the evening news tonight."

A world of autowinders and TV cameras and police cars and flames shooting upward comes to me, the first time in a few hours I've even thought of it.

"It was an unfortunate thing," I say.

She touches my forearm, says, "You will take care of yourself. I know you'll get yourself in control."

And when I begin to say why I'm giving her the money, when I start the awkward way of explaining that I believe I treated her poorly, an angry male West Virginia voice sounds from inside her apartment. "Leslie, just who you talking to," the voice says.

A silence then, tiny water droplets falling around us, engines droning off in the distance. Near, I detect her crinkling the money in her pocket.

"Must have a new head for the wall," I say. Dewy's

coconut likeness crosses my mind, my memory of its exaggerated lips and eyes bringing a smile to me, and I guffaw quietly and sadly.

"Well," she says, and places her hands within mine. "I gotta do something with my spare time. You understand."

"Of course," I say. And whatever she does, I'm thinking, is all right with me. After all, I will never see this woman again.

The hard hill-man voice shouts again from inside. "Do you need any help down there?"

Leslie slips her arms around my gut and squeezes in a gentle way. While we hug, I breathe deeply through my nose, implanting in my memory the precise character of her smell, sandalwood and tea and dope.

"You're a good man," she says.

"And you're a good woman."

Then in one movement she's inside her apartment and gone. I hear her climbing her staircase and saying, "No problem. Just the Crown Rental man stopped by for his payment."

I turn and actually laugh. Funny, I'm thinking, exactly how much a man can let go in a day. I begin walking with loping strides, feeling lighter somehow; only memories make up my weight.

When I open the van door, Fred stares at me, an angry look, the kind of expression his mother often gave me, something twitching about the nose, the split in the bulb like a rodent nose. Fred holds his bag of chips in a such a way that makes me think he might throw it at me, the bag in his hand raised from his knee.

"Mom was right," he says. He squares his shoulders toward me, the fighting posture of a grown man. "You did have another woman."

Under the dome light Fred's face and its fury sends shudders through my body. I quickly shut the van door, return the cab to darkness so I don't have to look at the boy or his mother's face in his. My first impulse is to deny it, make up some cock-and-bull that Leslie Britton is an old friend or a relative. Winky says, *Lie only when you're certain the customer will believe it*. I fire the ignition and begin rolling the van down the street.

"When you're my age," I say, "you'll understand what I was doing."

"Mom said you were an asshole. Now I know it's true."

"Maybe so," I say. I produce a cigarette from my shirt pocket, cram it in my mouth, and bite the filter. "I never said I was a decent man, Fred. Sometimes things happen to a guy and they're hard to control."

"That's crap," Fred says, and he crumples the Frito bag.

"It probably is," I say.

Up ahead, I see Dublin Road, an even line of street-lights and moving cars, the river of the big city, and I run through the drive to Milwaukee: eight hours in the dark with Margaret's son, who has found me out for who I am, which is a man who's lived some secret life full of lying to people, hiding from people, taking people's furniture away. Nothing about my repo life, this kid knows, was worth laughing over at the end of the day.

"Whatever's happened," I say, "there's not much we can do about it now."

Fred grumbles to himself, maneuvering his body loudly about in his seat, but he says nothing to me.

Then I turn on Dublin, the van taking this route as if my hands are not these hands gripping the steering wheel with nerves and sadness. Three months, I have been driving this city in this van, and I cannot escape thinking I'm leaving home now. Ohio, the hood, and the endless dark faces staring at me, Dewy, Leslie, Chareesa in the rain, the plume of fire shooting from Margaret's body—all this is forever stuck in my memory, moments that I might talk about some early afternoon, tap beer and a boat of peanuts in front of me, when the only thing the drunks at the bar will know about Ohio is that there are two professional football teams there and two professional baseball teams. That's what Ohio will become, something to talk about, just as Wisconsin, while I've been here, has been no more than some obscure part of me, a place I can mention in random tidbits, and people might smile for an instant and be entertained. I am driving this van in the dark, turning onto the I-70 bypass, turning to the West. I am leaving Columbus as a thief, a quitter of jobs, and the indirect cause of the fiery death of a woman, whose son won't speak with me now.

And the world in front of me is in the beam of the headlights.

A mile from the Ohio border, I see the lights of the big blue archway spanning I-70, which, in August, when I entered the state, displayed the words WELCOME TO OHIO. Margaret and I were in the car alone that day, the last stretch of Indiana sun fading into the late afternoon. I remember Margaret lighting a cigarette when we passed underneath the arch, saying, "And a welcome home it will be." I had agreed, without saying a word. A new home, I was thinking, a fresh start, the years of factory work and booze and cheating on Sara about to be forgotten. Nearly eleven o'clock now, the archway vivid on the horizon—the van approaches the arch at seventy miles per hour. I hear nothing from Fred, only him breathing next to me; he hasn't spoken since we began this drive.

I say, "You remember the arch up here, Fred?" Then I force a chuckle to humor him.

He shifts his weight, grumbles and snorts. Fred's arms are green folded sticks in the dashboard glow.

"Come on, Fred," I say. "You must have seen it."

"It was stupid then. It'll be stupid now," he says.

When we are a hundred yards from the archway, I see these words: THANK YOU FOR VISITING OHIO.

"Look at that, Bud," I say. "Some vacation this has been."

And I glance over at Fred. His palms are over his eyes. When I look up at the archway again, we have already passed underneath, the road pure darkness and thin headlights, trucks moving along the eastbound lanes.

"In time," I say, "you will be sorry you didn't look at that sign."

"Whatever," Fred says, and we resume our silence.

Midnight. Six miles east of Indianapolis there is an enormous truck stop called Grandma's, which is a restaurant and gas station and gift shop with showers, phones, and probably prostitutes working the sleeper cabs, like big truck stops on interstates everywhere, and the complex is built on a raised piece of earth, dirt that surely was hauled in during its construction, given the flatness of Indiana. Grandma's concrete lot is big enough to hold, my guess, two hundred trailers. Maybe fifty trailers are parked around the lot's perimeter now. On the east side of the complex stands an aluminum-covered series of diesel ports, each occupied. Half of the ports have trucks waiting in line, engines running, exhaust streaming into the night sky. On the west side a smaller line of automobile fuel ports is practically empty. Two other cars are here: a rusty VW microbus and a Ford Pinto. I see no one walking nearby while I fill the Crown Rental van tank with gas. And I am watching the lot carefully for people watching me—police more than anything—because I am a man with a stolen vehicle and a bankroll of stolen cash and a ten-year-old, I'm figuring, the cops could believe I've kidnapped.

I fill the tank as full as it can get, foam splashing my hand. Just to make sure I've maxed out the tank, I give it a few more experimental squirts. The gas smell is powerful and all Margaret in a circular gap in a crowd. I twist the cap back in place, cranking it down, trying to forget what gasoline does best, catch fire.

Before walking in the building to pay, I rap on the passenger door, one solid thump. Fred rolls his window down, leers out at me, his black eye in this light making him look like an old-time cartoon character.

I say, "Fred, it's time to take a piss."

"Maybe I'll just piss myself. What are you going to do about *that*?"

In his eyes, I can tell his anger is weakening some, something watery around the lower lids, something blank within the pupils. Fury works in short bursts, not over hours.

"I'll buy you whatever you want," I say, but I do not smile. I'm growing weary, aches in my back, my elbows swollen, parts of my face slightly singed. The itch of bloodshot paints my eyeballs. "You want a new T-shirt or something?"

With a sigh he opens the door and steps out, stretching, and he says, "I suppose." Then he holds himself still, his face wincing up at me. "That would be nice of you," he says. This is his mother's training: Be polite and grateful always. I've heard her bitch at him about gratitude a hundred times.

"I couldn't think of a better man to blow my money on," I say, and place my arm around him. He doesn't shrink away, merely accepts the gesture, leaning a half portion of his weight into me.

We shuffle to the building together, each of us look-ing like hayseeds—my hands in my coverall pockets fin-gering the bills I've stashed there, Fred's loose at his sides—walking at such a casual pace, with such indiffer-ent looks on our faces, a stranger might think we've both spent the day rebuilding a combine. To boot, we are grimy. I stink, have been wearing the same clothes for days. Fred's covered with a film of apartment dust.

But when we walk in the glass doors, nobody looks at us. Business, brisk for this time of night, goes on as usual. Feed-capped men in cowboy boots and jeans and black T-shirts mingle by telephones or sit off in the row of booths drinking coffee or spooning soup. Some thumb through magazines. Some stand alone by a win-dow, staring out at the busy night. The place smells like cigarettes and freshly deodorized armpits. In the middle of the complex there is a circular enclosure surrounded by cash registers, all of which are manned by white women in their twenties with poofy hair and excess trashy makeup. A steady ching fills the air, money changing hands. Fred wanders directly to the gift shop, mostly hats and coffee mugs, positions himself in front of the T-shirt rack, flipping them.

"Piss first," I say, and coddle him with an arm around his shoulder.

He sighs but walks with me to the bathroom.

While we stand, man and man in the posture of porcelain and letting go, I say, "Hell, we just rent our coffee. Drink it up and give it right back to the city."

Fred says nothing. He doesn't get it. But a man

behind us laughs out loud. "That's the goddam truth," the man says in a middle-range voice without twang, a voice I recognize as one from the Far North. "You never get to keep anything."

When I turn and zip up, I see this man is short and chubby, with a sizable gut hanging over his buckle. His buckle is rectangular and brass, has the words ACAPULCO GOLD written on it. The man nods to me, the hey sign, and while he assumes his position at the urinals, Fred and I saunter back to the T-shirt rack.

Out of the three dozen or so shirts on the rack, only four are any color other than black, and those four are navy blue. I watch the shirt designs while Fred examines each: menacing Harley Davidsons blowing smoke from their tailpipes, International Harvesters with living eyes for headlights, leather-clad blond women with mammoth breasts, and so on. About three-quarters of the way through his search Fred selects one he likes. This black shirt contains a colorful silk screen of a red-haired woman with whopping bare nippleless boobs. Her head is flat as a kitchen table, and on top of that flat surface rests a full mug of frothy beer. Her lips are full, bright red and formed into an O. This is what the caption reads: I MET THE PERFECT WOMAN IN INDIANA. On the back of the shirt is a cartoon of a grizzled old man with a red nose and a one-tooth smile, and these words: AFTER MIDNIGHT SHE TURNS INTO A ROAST BEEF SANDWICH.

"I want this one," Fred says, and he flashes me the first genuine smile of the day, a grin that displays the barely noticeable crooked smile of his mom.

Out of reflex, I say, "Are you sure?"

"I want this one," he says again, grinning his mother's grin, then removing the shirt from its hanger. It strikes me that Margaret would blow a gasket if she saw this shirt. I remember her sitting Fred down on certain nights and telling him when he grows up he should never look on women as anything but equals. Women, Margaret would say, are not mattresses; they are minds. Certainly, I never cared less what happened in Margaret's head, unless it got me into trouble. My whole attraction to Margaret centered on the way she felt in my hands, pure and simple—I knew that from the start—and it could be she's dead for it now. And this is her child with me, my responsibility for the next few hours. What respect am I paying her memory if I buy this shirt for her boy? I might as well tell Fred I've always looked on women as holes to fill and because of it I'm committing multiple felonies here on freeways of the Midwest. I might as well say, *Look, we're all assholes, and I'm happy I've been one to your dead mother.*

Fred now holds the shirt free from the rack, waving it in front of his face. He looks at the shirt solemnly. I am more than a foot taller than him. I have nearly two decades of hard living on this kid. I am a man. He's ten. No decent man, I'm thinking, whatever he thinks about women, would let a ten-year-old boy run around in a shirt like this.

"I think you should pick another shirt," I say.

In a snap, Fred folds the shirt into his chest, says, "But you said I could get whatever I want."

"The shirt isn't decent." I reach for the shirt, close my fingers about its cheap fabric. "You're too young for it."

"I seen boobs before." He tugs at the shirt with surprising strength, pulling it from my grip. "This is the shirt," he says.

"Your mom'd be pissed if she saw you in that goddam thing."

At this, a prolonged relaxation passes through Fred's body, the shoulders going slack, the arms lowering down so the T-shirt touches the floor. He looks downward for a moment, then wobbles his tennis shoes. He breathes at the same rate his feet move.

"Whatever," he finally says. Without blinking, he drops the shirt to the floor.

And I wait for him to glare at me. Instead Fred wanders to the snacks, shuffling and indifferent again, and removes a big bag of licorice. I follow, feeling for the first time in my life like a grown man and a father, like someone with standards and decency. Along with his licorice he grabs a quart of chocolate milk from the cooler, and I fill an immense plastic mug with black coffee, fuel for the drive.

When I pay, I glance nervously around, pick a twenty from my pocket so nobody will notice exactly how much cash I'm carrying. The woman who takes the money is tall and brown-haired and thin, though her lips are unusually thick, like they're bug-bit, and she has a wide gap between her front teeth. During our transaction, she bats her eyes like a clock ticking.

"She was freaky," Fred says when we step out into the parking lot.

"Everybody is," I say.

Then we're on the road again, the skyscraper lights of Indianapolis in front of us, towers of glass as in Columbus. Fred chews and doesn't speak. I mouth a cigarette, content with knowing soon this boy will have a home.

Winky says, *You can always be proud of a good day's work.*

Thursday morning early, 6:15 A.M., the sky pale blue and brightening—this is Wisconsin, land of cheese and happiness and the Sunday noontime observance of the Green Bay Packer game. This is Germantown, a far-northern suburb of Milwaukee, and this is the condominium complex where Fred's father lives. The parking lot is full of new cars—Ford Rangers, Honda Preludes, Pontiac Bonnevilles—windshields covered with dew. Sometime during the night, when I drove us north on I-65, Fred fell asleep, a ten-year-old quietly snoring over the freeway whine, and he slept through Gary, Indiana, through South Chicago and the tollbooths, through the miles north of Chicago where the billboards say WISCONSIN AWAITS YOU. Minutes ago I woke Fred with a nudge so he could direct me to this spot.

"Go on," I say, and I don't watch him. I scan the upper windows of the condo units, my repo habit. My hands feel in the steering wheel the van engine rumbling smoothly. Winky says, *You must have control of your actions in the field*. Winky says, *Know what you're getting into*. Winky says, *Pay attention to the customer and avoid trouble*. Winky will be part of me forever, like gasoline fumes and a shotgun blast in the night and the raining cold day Chareesa put her mouth to me in the back of this van.

"Aren't you coming in?" Fred says, his voice bright and excited, maybe his mother for the moment forgotten.

"I don't think so, Bud," I say. "Somewhere up north there's a beer with my name on it."

Fred opens his door, turns to me, his face now like any other ten-year-old with a black eye, a face that's smudged a bit with red licorice, a kid who needs a bath. I extend my hand to him and we shake, once up and down, and he steps out into the morning.

"Have a life," I say, and I give him a tired smile.

Without saying anything, Fred closes the door. I watch him walk in front of the van and onto a concrete sidewalk. His steps are loose and bumbling, not hurried, not the run I might expect from a kid going to see his father. Fred squares himself in front of the second condo in, strides to the door, and knocks, five sharp raps, the standard repo knock. A pause, that wait a good repo man must always endure, then the door opens. When I see that it's his father there, stocky and with curly blond hair, I do not wait for Fred to look back. I flip the van into drive and cruise off.

All around me there are echoes, voices I've heard in

this van, things I've done in this van, and I drive north toward McCutcheon. I will wait there till the police find me.

The Liquid Forest is a narrow tavern with a long mirrored bar, picture windows in the front, and not much room to move around, a tap-beer-and-peanuts place that on a good night can hold seventy-five people. It sits on the eastern edge of Mitchell Street, the university-tavern district of McCutcheon. This is where I met Margaret and where I met the women, over the years, I slept with to make myself feel better, when the grind of loyalty to Sara Weber was too much for me. This is where I came after work, after deer hunting, after fishing, after lazy summer barbecues, after I drove Sara to Minneapolis for her abortion, and so on. In the ten years I drank in this bar I'll bet I spent twenty grand, probably a lot more, every penny of which seems lost in my endless list of things I should not have done. I have more than three grand with me now. When I stopped for gas ninety miles south of McCutcheon and added up my pile, I quit counting when I reached three grand. It doesn't matter how much I have, because I know it will be enough to drink and eat and forget till I'm taken away. It is 10:45 A.M. If this only were Sunday, the Packer game would begin precisely at noon, like it always has, and the bar would be full of happy talking folk.

I have pulled the van to a stop directly in front of

the Liquid Forest window glass, and I stand here on Mitchell Street, sniffing the pine in the air, feeling the cold fall wind of the Far North. This is my home.

When I swing the glass tavern door open, I hear Patsy Cline on the juke, absently droning about a man and the wrong he's done her, and the stools along the bar are empty, save for Billy O'Donnell, the bartender, who occupies the last stool by the back door, near the pool table and the dartboard. He's got a cup of coffee, a lit cigarette, and a thick paperback. He closes his book, stands and unbends himself like a man twenty years his senior, then hobbles to the middle of the bar to greet me by the taps. Last night was a rough one for Billy. Since I've known him, all his nights have been. Billy is six feet tall, bony and freckled, has long red hair in a ponytail, and wears vaguely horn-rimmed glasses, which make him look, the joke's always gone, like northern Wisconsin's Elton John.

"Hey, Gunnar," he says, and I tip my head.

Without me saying anything, he flips on the bar TV with the sound off and he swiftly fixes me a double gin bloody Mary, my daytime drink for years. He pours me a Leinenkugel's chaser, fills me a boat of peanuts, and sets the stuff up in front of me. I place a twenty on the bar.

"You just get off work?" he says happily, the bartender's expert conversation tone. He grabs the twenty, his hand quaking as I remember it quaking, nerve endings shot from booze, and he turns to the till. While he fumbles to make change, I watch him in the mirror. Three months I've been gone from McCutcheon. He hasn't noticed me missing. Ten years of me drinking in this bar, afternoons here talking with Billy about this or that, secrets told, lies revealed, the whole world of bar buddies and everything that when I was away made me believe in who I was—he remembers only what I drink first in the daytime.

He sets my change down, and I say, "Just got off work all right."

"I sure hope the Pack beat the point spread Sunday," he says. His voice is every bit of Wisconsin that I remember, nasal and staccato with the consonants. "Been playing like shit, they have been."

I rub my forehead and exhale. "They sure have, Billy."

Then I gaze up at the television, cable news, and out of the corner of my eye I watch Billy returning to his seat at the end of the bar. I slurp my bloody Mary, sharp and mealy, the house specialty, but I don't taste the booze. Behind me Pasty Cline sings something about a man in a checkered shirt. Pine trees not fifty yards from this stool are slowing their sap, seizing up for winter coming on.

For a few minutes I stare blankly at the news—insurgents in fatigues running down a dirt road, a picture of the White House, a train wreck in Arizona—and my body loosens. I am not a thinking man. I am a man who has made his way home. Now on the television I see a street scene, a circular gap in a large crowd, the thick shoulders of a man in coveralls waving his arms. And the camera pans back, reveals a woman sitting with her legs splayed out, holding a can of gasoline in her lap. Just like that, when I realize the woman is Margaret and the man in coveralls is me, the flames begin, a huge plume that looks from this angle different than I recall, brighter orange, and the camera wavers. People run. Firemen spring into action. I see myself lying on the asphalt, pointing at the sky. Then it's the news studio again, a clean-cut man in a blue suit saying something I can't hear. This is all: my throat tightens. I swallow three times and look away to the outside world, this Wisconsin I drove 770 miles to fix in my eyes.

Through the bar window I see the side panel of my Crown Rental van. On this side panel is an airbrushed picture of Winky, bright yellow and smiling. In the line of his smile I believe I see a perfect row of teeth.

And for all the world I can't remember what Winky says.